OPENING LOVE'S DOOR

8-14-05 · OK

OPENING LOVE'S DOOR

The Seven Lessons

Diana Kirschner

iUniverse, Inc.
New York Lincoln Shanghai

Opening Love's Door
The Seven Lessons

iUniverse, Inc.

For information address:
iUniverse, Inc.
2021 Pine Lake Road, Suite 100
Lincoln, NE 68512
www.iuniverse.com

ISBN: 0-595-33386-9 (pbk)
ISBN: 0-595-66888-7 (cloth)

Printed in the United States of America

For Sam

Contents

Acknowledgements

To my family and friends: Concetta Kirschner, Jason Kirschner, Blessed Mama Concetta Adile, Clara Lorentz, Nancy Delisi, Dr. Rosalia Van Tichelt, Camille Dull, Belle Grubert, Sonia Kirschner, Sandy Robertson, Jane Firth, Hildy and Stan Richelson, Susan Shapiro, Jana Nestlerode, Gloria Lutz, Susan and Ona Unger, Helene Abrams, David Giller, Betts S. Gabrielsen Mayer, Dr. Joel Bergman, Dr. Howard Horowitz, Anne and Jim McGee, Dr. Rick and Judy Rappaport, Dr. Sig Van Raan, Dr. Susan Rosbrow Reich, Anastasia Furst, Jessica Dworkin, Dr. Florence Kaslow, Larry Freundlich, Janna Guidas, Marie Maguire, Beth and Tedd Koren, Special Agent George Muller II, Lynya Floyd, Joie Lee, Alex Ross, Lydia Ash, Barbara Donahue, Liz Trupin-Pulli, Brian McCafferty, Susan Batson, Carl Rumbaugh, Pamela Hunter and my mentors, Arthur Stein, Ph.D. and Lew Hunter.

Thank you for your many blessings, your ideas and suggestions, and above all for your loving support and belief in me and the project.

Prologue

He came to me in the middle of a restless night.

His seeking lips, his hands trembling with gentle urgency. I held back and stiffened, but my renegade hands took on a life of their own, exploring the solid sculpted terrain of his back and shoulders. The touch of his hardness filled me with sweet sensations, irresistible quivers. As I drew him down on top of me, seismic pleasures shook me, sent walls cracking, falling, chunks of my self, my rigid vigilant cage, tumbling away in violent surrender. With one time-less kiss he took me where there were no walls; only delicious rivulets, the divine co-mingling, male into female into male.

Until it was all over.

CHAPTER 1

No Shoes for the Shoemaker

On the other hand there was real life.

Scintillating dinner conversations over Lean Cuisine with my teacup yorkie, Milo. The intimate camaraderie of *Queer Eye* or the *E! True Hollywood Story* during the long night hours. And, of course, making the weekly run to Video Village to stock up on DVDs for the weekend. Preferably starring Jude Law, who bore some passing resemblance to my dreamland lover.

It was Monday afternoon and I revisited memories of my sweet incubus while I sat at the paper-strewn desk in the sanctuary of my office. The suite, on the first floor of the high-rise affectionately known as 191, was situated on Presidential Street in the old-moneyed Main Line section of Philadelphia. It was part of a three-room complex that I shared with my best friend Sooze.

A tight budget had forced me to decorate in early Staples: a simple particle board desk covered in alluring faux oak, two sturdy chrome chairs with beige padding, a brown tweed couch and my prized possession, the rust colored leather therapist's chair that Uncle Morty and Aunt Irma had brought to celebrate the opening of my practice. Three large low light palms, a pair of hanging philodendrons and an assortment of beige, orange and brown throw pillows warmed up the space. A tiny nested doll set from Russia, my favorite gift from Babba Pearl, sat on the bookcase, along with tomes of the masters: Freud, Kohut, Minuchin and Lazarus. The only downsides to this healing haven were the chemical smells wafting in and out from the beauty salon next door.

I peeked through the blinds to see if my clients had arrived. Couldn't spot their Jeep so I threw off my loafers and jumped on the couch to look at my legs in the large mirror on the opposite wall. My slip was peeking out below the hem of my Loehman's Back Room special. After pulling it into place, I smoothed the gray wool suit and stepped down to study my face. Pink lipstick emergency time. I pulled out a tube and crayoned it on to brighten the shadows. It's what's inside that counts, I mouthed to myself, not feeling it one bit.

Shrugging to myself, I pulled out the latest gift from a thankful client—one who ended up with the plum job, the divine husband and a pea in the pod to boot. It was a Harry & David tower of treats—a few creamy caramels later I was in a good mood.

A loud noise from the waiting room startled me and somehow I managed to dump my H & D treasure trove on my lap. My clients, Rhoda and Jim had arrived. As I giggled at my undoctor-like predicament, I could hear Rhoda, half-crying, half-screaming at her husband, through the double doors. Quickly propping up dignity, I got up and hurried over to welcome them into the office. They settled down on the couch while I sat on the chair that meant so much to me, half-praying, even though I didn't believe in God, that I could help these people. They were tough.

Each one of their last ten sessions had opened in the same way.

"He gives me nothing, Janna. He never touches me!" Rhoda wailed. A 38 year-old self-absorbed redhead, she elegantly used her carping to drive her husband away while she pleaded for him to come closer. Big tears made her mascara run black streamlets.

Jim sat in stony defiance. He had just turned 40 and lived in an immovable place, the great passive throne that kept him Rhoda-proof and safe. She would be critical and ball-cutting while he gave it right back to her with his silent, demeaning eye-rolling gestures in the super-analytical style of an engineer. They consulted with me to fix their marriage but did none of the assignments I suggested.

I was missing something. But I knew I would get it sooner or later. I usually did, even under the tyranny of managed care. That is, for everyone but myself.

The insurance carriers expected us to produce a magic cure for Sisyphus level problems in just six sessions. But I would end-run them by continuing to see my patients after their insurance had run out at reduced fees, feeling it was the only way I stood half a chance at making a difference in people's lives.

Because I practiced long-term therapy, referrals had dried up. The HMO gatekeepers, the internists and family doctors, were rewarded for not sending patients to specialists like me. After all, the more they could feed patients

Prozac right in their offices and not refer them for therapy the more money they made.

Bottom line: lower fees and fewer referrals left me struggling to pay the mortgage of my cozy nest in Flourtown. At least Rhoda and Jim were private payers, a dying breed who could afford long-term therapy.

"You never come through for me," she complained.

I stopped her. "Never use never. That's the 'awfulizing' word. Focus on how he's behaving in the moment. What is he doing right now?"

"He's not looking at me and his hands are folded across his chest."

"Good. Now ask him for what you want. From a win-win position."

"I want you to look at me, to unfold your arms and..." Her right leg began to tremble.

"Then you'll have another complaint. You're never happy," Jim rolled his eyes.

Before I could speak, Rhoda jolted me as she suddenly stood up and assumed the demeanor of a CNN reporter at the scene of a terrorist massacre. Nervous attempts at composure flitted through her face. "It's a train wreck. We're a train wreck. You know the last few weeks I've worked on the Cigna project every night? Well, Tony is the Cigna project."

The energy in the room shifted like storm clouds brewing on a sickeningly hot day.

Finally, Jim croaked out, "Your boss?"

"I've been living like a mummy, like they took out my heart and put it in a jar. He makes me, makes me feel."

The odors of the hairdresser's noxious perm chemicals wafted in from the hall and commingled with the smell of fear.

Long and painful minutes later, Jim's face turned beet-red and contorted. "That fucking Wop!" Then, without warning, he let out the eerie moan of a mortally wounded wolf. Rhoda moved over and put her hand on his arm. But Jim angrily pulled away, unsteadily rising to his feet.

"Write the check," he spit out, as he opened the double doors and stomped out. Barely maintaining my composure I suggested to the suddenly stricken Rhoda that we meet again in two days. I also promised her I would call Jim.

The feelings that filled me as they left took me back to the heartbreak ravages of Abel land. My parents' wars about money, Babba Aydel, Uncle Morty and Aunt Irma. And hiding while they went at it. One time I crawled into the safety zone of my closet and cowered there for a whole afternoon until my sister liberated me. I'm sure that's why I grew up to be a therapist—to learn how to fix this dreadful feeling, to fill this emptiness.

I finished my Monday hours late as usual, because I tacked on extra time with each client, holding them to me, hoping some last minute inspiration would create a greater breakthrough. My three o'clock just fell in love with the right guy. My six o'clock couple decided to renew their 20 year old marriage vows. By 7:15 PM I closed up feeling exhausted but satisfied. Got into my rusty '89 beige Volvo, turned on MGK and listened to the Spinners sing Rubber Band Man while I wearily drove home.

The route took me first onto Lincoln Drive, the undulating tree-lined speedway that ran passengers through the heart of Fairmont Park, emptying them onto the streets of Germantown and Chestnut Hill. I was mulling so deeply over the best way to handle the erupting affair that I seemed to arrive at my two-story clapboard haven on Wissahickon Street in Flourtown in three seconds flat.

Milo greeted me in a wet whirl of excitement as I walked in the front door, turning this way and that, hopping up and down like a black and tan wind-up toy; a five-pound stuffed animal come to life. Dancing over to the kitchen, he woofed at me to feed him his favorite liver treats. Tossing aside my fatigue, I nuked a Lean Cuisine chicken and rice dinner and poured tiny dog bones into my hand so I could hold Milo while he ate. He wagged his nub of a tail furiously and licked each one of my fingers clean with his sandpaper pink tongue. Then he snuggled into my chest, staring into my eyes adoringly.

"The true love of my life!" I giggled as I planted gentle kisses on his tiny nose.

The rest of the evening was punctuated by constant thoughts of Him. What does he symbolize? Am I that love-starved? Maybe the dreams are sent to liberate me from the walls of fear, my fear of men. Maybe they're meant to teach me about passion, the freedom to feel sexual, the openness I can never seem to have in real life. On the other hand, maybe they're just cruel gifts from the unconscious. The thoughts nagged me as I got into bed late that night. Clutching a pillow and touching myself, I hoped to dream of Him. I slept fitfully and could not remember any dreams at all.

❦   ❦   ❦

"He's the One," I quipped to Sooze, the next day. "I just know it. Only one small problem; he doesn't exist. Other than that…"

Sooze was an old soul wrapped up in an XL 35 year-old body. "Five feet tall and five feet wide" she was quick to say with a sharp-edged laugh. But to me, she was a safe warm harbor.

Sooze had been my anchor for ten years. Though our backgrounds were vastly different, we were a matched set of bookends. We had ended up in the same place, hiding from the world inside our offices as we traded devotion to our clients in exchange for their reassurance, admiration. Even love. In the absence of intimacy with real men, the therapeutic relationship was a powerful substitute.

We talked about it a lot—the countertransference, which kept us out of trouble. Amazingly enough, our dramas could all go on while we were helping people.

"This mystery lover, he sounds like the perfect man—moldable, no moods, no dirty underwear on the floor." Her round face broke into a sweetly mischievous grin. I flashed a smile.

We sat in Flakowitz's hole-in-the-wall bagel restaurant near 191, two 30-somethings, in a barren place of no love, no prospect of children, the clock counting down, and nothing on the horizon. Outside the window life cruelly re-birthed itself, with a spring parade of pin oak and red maple seeds floating down from the sky.

I broke the silence. "With my social life, having a kid would require an Immaculate Conception. I haven't been in a relationship in six years. At least you have Fred. He beats Mystery Lover."

"I don't think so. The drinking has finally pickled his penis. Once a week he closes up the dental office, we meet at the Red Tavern for dinner, he belts down a few rounds of Glenlivet and soda, we go back to my place or to his hole-in-the-wall apartment, and watch TV."

"Maybe he's guilty?"

"Yeah, I'm wondering just how separated he really is." Tension lines etched Sooze's face as she bit into her sesame bagel.

I jabbed my fork at the coleslaw. There was no way to help her find the strength to deal with Fred. But I tried. "Sooze, promises, schnomises. Feels to me like he's still got the old ball. Not to mention the chain." She nodded. "We're heading to Aunt Harriet and Miss Louise territory."

"Ah, yes. Two Main Line biddies getting it on the side from the gardeners at Gladwyne Assisted Living."

❀   ❀   ❀

Tom Cruise was my first client that afternoon. That's what I called him, anyway. Actually Bob was taller and had a more sculpted body, with beautifully formed hands Rodin would have immortalized. Not that I was noticing…

Bob came in for his session smelling of beer. Oddly enough, he looked even more handsome with a little help from Dionysus. Those limpid baby brown eyes were more open and vulnerable and they held mine in dreamy contact.

In previous sessions Bob exhibited the personality of a rock. But this time he carried a Cruise-like charm and a half-cocked grin that drew me in as he came on to me throughout the whole session. In the past, I had no problem dealing with a therapist-patient transference reaction but those damn dreams about Him were driving me crazy with all kinds of longings.

At the very end of the session, Bob stared at me.

"You've shown me more caring than any other woman." His grin spread slowly into a self-satisfied smile. "And I know you're attracted to me too." I jumped up and fiddled with the blinds and then returned to my leather chair red-faced. "Janna, do you believe in destiny?"

I hesitated.

"What do you mean?"

"We are meant to be together." Bob lunged forward and kissed me. I held his hands down, my slender fingers wrapped around the rough skin of those magnificent paws. But as we made contact an electric current coursed through me. I was so shocked by my reaction that I froze when his lips met mine. Their feathery touch felt like a cool breeze on a sweltering day. Finally, and reluctantly, I jerked away.

"This can't be, Bob." I struggled to put on my best therapist's mask. He half-listened as I gave a shaky rendition of the proper therapeutic speech. "Patients become attracted to their therapists the same way that boys 'fall in love' with their mothers at a precise point in their development. Perhaps your feelings for me represent unfulfilled Mother longings. After all, you describe your mother as a cold, abandoning woman."

I could tell Bob didn't buy the psychoanalytic explanation but he dutifully left the office. But that moment, that kiss, wouldn't leave me.

My countertransference took on a life of its own and, as torrential spring rains started to pour out of the sky, thoughts about Bob and his damn hands swarmed around my brain like bees on a honey pot. Despite all of my training,

I couldn't stop the luscious yet dangerous thoughts. Worst of all, my special, sacred dreams of Him became colored with tidbits of Bob. In the tainted dreams, the warmth of a flowing open-mouthed kiss enveloped me and then suddenly the lips became Bob's. Massive sinewy arms snaked around me and Bob's hands cradled my back, pouring sheer shameful pleasure into me.

"You better get into supervision fast, girl." Sooze insisted that weekend at her apartment. "For his sake and yours. Remember when that patient complained about Murray Johnson to the Pennsylvania Board? Claimed he French kissed her one time and he lost his license to practice for two years. They made him go into therapy and supervision. It was a freakin' mess."

"Sooze, don't lecture. You know damn well I would never act out with a client," I maintained.

"Well you can't see him in your condition."

"Look, we've only had four sessions. Why don't I transfer Bob to you? Wait 'til you see him," I snorted.

"Wait 'til he sees me," she guffawed. "He'll be out of the oedipal phase in no time!"

I drummed my fingertips nervously on the arm of my chair while I discussed the transfer with Bob.

"You know best," he said.

Naively, I thought the matter was resolved.

A few nights later I was cooking shrimp stir-fry and preparing for another quiet evening alone when Milo, who was peeing outside, began barking furiously. I looked over and saw the back of a man's legs in the light streaming out of the large window right next to the back door. He quickly sidled away into the darkness, but not before I caught a glimpse of him. It was Bob, peeping at me while I cooked. Horrified, I called Sooze in a panic and learned that Bob hadn't called for a first appointment. There was nothing she could do.

A glass of merlot later I picked up the phone with trembling hands and called Bob, pleading: "You need help."

"I'm so glad you called. Is there something wrong?" His voice had an odd, controlled hollow sound.

"Um, yes, you…you're spying on me." My head felt like a pressure cooker on high.

"Janna, how could you say that?" His voice cracked and trailed off.

Stupefied into silence, I helplessly held the receiver to my ear. Finally, I hung up, a brew of fear simmering in my belly.

Desperate, I called and insisted he go into therapy, if not with Sooze then with someone else. He 'yesed' me unconvincingly.

The stalking was suffocating. He sat like a vulture in his dented green Toyota across the street each night. Somehow he got hold of my home number and kept calling and hanging up. I'd take my messages only to be ambushed by his drunken words, "You and you and only you can complete me…So low without your smell…I know the sweetness…I crave the sweetness, your touch, your smile…Seeing you I will be filled, yes, yes, yes." I came to hate calling for voice mail.

Afraid for his safety and my own, I became terrified of being home alone. All those romantic thoughts had evaporated into a noxious haze of dread.

Bob had a violent father and a mother who had deserted him when he was ten. He hadn't shown any anger towards me. Yet. My ruminations took off from there, dredging up all sorts of stuff from my past. I would jump when the doorbell rang or when a car pulled up to the house.

Even the weather continued to work against me. Each spring day delivered wind and rain, wind and rain, gray and black, inside and outside. Loud storms brought the thunder and lightning to attack my frail wood frame house.

And Mr. Milo? He was no help. The tiny traitor had stopped barking whenever Bob came near. I installed an alarm system and a door lock with a deadbolt. But I continued having trouble sleeping at night.

After three long weeks of being under siege, I poured my heart out to Sooze over lunch at the bagel restaurant. Sheets of rain covered the bay windows and it was dark and suffocating in the closet dining area. I picked at my whitefish special. "Sooze this is wiping me out. I can't sleep. I'm always sick with sinus infections."

I cradled my aching head in my hands.

"What about the police?" She wiped sweat droplets off the red ringlets around her forehead with a folded napkin.

"The Montgomery County cops told me these cases are hard to prosecute. They did put a restraining order on him, though."

"And?"

"And he just randomized his stalking."

"Jan, you need to get away. Listen, I got this brochure in the mail. You fly to San Juan and then take a singles cruise over to St. Thomas, US Virgin Islands for four days and three nights of El Paradiso. Let's go. The last sailing is April 30th."

"But that's only a week away. Besides, I just paid my estimated taxes and I'm broke," I protested.

Sooze was firm.

"You need to escape and so do I. Fred disappeared on me last week," she added morosely. "It's meltdown season."

"But you know how I hate to leave Milo! He won't eat when he's away from me." I took a bite of the whitefish as horrifying images of me parading around in a bathing suit in front of strange men swam before my eyes. Even though I had lost five pounds in the last few weeks, the thought almost made me upchuck—the legacy of a chubby childhood. But I was sure Sooze felt even more insecure, so I didn't dare bring up my size 10 blues.

"Your neighbor's daughter, what's her name, Brooke, loves Milo. She can take care of him. And today's your lucky day. I just got a dividend payment out of the blue."

"I've been barricading the back door every night." My eyes moistened.

"That's it. Dr. Banks has prescribed the tropical rest cure. You're going."

CHAPTER 2

The Meeting

The gauntlet of *The WindSong's* welcoming cocktail party seemed mild compared to the ordeal I had just escaped. I had poured myself into a black sleeveless sheath made of a thin jersey material that showed everything except my I.Q. Regretting this decision, I worried my bulging upper thighs were jiggling like molds of Jell-O. Trying unsuccessfully to pull down my control top pantyhose, I cautiously moved into the danger zone on the aft deck where drinks were being served. Sooze was still in the cabin in her endless getting ready ritual.

The deep blue water rocked the boat and my stomach responded with waves of its own as I checked out the group of 100 or so. Even a stiff Appleton Estate and coke couldn't change the odds—there were twice as many women as men. Balding and paunchy men at that.

Laughter drew my attention to a small group at a white metal table by the railing. Silhouetted against a watercolor swash of sunset was a group salted with all of the eligible men. Three had possibilities; a bronzed rugged-looking guy, a wiry fellow in a Hawaiian shirt and a Mel Gibson look-alike. Two aging Cosmo model types posed siren-like on their perches, holding the men spellbound. I stood awkwardly at the bar, staring at them in my slightly inebriated state and managed to knock over a glass with my elbow. 'Klutzy,' I thought. I had such great self talk.

Just then Sooze made her grand appearance and immediately started flirting with the mustachioed bartender who looked sharp in a Coppertone tan and his dress whites. I shot her a hostile look and said, "What were you doing, preparing for a role as Carmen?"

I felt guilty and contrite almost immediately.

"You know how I hate comparisons to my mother," she snapped back.

When I first met Sooze at the Temple Social Work program I was jealous of her "perfect" family. Suzanne Marie Banks' mother was an impossibly gifted opera diva, both on and off-stage, a dark-haired beauty painted by Guy Buffet to grace the millennium bottles of Perrier Jouet. Her father had a real estate law mega-practice on Rittenhouse Square, the most exclusive address in town.

But there was a tragic flaw. Sooze's weight was the single greatest heartbreak of her mother's life. It couldn't be disguised. It couldn't be ignored. It couldn't even be starved out of her. Sooze suffered from a strange metabolic condition that defeated her mother's every effort. And the diva never forgot it. Screaming matches between them sent Sooze's father ever deeper into the burrows of his work. No eating disorder clinic, no fat camp, no therapist or nutritionist could help.

"Sooze, I'm so sorry. Bartender, a drink for my friend, the mistress of wit."

"What would m'lady desire?" He flashed a pearly smile at Sooze.

"Sex on the Beach," she chortled. Even though I was afraid of being alone on the cruise, I continued to praise Sooze, setting her up with him to offset my faux pas.

A long history with a favored sister had left me testy in triangles. I was the chubby, klutzy one with mouse-brown hair, buried by God's gift to mankind, my older sister Doris. In a bizarre self-hating way, my Jewish mother was crazy about Doris, with her honey-blonde hair and blue eyes. She embodied the consummate *shiksa*. My mother named her after Doris Day and spent hours setting her golden locks with jumbo red rollers. She never brushed, much less set my hair: "That rat's nest is too thick and curly."

Doris ruled over my hausfrau mother; she even named me. In her two-year old vocabulary, Joanna became Janna and the name stuck because both my parents thought the moniker was cute. Anyway, that's why threesomes didn't work for me.

My matchmaking was successful as Sooze arranged to meet the bartender after dinner. At the ridiculously sumptuous buffet I developed another head-ache and couldn't eat much, but Sooze made up for me. Several helpings of mahi-mahi, fried plantains, mango soufflé and pineapple tart later, she went off on her date while I got myself some coffee with pineapple cognac and wandered down to the casino. I was annoyed to find the same group of beautiful people near the blackjack table conspiratorially tittering and telling stories. Nursing my coffee, I sat at a slot machine half-facing them. I studied the tableau: one of the Cosmo girls sat in her white slip dress, bronzed legs crossed, right foot dangling a baby pink Prada sandal as bait for Mel Gibson. The sloe-eyed beauty held the rugged fellow's eyes as she smoothed platinum locks repeatedly like a female macaw. The third possibility, the lean guy, was alluringly unattached.

But I was more comfortable as a therapist than I was socially. And these Palm Beach types were people from the world of my Aunt Irm—a world of ease and entitlement. Socialites, wunderkinds and movie stars in my child's eye.

Mindlessly I began feeding quarter after quarter to the slot machine in front of me until a cache of booty noisily spilled out. I cajoled myself: Janna, if your client was having a flashback you would tell her 'that was then, this is now' and to march over and join the party. Now do it. The therapist inside forced me to yank down the impossible-to-manage black dress and stride valiantly to the line of fire. The boat rocked nervously in response.

I inserted myself near the macaw and said, 'Hi, I'm Janna Abel.'

The clique welcomed me with deafening silence. Eons passed until finally they gave up the faintest of stiff hellos. I nodded, only to be met with subtly downcast eyes and barely perceptible shifts of posture. The next round of silence was broken only by the clink of ice in a glass. Mortified, I put on the blasé mask and stared out a porthole.

But when there was no respite from the fingernails-on-the-blackboard situation, I escaped to the upper lounge and ordered another coffee and cognac. There the evening's festivities reached a new crescendo when a hoarse voice whispered in my ear, "Hey there, pretty lady." With dread rising up my spine I turned around to fend off the ministrations of a brown-toothed septuagenarian. I slunk away to my cabin hoping to leave no scent for him to follow.

The rough starched sheets rubbed against my bare nipples, the sensation making me think of Him, as the boat gently rocked me. I couldn't get into a really deep sleep and I replayed the images, the feelings of His touch to console myself. But I startled out of my sweet reverie when Sooze entered the cabin and went into the tiny bathroom.

I must have nodded off because I was in a familiar place: inside the nightmare I've had since the age of ten. The scene was always the same: The family all together in bumper cars at a kiddy carnival, with Doris and my mother in one car, my father in another, and me in a third. We were bumping each other, laughing and carrying on like boisterous children. Suddenly, all the lights went out. Pitch black.

I lost control of my car and it went hurtling into darkness. It fell over the edge of a huge cliff. I called and called for my mother but she didn't answer. Thrown out of the car, I plummeted down. Falling. Endlessly falling. Panicked, I tried to scream but no sound came out of my throat.

Throughout my life I had awoken from this dream in a cold sweat. But this time, as I was falling, I heard a voice calling out "*Janna, over here.*" I floated in the direction of the call and I saw ahead of me a fine lavender mist. As I moved closer to the voice I could see a shadowy figure. It was terrifying. Yet I continued drifting closer and closer through the mist. When I was arms' length away, I flailed out feebly with my fists. But it grabbed hold and restrained me. I struggled to no avail, horrified, hyperventilating as the vapor began to penetrate my skin. But there was no escaping. The mist passed into me. I smelled the sweet scent of lilacs and slowly, fear drained from my body.

I could not make out the face of the figure that was holding me. Somehow it seemed to be made out of the mist particles. But it had a woman's voice, rich with overtones. "*Consider this: maybe you can go home again.*" A soft touch stroked my forehead and energy streamed from the base of my spine to my crown. The voice continued. "*So the shoemaker can make her own shoes.*" Laughing, I woke myself up.

Relieved but oddly unsettled, I noticed it was three AM. Sooze was snoring in the other bed, so I put a pillow over my head to get back to sleep. The distinctive fragrance remained.

"Sooze, the strangest thing happened. You know that recurrent nightmare where I'm falling? Well, I had it again last night, but with a crazy twist…a kind of visitation from a spirit who rescued me," I reported with some hesitation as we sat together the next morning at another buffet that could feed all of Calcutta.

"Call *The National Enquirer. Aliens Abduct Therapist From Singles Cruise: Many Were Good-Looking*," Sooze joked in between bites of mango pancakes.

"Right. I had sex with one of them and it was out of this world. Seriously, in twenty-five years of having that nightmare, no one has ever come to my aid." I played with the scrambled eggs on my plate and then popped a capsule of the new antibiotic that had been prescribed for my sinuses. "For the past two months Mystery Lover visits me, and now this."

"Wish fulfillment. It's wish fulfillment," Sooze pronounced.

"But why now? I can't think of any day residue that it would be based on."

"We did see *Schindler's List* on cable last week. It brought up your mother's family, how Babba Aydel survived the Holocaust, only to lose her daughter. Schindler was a rescuer. Maybe your mystery lover is Liam Neeson."

"No. He's Jude Law. I told you." I chortled and then became lost in the hypnotic movements of the gray-blue waves.

"Seriously, these new dreams are good. You're making progress on your mother wound. Let's face it, you're a survivor." Sooze tenderly touched my arm.

Survivor. Mother wound. Five long years in therapy obsessing about a single sentence. My final words.

I was nine years old. Mom was taking Doris to see *Hair* as a reward for good grades. My grades were average. As they walked out the door I ran into Doris' room, blind with envy and grabbed her hair rollers, her Maybelline pale peach lipstick, and her favorite Robert Redford poster and threw them in the Penn Fruit Company dumpster behind our house. My raging eyes locked on to my mother as she backed the car out of the driveway. "I HATE YOU!" I shrieked as loud as I could as they pulled away.

It was the last time I ever saw her alive.

The drunk driver hit their car head on. Mother died instantly. Doris spent three weeks in intensive care, bringing home a permanent limp and a wicked scar that marred her glorious shiksa face in spite of all the plastic surgery my father paid for.

After Papa told me, I found myself on the floor, crying and screaming. Then I remember punching two holes in our dining room wall.

The rest of my childhood was shaped by Doris' needs—doctor visits, physical therapy appointments and plastic surgeries. I don't know if my father was embarrassed or horrified by his marred daughter, but he gave her everything she wanted in order to make reparation.

Doris had the credit cards, Wanamaker's clothes and the country club Bat Mitzvah. Papa scraped to send her each summer to Ramah, the ritzy overnight camp. When she wanted a fancy prom dress and chauffeured limousine, he put in extra hours in his accounting office, hunched over his ledger books and pencils. He became washed out, as gray as the pencil marks he made so carefully.

And as Papa disappeared into his papers he put Doris all the way up there, into the fancy world of his charismatic brother, Morty, who not only created money, but married into it.

As for me, I paid penance by asking for very little.

Sooze's round, compassionate face swam back into view.

"How I prayed and prayed for my sister…I thought everything was my fault. When the doctor said she would never be the same…at first I was angry and hated God. Then I dumped Him altogether. I still hate those songs from Hair—dawning of the Age of Crap."

"Yeah, yeah. The Age of Aquarius will precipitate the decline and fall of the American Empire," Sooze recited from memory, with a full mouth of apple chicken sausage and scrambled eggs.

"Our lives were ruined because they went to a play about hope." I squeezed back the tears. "And I'm sorry for ruining this trip."

"Ridiculous. Hey, when we dock at St. John we should go exploring instead of shopping. I read that it's virginal land."

"Just right for me," I joked. "At least I've lost a few pounds. How about this for a book? *Seasick and Lovin' It: Seven Days to a New You.*"

"Six months on top of *The Times* bestseller list, guaranteed," Sooze mocked.

After breakfast we went for a walk on deck. The ship had cruised all night out of San Juan and we were finally docking at St. Thomas. As I saw the lush colors of the island in the glorious morning light, my mood lifted. The azure waters and tropic greens doted with red and gold-pink hibiscus flowers were a welcome contrast to rainy, suffocation of Philadelphia.

Our cruise mates went duty-free shopping in Charlotte Amalie, while Sooze treated me to a private sightseeing tour. Over the years Sooze's generosity included small luxuries and lending me money when times were difficult. She was a trust fund baby who had recently received the second installment of three disbursements from her grandparents. The money was a boon to both of us.

The cabbie dropped us in the quaint town square, a dirt lot dotted with ramshackle kiosks filled with brightly colored pareos and island dresses. In the middle of the mélange of reds and oranges, corals and blues was a magnificent stone statue of a native blowing on a conch shell. It said Freedom for All.

"Freedom from Bob," I declared.

"And Fred," Sooze added. We stood staring at the sculpture.

Just then a Calypso song blared from the boombox of a Black Adonis seated in the square. "Viagra, wake up the living dead. Viagra, make a white man into Africa!" Cackling hysterically, we sang along: "Viagra, wake up the living dead." Adding: "Give it to Sooze's Fred."

Sooze's rest cure proved successful. I unwound, lost a few more pounds and my sinuses cleared up. But the moment the plane touched down on the Philly tarmac, a familiar nausea hit me.

At home, I locked myself in and forced myself to sit on the living room couch to listen to my messages. Mercifully, Bob's voice was not on the tape. There were, however, an endless series of frenetic calls from Rhoda and Jim.

"The son of a bitch choked me," Rhoda screamed. The next two messages were hang-ups.

Then, "Janna, it's me, Jim. She stabbed my thigh with a serving fork. Please call." And so on. They had never called the back-up therapist covering my practice. An exhausting hour on the phone with both of them ended with a cease-fire.

What can I do to get these folks moving in the right direction? I wondered in exasperation.

Milo had waited, studying me attentively while I worked on the phone. When I finally reached for him, he jumped on the couch and snuggled his shaggy body into the folds of my lap. I was so tired I dozed off. There was a hazy blur of images and feelings as I passed into a hypnogogic state. I was dreaming that Bob was chasing me and like a child I could only move in agonizingly slow steps. He was gaining on me. I tried to put one leaden foot in front of the other, but it was too hard. He was coming, coming to get me.

Suddenly the smell of lilac perfumed the air. It was the spirit again. I heard her voice: "*Turn and face him. Fear leads to mastery.*"

A clap of thunder erupted and I was sent flying back towards Bob. As he saw me approaching, Bob started changing shape. I stared with fascination as his face and body metamorphosed. I flew closer and closer until finally I stood on the ground face to face with him. Bob had become me.

CHAPTER 3

An Unwanted Gift

On Friday morning Milo sat, his fuzzy triangle ears on alert, while I brewed the only luxury in my life—Jamaica Blue Mountain Blend. I bent over him and triumphantly announced with a very bad Jamaican accent, "Don't worry 'bout a thing. Cause every little thing is gonna be all right!"

In the few days since the cruise Bob had not appeared once and my relentless headaches had lifted. Loafing on a Hitchcock chair at my oak dinette, I gazed out the window, taking in the cloudless cerulean May sky.

After savoring the last drops of the morning fix, I quickly retrieved Milo's faded red leather leash and collar. He danced around with special enthusiasm because I had put a moratorium on our usual Valley Green excursions during the ordeal. We sped off in the Volvo to meander around the wide dirt footpaths through the budding greenery of Forbidden Drive. Happily I belted out the Motown ditty, *I Can't Help Myself*, by the Four Tops, to the mossy green boulders lining Wissahickon Creek.

When I got home the day's barrage of mail had arrived. I braced myself with another cup of the black elixir, settled at the dinette table and began the most odious chore: paperwork. There was a stack of inquiries from my client, Anne's, insurance company that immediately brought my mood crashing down. Her HMO wanted me to use CPT codes on her bills, the codes that describe the kind of visit the patient had, like individual, couple, or family therapy. They were refusing to pay me until I anted up the codes. This was one of the games insurance companies played to hold on to cash and maximize their float. Of course, I didn't have a current list of codes.

Dutifully, I called their information number and was politely told to call two other extensions, both of which were the wrong departments. Finally, a most helpful administrator gave me the number of the service provider liaison who could "definitely" help me. That number: not even in service.

Sooze phoned to say she wasn't going to Betsy's party that night. Betsy Goldstein, our old professor at Temple, was celebrating the opening of her new Chestnut Hill office. Sooze and Fred were in a spat. After spending an hour on the phone listening to the latest installment of The Fred Show, I noticed five o'clock had rolled around. A nuked turkey tetrazzini dinner later, I threw on a tan cotton turtleneck and a houndstooth jacket with khaki slacks, and took off for the party alone.

That evening the starry skies were clear and a full moon graced the short drive to the quaint cobbled streets of the Hill. The office on Mount Airy Street was in a charming old stone building dating from the 1800s, but the darkness of the parking lot prompted me to move as quickly as possible once out of the car. I ducked into the building and squeezed into the group of twenty or so crowded into the postage stamp party space.

I sat near the antique desk that served as a wine bar, chitchatting away, and sipping a buttery Napa Valley Chardonnay to calm my nerves. As I was pouring myself a second glass, Ron Morgenstern, the burly psychiatrist who handled my medication consults, remarked to no one in particular, "Hey, someone's been sitting in that beat up car for the last hour. I wonder if he's OK."

The telltale Toyota was parked directly across the street but his face was obscured since the street lamp was out. We called the local police but Bob was gone by the time they arrived.

Betsy, seeing I was shaken, took me by the arm into an adjoining office. I had always gotten on with her, I think because she was an older, wiser version of me. Betsy took her trademark orthopedic pillow, positioned it carefully on the couch so she was comfortable, and turned to me attentively. She carried all her tension in her shoulders, held up close to her neck as if braced for attack. Betsy adjusted the jacket of the boxy, checked gray suit she was wearing, folded her arms and listened carefully while I recounted my tale.

"I had consults with Milt and Arnie. They just psychoanalyzed the situation to death. I'm desperate." I choked back tears and cleared my throat nervously.

Unexpectedly, Betsy offered up a solution.

"There's this woman I met years ago at a Temple colloquium who may be able to help you. I'll never forget the title of her lecture—'Coaching Tyrants:

the Difficult CEO.' She was more than brilliant. At the time, my niece worked for a Fortune 500 president, a narcissistic character, extremely powerful and clever. Long story short, he was married and in love with my niece. A man used to eating his cake and having it too. Could have destroyed her whole career. And his too. But after the colloquium, I arranged for this woman to coach my niece and she came out way ahead with no bloodshed. That woman worked wonders."

"What's her approach?" I asked.

"I never did understand it. My niece was secretive about their work together. All I know is that she was promoted to take over one of his subsidiaries without threatening him or sleeping with him."

Desperate, I asked for the woman's name.

"Dr. Raphaela Love," Betsy said, as she shifted her back uncomfortably. "I hear she's odd but don't let that stop you."

According to Betsy, Raphaela was a therapist turned management consultant, who had sold her business and retired to a life of philanthropy. "I may still have her card in my briefcase." She fetched a worn leather satchel from the closet and busily rooted through it. "Here it is. For some reason I held on to it. I hope you can still reach Raphaela at this number."

Betsy handed me a bent lavender card. I grabbed hold of her shoulders and gently hugged her.

Betsy went back to hosting as I made a beeline for the bar. Herb, one of my long-time buddies from graduate school, poured each of us a Chardonnay. I had always liked Herb, even though he was older and a self-proclaimed New-Ager complete with Jerry Garcia beard, wire-rim glasses and a perennial pony-tail of prematurely gray hair. Herb's office was down the hall from mine and we often got together to commiserate about the insurance companies and the modern practice of psychotherapy. His income was way down because, like me, he practiced long-term therapy. Herb liked to pontificate about organizing a group of therapists to go after the insurance companies in a class action suit. But I'd known him for a long time; he was a man of words, not actions.

Herb could see how upset I was about the stalking. As he sipped his wine, he looked at me earnestly. "Maybe you're sitting in this place of fear for a reason, to help you move to a higher spiritual level."

I shot him a dirty look. "Oh please. Don't give me that Mother/Father God loves you; everything has a benevolent purpose lecture. Random shit happens and if you're in the wrong place at the wrong time, you're S.O.L."

"That belief leads to great suffering. Are you sure you want to keep creating that in your life?"

"What choice do I have?"

"Well, the reality I choose to live is that my life is unfolding according to a Divine design. Which means that even when things look bad, they could be good. At least in the long run. So even this crazy guy could turn out to be an unwanted gift."

"Prove there's a plan," I challenged sadly.

"I can't. It's a leap of faith." Herb put his arms around me and offered to follow me home. When we got to Wissahickon Street Herb drove around to check for the Toyota and I was so thankful, I invited him in to have a cup of tea. His presence was like a warm blanket as we sat together in my sparsely decorated living room drinking Earl Grey. He draped himself on my brown corduroy sofa while I sat and rocked in an aging white rocker.

Maybe it was the alcohol. I didn't know who started what; I did go over to the couch to ask him to hold me because he's a good hugger, but the embrace turned into a quick lay on my living room couch. The sex was like masturbation; we just pawed each other more than anything else. Even with a condom he came in three minutes; amazingly, I came a minute later.

Afterwards, Herb kissed me awkwardly on the cheek and told me he couldn't stay over because he had sessions the next morning. We said goodbye and I bolted the front door, wondering about what had just transpired. I worried that the sex, as lousy as it was, would mess up our friendship.

Rather than soothing me, the impetuous episode served to fray my nerves even more. I found myself wandering mindlessly around the house, checking and rechecking the window and door locks. That night, I had a nightmare in which I was surrounded by a group of ravenous wolves staring at me. I woke up. A booming clap of thunder loosed its cannon shot directly over my roof. The digital alarm near my bed proclaimed in an eerie green light that it was 2:45 AM. I padded down to the kitchen to eat a peach hoping food would soothe me back to sleep. The heavens finally quieted and I was pleased to see Bob's car wasn't parked on the street. I thankfully crawled into bed and tried to fall asleep.

The inner storm resurged as I drifted back to being a 15-year old sophomore at Northeast High. That pivotal year a group of boys had made me the butt of their juvenile jokes. They called me "Fumbles" and "Bumblestiltzkin" and teased me unmercifully. At first I liked the teasing. At least it was attention and in my own stupid way I hoped Eric, their leader, actually liked me.

One spring afternoon, I rushed to the girls' gym after school as I was late getting changed into my swimsuit for team tryouts. Aunt Irm had always said that swimming was the perfect exercise for weight loss and down the shore she had arranged for private lessons that had trimmed down my childhood chubbiness. The rank-smelling locker room was unusually quiet since the others were already in the pool. Suddenly, from out of nowhere, I heard Eric's voice. "Hey, Fumbles, what's going on?" I turned around blushing and yelled, "Get out. You're not supposed to be in here." I was shocked to see that he was not alone—we were not alone. The whole gang was leering at me with their beady eyes. Before I could react, Eric had jumped over the bench, grabbed my top and pulled it down, exposing my none-too-developed breasts. I was mortified, shaking so hard I was weak in the knees. He murmured something I couldn't hear—his hot, smelly breath and spittle spraying onto my cheek. Earl, his main sidekick had exposed himself and was stroking his penis. I gurgled out a scream and they scurried away like rats.

They never stopped teasing me and I never did try out for the swim team. Afterward, I became mousy quiet and started getting sinus infections and the flu. When I wasn't sick I began pretending that I was, so I didn't have to go to school. My grades, which used to be all As, began to suffer. Finally I convinced my father to transfer me out of Northeast High.

By six AM the bedclothes were wrapped around my neck and my feet were freezing. I punched my pillow vowing to call Raphaela Love, though I doubted she could help me.

When Raphaela answered the phone later that morning the music in her voice reminded me of the operatic Mrs. Banks. I told her the problem and all Raphaela said was, "Yes, I know. Come tomorrow at 3:00."

CHAPTER 4

Opening Love's Door

Raphaela's careful directions led me through Chester County, a place of lime green forests dotted with early bursts of purple azaleas. Each turn of the road showcased tranquil gentleman farms or still ponds filled with ducks, Canadian geese and a stray swan or two. The chocolate-colored thoroughbred horses gamboling in fenced pastures and the cows grazing in rolling green meadows were as perfect as background movie sets.

Finally I came to the house in Chadds Ford wrapped like a gem in a setting of emerald-green hills. A restored farmhouse with a stone and glass addition, it was a seamless melding of old and new. White-tailed deer fearlessly grazed on the front lawn and three tiny fawns stared at me as I drove to the center of the circular drive in front of the house and parked the car. All the pastoral beauty was somehow annoying.

As I sat there gathering my thoughts I saw an elegant, older man come out. He was slightly graying and carried himself like the rakish officer played by Steve McQueen in The Great Escape.

I immediately felt the uglies kick in: my body image grew chunky. I went to get out of the Volvo and managed to trip and fall right on the driveway. He gallantly came over to help me. As the stranger offered his hand I was touched by his gentle manner and lured by a flirtatious twinkle in his eyes. He proceeded to brush the dust off my corduroy jacket but a quick glance at the wedding band on his left hand ended my fantasies.

I walked over to Love's ornate glass front door and pressed the chime. It was then that the fragrance reached me—lilacs. Two gigantic bushes planted on either side of the front door. Both were in full lavender bloom and their perfume was redolent in the air. A wave of sadness hit me as I remembered my mother's white lilac bush in the postage-stamp garden in front of our rowhouse on Green Street. Each May she would bring in a frilly bouquet and set it on the red brick fireplace mantle in the living room. Maybe Sooze was right; the dream on the cruise came simply from a wish to have my mother back.

Raphaela opened the door. An ageless woman with jet-black shoulder-length hair, her charisma extended outward like the gravity field of a large planet. Raphaela's beauty was accented by a fitted St. John suit with a retro look—an elegant ankle-length outfit designed to show off ample breasts that tapered to a slim waist and long lean legs. Diamonds and gold finished the look.

A wave of disappointment hit me. We're apples and lemons, I thought.

I started to wiggle out of what now seemed to be a ridiculous waste of time and money. "Well I'm not really sure...."

But then I gazed into her eyes, these eyes that took me far away. I stood there fixed like a moth pinned to a display mat. Contessa-like, the woman put out her hand. "I am Raphaela."

I croaked out my name and then stood feeling like a young schoolgirl. Raphaela ushered me in and as I followed her I managed to knock over a small Chinese jar with a golden floral motif that was sitting on a Queen Anne table by the front door. I blushed and apologized but she ignored the mishap. Luckily the urn didn't break.

Raphaela silently motioned for me to sit on a sofa in the living room, as she sat on an overstuffed brown leather armchair. The space was beautifully furnished with highly polished antiques, oversized leather furniture and early Americana knickknacks. Old bridle bits and railroad ties were done up into contemporary sculptures and dried flowers were hanging from weathered barn wood ceiling rafters. Rich brocaded throws in tones of gold, turquoise and magenta set a warm tone. In the center of the floor lay a spectacular navy blue Persian rug.

Raphaela looked at me in a totally focused yet unfocused way. I blurted out my troubles, the stalking, the sleeplessness, the hiding and fear, the high school sexual abuse, and that I had spent about five years in therapy. Raphaela sat motionless, not uttering a word. I noticed she had long fake nails. A marquise diamond ring that must have weighed in at four carats sat prominently on her right hand.

She's so superficial and Botoxed out…ridiculously expensive too, I thought. Maybe I can cut this short.

As I shifted uncomfortably in the seat the diamond, so oddly beautiful, like a lighthouse lamp from another world, drew my attention and held it. Within moments, relaxation and then serenity washed over me.

"That ring. Where did you get it?" I asked Raphaela.

"A dear friend saw the gem in meditation; saw that it was meant to help me in my work and where it was to be found. He went and bought the ring for me."

Oh please, I thought. Some people go to Tiffany's and brag but this woman has to make up elaborate New Age bullshit.

Yet, an odd peaceful feeling persisted. Then I noticed she had a rainbow of nail polish bottles on the table at her side. Raphaela opened a bottle of neon yellow nail polish and began to carefully paint the tips of her long tapered fingernails.

"What…" I asked, unnerved. "I think I have to go." I got up to leave.

She waved the polish brush at me. "Not if you really want to change your life."

I stood staring at this strange creature of a woman, uncertain of what to do. She quietly painted a thin line of orange polish next to the yellow on each nail.

"I have gifts."

"You look busy."

"Especially for you." She pointed the orange brush at me. "Sit."

So I'll give it five minutes, I thought, as I sat back down on the couch.

"We begin with Lesson One: *Fear lights the way to mastery.*"

"That seems familiar." My feeling of discomfort grew as Raphaela continued painting her fingernails into mini-rainbows.

Finally she spoke. "Do you want to know what that means?"

"Yes, if it'll help me stop Bob."

"That and much more."

I nodded.

As she started applying topcoat she continued, "When we are adults, fear is a signal, the alpha point, while mastery is the omega or end point. Fear tells us where we need to rally, what we need to do in order to build courage, personal power, and freedom."

"Oh, come on! Aren't some fears reasonable? I mean you wouldn't walk out in front of a speeding freight train."

"Fear is a scout that plays two different roles in our lives. When we are children it teaches us about the rules of safety and survival in the world. It is the scout who says, 'Back off. Don't go there'. But later on fear can play a whole new role. Can you guess what that is?"

"Freud said that the fear is the wish," I responded.

"Freud teaches that we often long for what we fear, especially in the sexual arena. That it can serve as to uncover what we truly desire. But it is more than that. Fear can be the beginning of a call to right action. And that, my dear, is a spiritual gift." Raphaela wiggled her rainbow fingertips at me. "Bob is bringing you a gift."

I rolled my eyes. "Please."

Raphaela remained unfazed. "A gift that comes not consciously from him, but one that you may consciously give to yourself."

"How?"

"By stretching and moving outside your comfort zone. And thus, healing yourself." She finished her second coat and closed the polish bottle. Then she spread her fingers, admiring her artwork. "For you it is a singular opportunity. After all, you have spent your whole life in hiding."

"How do you know that?"

"It's written all over you. You've been stunted in your growth—acting like a fearful child." I was stung by her words, knowing what she was saying was true.

Raphaela continued, "What you have missed out on is a full life of mastery."

"I'm pretty damn proud of my social work degree. And my clinical work. I'm good, really good at what I do."

"For other people. But for you?" Raphaela cocked her head. "You wanted a Ph.D., right?"

"How did you know that?"

"You fail yourself because you are plagued by inner and outer demons that you have not confronted."

She can't be reading my mind, can she? I wondered anxiously.

Raphaela continued. "The extraordinary life is one in which we continuously take on higher and higher challenges by overcoming our inner saboteurs and outer enemies. To do this we must transmute discomfort, scary situations and difficult people into guides that can ultimately lead us to freedom." Raphaela crossed one slender leg over the other and jiggled her pointy-toed navy Jimmy Choo in my direction.

"What about just being? Just reacting? You can't always be stretching." I noticed I was digging my fingernails into the palms of my hands.

"You have received a wake-up call from Bob. Just as many of us did with the fall of the Twin Towers."

I crossed my arms over my chest and glared at her. "A lot of people were traumatized by that senseless brutality."

"Yes, they were. But many heard the call and changed their lives. You didn't."

"I counseled a bunch of people with post-traumatic stress after 9/11…"

"But how did you change?" she prodded.

"I was shaken."

"Not woken up."

"Well…" I frowned.

Raphaela stood up, clapped her hands like an opera diva and recited,

∾

Friend, wake up! Why do you go on sleeping?

The night is over—do you want to lose the day the same way?

Other women who managed to get up early

Have already found an elephant or a jewel…

So much was lost already while you slept and that was so unnecessary…

In your twenties you did not grow

Wake up! Wake up!

Kabir says: The only woman awake is the woman who has heard the flute.

"I don't understand," I admitted.

"It's about waking up, rising out of the day to day auto-pilot chatter that runs our lives, the unconscious state in which we avoid what that which makes us uneasy."

"I've done a lot of journaling…"

"Not enough to awaken yourself from your basic denial."

"OK. What denial?"

"The denial of loss. Of death, your certain fate and your greatest fear. Facing that death is always at your shoulder would give you life. The precious gift of each hour, each day, each month and each year. Instead you are mindless, unconscious, forever preparing to live tomorrow but never today. In the flow of the present. As a result you squander precious time in activities that don't really matter."

"Counseling people is not exactly squandering…"

"That is for others. What do you do for yourself? You live in the cursed pettiness that belongs to women who live their lives as if death will never touch them."

"It's depressing, Woody Allenish, to dwell on death."

"Death is the biggest ally, the wisest advisor, we have."

Let me out of here, I thought.

Raphaela's eyes flashed as she leaned forward and grabbed my arm with her rainbow-colored fingertips. I broke out in a sweat.

"You can get away from me. But not from death. Or your destiny." Raphaela's grip tightened on my arm. A shiver sped down my spine. "Begin the heroine's journey."

"I guess I'm afraid that Bob…well, his father used to beat him with a belt buckle. I'm afraid he might take out a gun and shoot me in a drunken rage…" I began to feel faint.

"Good. Face it. Your healing journey starts in the darkness of your worst nightmares. Anger. Power. Self-protection. They scare you."

"Not completely."

She laughed. "You get lost in the 'what ifs'. You sacrifice your attention, your best self to the demon that lies within, by not acting. For yourself."

I nodded, blushing.

Raphaela's eyes twinkled. "You are a Jonah."

"What?"

"In the bible Jonah was terrified when God called him to become a prophet and save the pagans of Nineveh."

"I just love the bible," I said wryly.

She ignored me. "Instead he fled on a ship. After a storm he was swallowed by a whale. For three days he was stuck deep in the belly of the giant, hidden in fear.

"But he got out, didn't he?" I asked.

"Only when he recognized he had fled from his true purpose and asked for a second chance. Inside the whale, that is, in his darkness and in his absolute terror, Jonah experienced a transformation. And then the whale released him. He went to Nineveh, began preaching and helped the Babylonians repent for their sins. Because of him God spared the city."

"Well, I'm no prophet," I muttered.

Raphaela's eyes met mine. "We are all called to be prophets in our own lands, be they big or small. You can avoid the message and risk living in the belly or use it to enter the world of possibility."

"I just want to get away from Bob."

"Hogwash. I know you want to play full out for yourself in the world. It's an illusion to think that you can't."

"I, I…," I stuttered.

"It's time for you. I will help you reclaim the power you have given away."

"But how?"

"We'll start with Bob. I know how you can be a Jonah, how you can liberate yourself and him." My ears perked up. "Then we can handle the others."

I wondered who she had in mind, but I figured we better get right to Bob. Anxiously, I folded my arms.

"What do you suggest about Bob? The legal system has been useless and I don't have a clue…"

"Lesson one implies that your strength lies in facing what you fear. You can't run and you can't hide."

"And…"

"You must take action with all your cleverness and might, action that brings a win-win solution to all." Raphaela stared at me with fierce intensity.

"And your suggestion is…?"

"Will you do exactly what I suggest?"

"I don't know. What is it?"

"I will not tell you until you agree to follow through."

"This is a ridiculous leap of faith you're asking for." I began to worry that she was a weirdly insane. And a control freak to boot.

Raphaela grinned. "Faith is precisely what you need."

"Right," I said sarcastically.

"You are not sincere. You can leave now."

Bitch, I thought. But I was desperate. "OK, I swear I'll do whatever you say."

"Call Bob on the phone and arrange to meet him."

"What, are you crazy?"

"You have to look fear in the eye and conquer it—in a safe way of course."

"How in the world…"

"Bob is acting like a boy who is lost and out of control. You must confront him, discipline him and set him on the right path."

"I tried that already."

"Please," Raphaela smirked as I turned beet red. "You had no vision for an outcome that encompassed both your safety and his healing."

"You're right."

"We're going to role-play so that you understand what I mean. You play Bob and I'll be you. Ready?" I nodded. "Bob, this is Janna. Your behavior is completely out of control and you need help. Do you want to wind up in jail and ruin your whole life?"

I thought to myself, be Bob. "No, Janna, I…"

Raphaela interrupted. "Bob you are at a turning point. This obsession could escalate way out of control. Do you want to destroy everything you have?"

"I've already told you it's not me," I/he said defensively.

"That's absolute bullshit. Look Bob, I care about you and want to help you straighten this mess out. But you must stop the path you're on right now before you hurt yourself any further."

"You care? You threw me out of therapy."

"You cannot see me. It won't work. But what I'm willing to do is to come with you to a great psychiatrist who can help you. You need medication for your depression and AA to deal with your alcoholism. If you agree to this program, I'll meet you at the psychiatrist's office for the first session. And if you, in good faith, work hard on yourself, you can email your progress to me monthly. Are you game?"

I was stunned by her direct and confrontational approach. In my role as Bob, I felt grounded and more stable.

"Yes," I/Bob replied.

"But this stalking behavior is disgusting and completely out of bounds. It has to end. Now."

Raphaela arose abruptly. "Our time is up." She paused and looked at me intently. "I know you can do this. You're more special than you know."

I smiled nervously as stood up to leave. She beamed at me. "Come back. I have more for you."

"I don't know…"

"My fee for today is $200."

I gulped, paid her and left. My stomach was in knots and I couldn't eat for the rest of the day.

CHAPTER 5

Staring Down the Demon

Thursday afternoon I sat in Sooze's roomy two-bedroom condo at 191 that was my nest away from home. On the 20th floor, its huge windows opened out over a green sea of treetops. I loved sinking into the overstuffed sofa she had strategically placed overlooking the soaring expanse of sky and forest, loved the warmth of her book-strewn hodgepodge of pine tables and bookcases. Sooze had two Georgia O'Keefe prints, larger than life pastel flowers, across from the sofa that imbued the room with stillness. And she always had Sarah McLachlan or Alanis Morissette serenading in the background.

As we lounged on the sofa noshing on bagel chips and cheese dip, I told Sooze about what happened with Bob. "After I left Raphaela's, frugality finally pushed me over the edge. $200! $200 would go to waste if I didn't act. First I lined up Morgenstern, who agreed to meet with Bob and me. Then I called Bob and it worked!"

"Unbelievable." Sooze mopped sweat droplets from the side of her face with a folded napkin.

"Besides therapy, Bob has agreed to go to AA." I scooped up a big dab of dip and stuffed it in my mouth. "I think disciplining Bob helped him contain his feeling out of control so he could stop acting like a jerk. He needed a strong parental figure to stand up to him. But it was corrective for me too. At some level, I've been afraid of men my whole life."

"Who isn't?" Sooze chortled.

"Thinking back, I can see that Raphaela disciplined me and that made me feel stronger."

"She still should have subtracted her manicure time from the fee."

"I giggled. "She is one tough bagel. She insisted, in advance of any recommendation, that I promise to follow through on her advice. Then, when I spat out a bullshit half-hearted 'okay', she told me to leave the office."

"Wow!" Sooze said as she opened a new bag of chips along with smoked Gouda. "Thank God I didn't have to see Bob! He reminded me of that creep, Dennis, who left you standing in the middle of Walnut Street on Christmas day." She pulled the hem of her blue floral print shift down over her thighs.

"Yeah, at least he only lasted six weeks. I manage to fall for the sprinters."

Sooze wiped yellow crumbs of cheese from the front of her dress. "By the way, I heard Raphaela Love studied family therapy in the early '70s with the founders at Child Guidance."

"Well I've nosed around too and got all kinds of rumors. Phil at Child Guidance said she had some unbelievable family tragedy that ruined her—she lost her whole practice and became a total recluse. But she managed to pull herself out of the hole by going to India and studying with gurus. Supposedly Love has mastered the siddhis."

"You mean she's taken Philadelphia by storm, not to mention New York or LA?" Sooze twinkled.

I smirked. "Not cities, 'sid-hees'. Herb told me they're super powers that were given to advanced meditators and seers. Patanjali, a Hindu sage, one of the originators of Yoga, supposedly described them about 2000 years ago. According to legend he developed exercises that led to the cultivation of telepathy, astral projection, clairvoyance and levitation."

Sooze affected a stuffy British accent. "Naturally. All those Harry Potter books are true, you know."

"But she did give me some wacky story about her ring."

"Tolkien's magic ring of Mordor, no doubt."

I quickly changed the subject. "What's doing with Fred? I thought you two made up last Friday."

"Sort of. But he didn't call me this week. So he must be with the wife." She jabbed at the Gouda with a small knife. "I'm going on Prozac. It'll pick up my mood and may help me lose some weight. Anyway, I don't have sex often enough to worry about arousal."

"What about St. John's Wort?" I suggested. "I've been reading up on herbs. Better to go natural—less side effects. One of my clients is taking St. John's Wort and she's definitely less depressed. Might try it for my moodiness."

I took a bite of the smoked cheese.

"You know," she continued, ignoring my remarks, "work used to make me happy. Now with ignorant 23 year-old HMO case managers dictating what problems are or aren't covered, it just makes me feel screwed over. Just last week this caseworker told me, ME, that helping my patient through a painful divorce would not be covered by insurance. 'That's a problem of everyday life,' she insisted. I yelled back, 'And what about the bottle of Xanax she took?'"

Sooze wiped some damp hair off her forehead. "She finally approved six sessions, but this is the daily serving of crap we get," she said bitterly. "Maybe we should move to England. There they offer 30 sessions a year to depressed dogs and their owners."

"You're damn lucky to have your trust fund. It doesn't matter how much you make from doing therapy. You can travel; do anything, including not working."

"That would be great. Then I could eat constantly and get more depressed. At least when I'm with my clients I'm too embarrassed to stuff food in my mouth, even when they offer."

"Did you speak to Fred about wakin' up da livin' dead?"

"I told him one of my clients turned into a love machine on the drug. By the way, Fred was Mr. Romance on Friday."

"No kidding?"

"Yeah, complete with roses. Probably felt guilty for sleeping over at the house with the wife. He promised he wouldn't do it again."

"And you believed him?" I asked skeptically.

"Well, that's the point, I didn't. I was still fuming but happy that he came over to apologize. When he started slowly kissing my neck, I melted. He worked his way down to my breasts, trailing soft kisses with just a hint of lust. It was so erotic, so titillating, so not Fred. And then the rage took over and I said something that destroyed the whole evening." Sooze teared up.

"What did you say?"

"I used the 'W' word."

"You brought up his wife again? That was bad timing."

"Yeah, he lost his erection." Tears dripped slowly from her eyes. "I did have an epiphany, though. I realized that we've been screwing each other over, tit for tat. He's probably been two-timing me all along while I emasculate him with hostile remarks when we start having sex."

I handed Sooze a tissue and hugged her.

I flashed back to my affair with a graduate school professor, Dr. Stokes. He was so sophisticated to my 20-something eyes, splurging on dinners at the

White Dog Café, sharing his research plans, the outline of his latest book. He took me to the ballet and the Barnes Museum. All the while I felt blessed and privileged to be in his company. He was all tall and lanky with sandy hair and a mustache that tickled when we French kissed. How great it was to make love right there on his desk in Solomon Hall! Stokes didn't even take off the corduroy jacket and cowboy boots he always wore. He would just take out this enormously long, thin penis and give me more pleasure than I knew existed. It was illicit, shameful, delicious. Until the end, when I got brave enough to start making remarks about how frightened he seemed in dealing with the 'W'. Then he dumped me quickly and unceremoniously. In hindsight, I think I ended the tryst with those not so subtle, ball-cutting digs. I resented his wife getting all the goodies and I sure as hell couldn't compete with her. Another triangle, another Doris, another loss.

God, I hated him. That prick exploited me and he knew better. He studied abuse, damn it. Of all people, he should have understood how reprehensible it was to take advantage of someone who has less power. At least Fred was just a regular shmo.

My reverie was broken by a sudden 'tap,tap,tap' at the window. Startled, Sooze and I looked up and were confronted by an enormous crow sitting on the windowsill. The glistening black bird cocked its head, looked in at us and then tapped rhythmically on the windowpane. We stared as the crow repeated the strange behavior. Finally it dropped one huge iridescent black feather and flew off into the air.

Sooze said. "That's never happened before. Crows don't usually fly this high."

"Maybe it was Raphaela, trying to tell us something," I added, jokingly. "Don't shamans and such believe in messages from power animals?"

"Stop getting woo-woo on me."

"The Raphaela raven says you're right. You're bitchy, bitchy, bitchy, with Fred." Sooze threw a couch pillow at me and missed. We shared a giggle.

"Seriously," I continued, "I am definitely whacked because…."

"You don't want to see Ms. Strangelove again?"

I shook my head yes. "There's something about her, about the way she looks at me. Or through me."

"She paid more attention to her nails than you."

"Did not. Anyway that's probably why I'm going back. I feel different with her, frightened, excited, I don't know. She's so supremely confident…"

"Transference, transference, I say. And she's too expensive," Sooze insisted.

"Yeah, but look where one consultation got me!" I protested, "Can I borrow a few bucks?"

"First you bust my balls and then you want money?" Sooze shook her head in a mock scolding. "How much?"

"Four hundred?" I asked in a suddenly tiny voice.

"It's highway robbery," Sooze teased as she went to the bedroom to get the checkbook.

"Maybe she was right that fear could have spiritual significance," I called out after Sooze. Herb had described the stalking ordeal as a 'spiritual crisis'. I shook the thoughts out of my head, went over to the window and opened the sash to retrieve the shiny black feather from the outer sill.

As soon as I touched the silky plume, my imagination turned it into a black arrow about two feet in length. Its diamond tip blinded me momentarily with a reflected flash of sunlight. Alarmed, I dropped the shaft and as it fell, it changed back into a feather that wafted slowly into the leafy canopy, out of sight.

❦   ❦   ❦

The next Sunday, I got lost on winding lanes, sliding this way and that on a rain-slicked day, as I drove to the second meeting with Raphaela. The pounding rain and the hammering slosh of wipers on the foggy windshield seized my neck and upper back into aching knots. Ambivalent and tired, I arrived fifteen minutes late. Looking out the window I saw Steve McQueen in the detached garage puttering over an old Porsche.

When Raphaela finally ushered me in, she looked completely different. Warmer, more down to earth. She wore little makeup and her ebony hair was pulled back in a loose ponytail, held by a gold-chained Hermes scarf. But even a plain denim shirt-dress couldn't hide the fact that she was still stunning. Raphaela motioned me to the couch while she seated herself on an elaborate rococo-carved wood chair with blue velvet padding.

"How's Bob?" Her gaze was intense as if she somehow knew of my ambivalence towards her.

"He's all set up with Dr. Morgenstern and I've been released from prison," I said as I massaged the spasms in my neck.

"The warrior marshaled her special arrows," Raphaela laughed. Chills went up my spine.

"Raphaela, for a moment I thought I saw a diamond-tipped arrow…"

"When you choose the path of mastery, you shift your path in the direction of beauty and magic." She beamed.

"But it was really a crow's feather," I insisted.

"Everything comes into existence as a result of consciousness," Raphaela said.

"What is that mumbo-jumbo supposed to mean? You can't create objects just by thinking," I challenged. "It must have been a stress-related illusion."

"And is that not as a result of consciousness?" She challenged. "For now, just relax and enjoy the journey. How did you feel after you left Dr. Morgenstern's office?"

"Giddy. Euphoric."

Raphaela laughed heartily. "When we break through the confines of fear, the energy patterns of our physical bodies shift into a more relaxed and symmetrical state. This happens with a great burst of light that we experience as joy."

"And since the confrontation I've been more peaceful."

Raphaela nodded. "You reclaimed something for yourself."

"I had a dream…Bob turned into me. I think it symbolized that I had put my own power onto him. After facing him, I feel stronger, like I've taken it right back," I said, gesturing at my belly. I studied her face. "Raphaela, I'd like to study with you."

Raphaela whipped out a compact and started applying shiny pink lipstick.

Here we go again, I thought to myself.

"Study what?" she asked.

"Well, living, I guess," I said sheepishly.

She blotted her newly pinked lips with a tissue. "Why should I take you on? You have lived narrowly and lost in judgments. You are closed off, afraid to speak the truth." Just then a thunderbolt boomed over the house and I jumped. Raphaela didn't react.

"But you said to come back. There's a void in my life, sadness, a hunger I need to fill." I countered. "And, look what happened to me after you touched on the first lesson."

"There are many more."

"I want to study them."

"If and when you master the first one," her jade eyes flashed. I trembled in response, afraid she was using hypnosis to control me. To regain my equilibrium, I used a clever trick honed to perfection by my clients: I started asking her questions.

"Is that your husband or boyfriend outside?"

"No, that's Bill Boros. We work together in a group called the Minyan on humanistic projects. And we just did a little Botox party."

"He's Boros, the philanthropist billionaire? I read about him in the papers," I straightened up to peer out the window. "What are you working on?"

"We may discuss that later." She dabbed at red marks on her face and then looked at me with her transfixing gaze. "Back to Lesson One, *Fear lights the way to mastery.* This is a central teaching for you because your life has been shackled by fear. What demons still frighten you? Who do you need to confront in your internal or external worlds?" Just then Raphaela's phone rang and she answered it. "Yes, I'll take the seaweed wrap at two and the massage at three. And I want the Photofacial." Here we go, I thought….wrong place, wrong time. She turned back to me and whispered, "Your demons—think."

She hung up and went off to the kitchen while I mentally went through a list: Dad? Doris? Mom? Baba Aydel? Stokes? Vincent? Vincent, yes, Uncle Vincent.

My thoughts drifted to the period after Mom died, when her mother, Baba Aydel, and Mom's much younger brother, Vincent, came over to help out. Vincent was just six years older than I was, dark, swarthy, with ugly horn-rimmed glasses. He took me down in the basement and played "horsy" with me on the couch that smelled like mouse shit. He bounced me on his leg, stimulating my crotch and then he took me on his lap to "tickle" me down there. Our playtimes seemed innocent enough, and at first I remember looking forward to his visiting. At first.

The sex play went on for a couple of years until I turned 12. I noticed something hard in his lap and he was pressing me against it more and more. That's when our play became wrong and shameful, but I didn't want to hurt his feelings so I didn't stop him. I just made myself scarce whenever he came over.

Only when I was 25 and in graduate school did I realize that Vincent's behavior was not normal. Ironically, it was Dr. Stokes' work with sexually abused children that opened my eyes. In class one day, he showed a videotape of a social worker counseling a family in which the 17 year-old was accused of peeping on his younger teenage sister while she dressed. The voyeur had drilled a hole in the bathroom wall that adjoined his bedroom and whenever the 13 year-old girl took a bath or changed clothes he had a ringside seat. The victim told the therapist and stunned parents that when they went out her brother would also get drunk, wrestle her to the ground and force her to have sex.

Watching the videotape brought memories of Vincent and me rushing back with a whole herd of bad feelings that threatened to trample me. After the tape ended, Stokes reviewed the statistics on sexual abuse. I'll never forget his words. "Russell's landmark study has shown that uncle-niece incest is the most common. Numerous therapists have reported traumatic effects for survivors, including nightmares, insomnia, depression and revictimization."

Revictimization. That's what happened in the stench of my high school gym with Eric and Earl. Holy shit, he's talking about me. The thoughts hit like lightning bolts as I sat stunned, stuck to my seat. After class, I dragged myself across the Quad to Stokes' office in Solomon Hall and choked out my shocking realization about Vincent and me.

Stokes referred me to a colleague, Dr. Jim Stellar, and that was the beginning of my therapy. Ironically, I wound up telling his friend more about the trials and tribulations of the affair with Stokes than about the incest.

When the affair finally ended, Stellar encouraged me to open up about the abuse. He assured me I was not alone, that one in five women have experienced incestuous behavior. Talking it out and being with a kindly father figure that wasn't repulsed by what I had done definitely helped.

It became clear that the affair with Stokes, a professor who had power over me, was a whole new episode of abuse. I was furious, but too weak and frightened to bring him up to the University Ombudsman on charges of sexual exploitation. I was 'busy' writing my Master's thesis on the consequences of sexual abuse, with another professor as chair of my committee.

At that moment in Raphaela's office, I acknowledged to myself that Vincent was still my demon. In spite of therapy and my thesis research, I realized I still suffered from post-traumatic stress disorder: that's why I reacted so strongly to Bob's stalking.

It started to pour heavily outside the farmhouse windows by the time Raphaela came back from the kitchen with an elegant, highly polished silver teapot and matching cups on an ornate tray. She poured steaming mint tea and I set mine on a small side table near the couch. Just thinking about Vincent turned my stomach. Raphaela looked at me with compassion and said, "Yes, what's coming to mind?"

"Uncle Vincent," I stammered.

"He abused you sexually. Tell me about it."

I was startled. "It's kind of a long story. When I was nine, my mother and sister were in a serious car accident. Mom was killed and my sister, Doris, wound up with a limp and facial scar. I spent a lot of time in therapy working through my guilt."

I'm sick of the whole saga, I thought to myself.

"So you were a motherless child, left unprotected." There was a profound moment of silence. "And what happened with Uncle Vincent?"

I told her the abridged version of Vincent and the games while I comforted myself with warm sips of tea. "It wasn't that bad," I said, "in comparison with the more gruesome incest cases I studied for my thesis."

"Vincent screwed you over when you were a child and you're still paying the price. It was that bad. You've been afraid to tell the whole story about what happened."

Man, is she different, I thought. Dr. Stellar was always damn careful to be non-judgmental.

Suddenly a violent pain arose in my throat and I fought desperately to choke back the sobbing. It was that bad. After a paroxysm of coughing, I regained some remnant of composure by sipping the tea.

Raphaela continued, "And what was going on inside you while he was using you like that?" Again, her pointed questions were cutting through my denial and minimization.

"He used to call me 'little flirt' and I felt like the games were my fault. I was afraid he'd tell Babba Aydel. When he started touching me…"

"Where did he touch you?" she interrupted.

"My crotch." I blushed.

"Lesson one means speaking the truth that you fear to say. At the right place and time. For you that is right here, right now. Tell me one thing you have never told anyone, including Dr. Stellar," Raphaela challenged.

Images of blood-spattered panties came to me. It wasn't my period, the symbol of beginning adulthood, but a loss, childhood's end. "Robbed, he robbed me. He took my virginity when I was twelve." There I said it, I thought, as shame kicked up in my belly.

Raphaela watched me with a nonchalant expression.

"He did much more, didn't he?" she said, not as a question but as a statement.

Vague alarm bells tolled, protecting a part of me that was dimly sensed, hated. I remembered nasty desires, the dirty flirt, hidden. My neck and shoulders tensed up with stabbing pain.

Wanting a place to rest, to hide, I curled up into a ball on the sofa.

"You're disassociating." Again, Raphaela was right. "Stay with me."

"I'm so tired right now," I croaked out.

"Janna, the shame-filled pockets are there." I was startled at how she saw into the core of me. She went on, "But you must lance them and let the poisons out." Her face radiated empathy.

"The night I found the blood, I was afraid something was wrong with me, but more scared to tell anyone. Afterwards, I made up all kinds of excuses not to see Uncle Vincent, pretending I was sick, staying in my room, going to the movies when he came over. But eventually he would find me. I started going numb, playing arithmetic games in my head while he fooled with me." Dredging up this crap made my head pound.

"You were innocent and unprotected, just like the fawns that play on my front lawn," she pointed out the front window, "and that bastard really hurt you."

"I understand what happened but still haven't healed." I sat up and implored. "Can't trust men, I act out sexually…half the time I disassociate and don't enjoy the sex. Women never really get over this."

"Yes, they do." She leaned over and took my hands in hers. "Tell me one more thing you've never told anyone."

Raphaela held me with her eyes.

"Oh, I, ah…" Speak the unspeakable? I fretted. "Give me a few minutes."

"You're in control, Janna."

I took a deep breath. It seemed impossible but I needed to rid myself of the plague, cleanse my spirit of him once and for all. "He, he…. fucked me one time." I whispered. I wanted to run out of the room.

"Say more. It's OK, I'm here." Raphaela squeezed my hands.

"Dad was away at the hospital. Doris was having a third round of re-con-structive surgery, the final operation that made her face look almost normal. Vincent came over to keep me company and we got into the cognac Dad kept in the kitchen pantry for guests." I felt faint but the nausea had subsided.

"How old were you?"

"Thirteen."

"Then what happened?"

"We ended up drinking on my father's bed. I was feeling dizzy and laughing at Vincent's stupid jokes. He started to tickle me, and then he grabbed me and jumped on top of me. When he pulled my jeans down and then my panties, I thought that he was going to touch me again. Instead, he pulled down his shorts, and then I saw his penis all erect. It looked huge and gross. Frightening."

"Go on."

"When he entered me it hurt…but then I didn't feel much. He grunted and made these weird moans. He wasn't that heavy, but I wanted him to get off me. I said, 'stop, you jerk.' Then suddenly, he pulled out. I ran to the bathroom and locked the door."

"That low-life loser!" Raphaela scowled as she sat on the couch and put her arm around me. "If I had been your mother I would have protected you, guarded my sweetheart. And your uncle would have been in serious trouble the first time he tried to touch you."

Raphaela remained next to me, utterly still and I became joined to her, like a boat in safe anchorage.

But the calm was quickly disturbed and in its wake arose self-condemning thoughts; how disheveled I must look, how ridiculous, with my face all red. As these lovely reflections began to torment me, Raphaela tapped my forehead. The inner haranguing abruptly stopped.

"Excuse me for a moment, I'll be right back." Raphaela went into another room and came back carrying a perfectly round crystal about six inches in diameter that sat on a filigreed brass pedestal with three legs. "Blow on it," she insisted.

This is crazy, I thought, but I complied anyway.

Raphaela instructed. "Watch it a few times and you will desensitize and detach from the whole story. Only you will see what you need to see."

As I stared into the glassy surface I was astonished to see holographic figures of Vincent and me enacting the drunken scene. The painful play repeated itself in the crystal ball in an endless loop. By the fifth repetition, my horror and shame had vanished along with the images themselves. She must be using a very powerful form of hypnosis, I thought.

Raphaela took the crystal ball back into the other room. Blinking back thankful tears, I felt awe and love for Raphaela. She returned, handing me a tissue.

"Good work, my dear."

I looked around and took in the tapestry of the room with its marvelous antiques and multicolored throws as if seeing it for the first time.

"You are in a state of mastery. Fear lit the way, yes?"

I nodded.

"Is there any more you need to say?"

"Yes," I heard myself say, to my surprise. I hugged the gold silk throw pillow that was next to me. "In the beginning I felt pleasure with Vincent."

Just then my elbow jerked and knocked over the teacup on the side-table. To my horror, the brown stain slowly spread out along the corner of the Persian rug. Nonplussed, Raphaela walked to the kitchen and brought back some wet paper towels. I took them and dabbed furiously at the stain.

"It's O.K.," Raphaela reassured me. I was shocked she wasn't angry with me; she kept right on going. "It's O.K. We were talking about being turned on with Vincent."

I coughed.

"Tell me about that." She kept drinking her tea in the most relaxed way, as if we were discussing the weather.

"I looked forward to him coming over and touching me during our special time." Nervously, I twisted a lock of hair around my forefinger. "Going down to the basement with him was the highlight of my empty days. In some odd way he taught me how to pleasure myself. Later, I had more ambivalence, more resistance. And in the end, only guilt and shame." The sentences emerged in staccato bursts. "There. Now you know the whole story. I'm not holding back unless I've completely disassociated any memories."

I went back to clasping my comfort pillow.

"Excellent. Now, I want you to write a letter to your Uncle Vincent, but don't send it yet. Call me when you're done."

I nodded, stood up unsteadily and reeled out of the room.

❀   ❀   ❀

That night I dreamed of Him again. We were dancing on a pink marbled patio near a circular turquoise pool surrounded by oleander sprays and bougainvillea. His sculpted body glistened in the moonlight with the aura of Michaelangelo's David. He pulled me closer and held the back of my head with his right hand. As we waltzed around in slow circles we floated in the moist tropical air.

The eeriness of being lighter than air both startled and charmed me. But then I remembered that I hadn't bathed. Desperately I checked myself for a whiff of bad odor. Instead, I smelled a luscious fragrance. Looking down, I saw I was wearing an exquisite gown made entirely of white frangipani petals. They covered my whole body except for my breasts. He leaned down and softly nuzzled my neck. Then his liquid mouth slowly tickled my shoulders with moist electric kisses.

I replayed the dream the next morning, during the sunny June is Bustin' Out All Over excursion to the airy greenery and sharp blue skies of Fairmount Park; while I swam through another dull white sea of HMO paperwork; and as I ate my skimpy no-fat yogurt and banana lunch.

But by afternoon, the Vincent assignment began to intrude as fragments of what I wanted to say to him floated up. So I decided to get on with it, bolstered by the Appleton Estate I brought back from St. Thomas. I sat at the oak dinette for an eternity, scribbling and sipping the rum with Coke, while Milo snored with his head on my foot. The ordeal was as grueling as running a marathon.

Finished, I called Raphaela with great relief.

But to my horror she wanted me to meet with Vincent. Face to face. "You have to encounter your demon," she repeated. A yoke of pain descended onto my neck. Raphaela suggested I call Vincent, even though I hadn't seen him for the past seven years, tell him I was suffering from depression and anxiety and ask for his help.

I procrastinated. Finally, sick of being tortured by ruminations, I called Vincent on Friday. Surprisingly, after few questions, he agreed to come in. Maybe he felt guilty, or maybe he was afraid word of the incest would get to Uncle Morty. Vincent managed the Rose Briar, one of Morty's properties in Bryn Mawr.

My reward for calling Vincent was culinary: Friday dinner at Sooze's. She was preparing her specialty, veal parmigiana. "What's new with Her Weirdness?" she asked as she breaded the thin strips of meat.

"You'll never believe this! I'm meeting with Uncle Vincent in Raphaela's office in about 10 days."

"No."

"Yes. Raphaela's helping me face the incest and the PTSD. Stellar just skimmed the surface; he never pressed me for details."

"Maybe Her Weirdness is worth it," Sooze said as she went into the living room and put on Moby's "Play."

Ironically, Sooze only knew the barest outlines of my abuse. She hadn't asked and I hadn't offered. This is my best friend? I thought. Maybe, I'll show her the journal that Raphaela asked me to keep. Maybe, later.

Sooze lumbered back into the kitchen. "Janna, I'm thrilled. But I thought she was a coach, not a therapist."

"I honestly don't know what she is anymore. She stopped practicing therapy long ago. But whatever she calls her work, it's miraculous." I stirred the thick plum tomato sauce with a wooden spoon in time to Moby's, *Nobody knows my troubles but God.*

"And she used a strange gizmo to desensitize me, a crystal ball," I continued.

"Sounds like a fortune-teller." Sooze tore up the arugula and tossed it in a bowl.

"I think Raphaela got me into an altered state. Must have hypnotically suggested that I 'project' Vincent onto the crystal and view the incest scene over and over again. Standard implosion," I added.

"That's as amazing as Milton Erickson's stuff."

"Speaking of mind-blowing, put your analyst hat on for a minute. After the session with Raphaela, Mystery Lover came again and in the dream, I worried that I smelled. Then I noticed that my body was covered with white flowers and this extraordinary fragrance was coming from my body. What does it mean, Herr Professor?" I asked as I put placemats graced by Monet's Water Lilies on Sooze's wicker and glass dinette.

"First you experienced the shame of a survivor but then you were pure and clean, absolved." Sooze was definitive. "That will be $5 please." Sooze chuckled as she held out her hand.

Ten days later on another sunny June morning I drove to Raphaela's to meet the hangman's noose. The purple, mauve and white phlox sprinkled throughout the sun-kissed Chadds Ford hills stood upright and perky, in stark contrast to my sorry procession. As I pulled into the farmhouse driveway I noticed splashes of white petunias and begonias near the front doorway that looked funereal. I sat in the car reassuring myself that Vincent couldn't hurt me.

When I entered the living room he was already sitting on the couch, so I plopped down on a blue upholstered armchair. Vincent was 42, still a geek, his thin bent frame accentuated by a wiry short Afro and Semitic nose. The same coke bottle glasses. My stomach turned.

"Vincent. Thank you for coming," Raphaela said, bonding with the scumbag. "You are in a unique position to help Janna. She has suffered for a long time and she needs to read you a letter to free herself from the past. All you need to do right now is listen without interrupting."

My heart jack hammered, my hands trembled as I opened the letter. Then I had a wild coughing fit. Raphaela brought me a glass of ice water and I sipped to calm myself. Without looking at him I slowly croaked out the words.

∾

"Vincent,

My nightmares began with you. I would dream that I was out of control and fall-ing, falling to a certain death, with no one there to help or to catch me. My fear of men, my attachments to men who are not available, my sadness and self-loathing, and above all, my shame came from you. Not all of it. But a lot. More than you would ever imagine.

Vincent, I was alone and I loved you when I was little. I loved playing chess with you and going on the rides at Hershey Park. But you took advantage of my inno-cence and my need. You used me. You fucked me and fucked me up in that damp smelly cellar on Green Street. And then I hated you.

I cannot tell you how many nights I didn't sleep, how many times I got sick to avoid you, how I felt dirty and damaged inside. I was so marked that I was sexu-ally harassed and abused at Northeast High and even exploited by my graduate school professor. I became bitter and hopeless about men.

I hate you for this.

But I will stop hating myself. What's done is done and I can only learn to forgive myself and honor my innocence. But, as for the future, my weakness and passiv-ity are done. From this moment on, I vow that no bastard will hurt, use or abuse me and get away unscathed. Never again."

I finished reading and cradled my head in my hands. Out of the corner of my eye I could see Vincent. He was as ashen as a corpse.

"Well, Vincent, what's your reaction?" Raphaela challenged.

"I…I…I don't know what to say. It happened so long ago, we were just kids, you know. Innocent horseplay. Playin' doctor and nurse, you know." He rubbed his thighs nervously. "Anyway, what does this have to do with her prob-lems today? It happened 25 years ago."

"What you call doctor and nurse, did that include fingering her and forcing her to have intercourse?" Raphaela shot him a steely look.

"She asked me down to the basement. She enjoyed it. Guess it was wrong but I couldn't help myself. Hey, I was only 16. But we never had sex or nothin'."

I sat there speechless. Raphaela got up, came over to my chair and, without warning, tapped me hard on the right shoulder. I don't know what happened, but in the next moment I jumped up and screamed at Vincent. "Don't lie! You fingered me until you broke my hymen, you scumbag. I found blood on my panties and I was so scared that I didn't tell anyone." As I spoke spittle flew from my mouth. My fear transformed into steely energy. Vincent slouched over in his chair and covered his head with his arms.

"Tell Janna how deeply sorry you are for fingering her and taking her virginity," Raphaela insisted.

Vincent looked up at me and whispered, "Sorry, Janna, I'm so sorry." And then a look of horror came over his face. "You're not gonna tell my wife are you? She might leave, take the kids away. I don't know…" Vincent turned green.

"First things first," Raphaela interceded. "We have the sexual intercourse to discuss. Then we can talk about your wife."

I jumped in. "Your wife and family? A drunk driver took my mother away from me when I was nine. And a perverted uncle took my innocence when I was ten! I've never even had a family. It would serve you right to lose them."

"Are we bein' taped?" Vincent looked wildly around the room surveying for possible hidden cameras or microphones.

Raphaela snorted. "Of course not."

"One time. Just once." Vincent hid his face in his hands. He continued in a muffled voice, "I swear on my daughters' lives, I never forced her. She was drinkin' and I was drinkin' and we were havin' fun."

"She was only 13 years old, Vincent. Can you imagine if a 19-year old did that to one of your girls, what you would do?" Raphaela pointed at him.

Stunned, he choked out the words. "I don't know."

"You'd want to choke him," Raphaela said.

I jumped in. "I wanted to kill you. Three years you exploited me. Used me. For three years you betrayed my childhood trust in you. And you walk away unscathed and unpunished while I'm scarred for years." I towered over him as he sat crumpled on the couch.

"What about making reparation to Janna?" Raphaela asked.

"Not like I haven't suffered about it too, you know."

"Stop! Vincent, don't make it worse. This is Janna's time. What can you do for her, to make it up to her?" Raphaela said firmly.

"Don't know."

"What would you like, Janna?" She turned to me.

So this is what it's like to have a champion, I thought.

"Give me a minute." I sat back down. I remembered Doris telling me about Vincent's mousy wife and their two young daughters. What a set up for abuse, I realized.

"Tell your wife so the cycle of abuse stops with me." I stared at him coldly.

"How would I explain…?" Fear screamed from his face.

Raphaela answered, "If I were you, I would tell her the truth, something like, 'I met with Janna's coach and some things came out that I did when we were kids. I sexually abused her.' And when she hits the roof, you may call me and I will talk to her and then refer you both to a therapist who can help you get through this crisis." She folded her perfectly manicured hands together, adding, "I promise you, you will wind up being a better man, Vincent."

Whether it was because he was beaten, whether it was because he was afraid word would get out to the family, or for some other hidden reason, Vincent agreed he would tell his wife. Raphaela acknowledged his courage and Vincent shuffled off.

I felt fearless. "Raphaela, I don't have the words to thank you."

She patted my shoulder proudly.

"I want to continue with you, be your apprentice, your student."

"You did well in completing Lesson One."

"Will you have me? I'll work hard."

"You may have to play hard too." She chuckled.

"No problem."

Raphaela shook her head yes. I sighed. "Now you must face your fear of loss. It's your Second Lesson."

"How?" I swallowed nervously.

"Write a truthful letter to your father, a letter from the heart to the man who didn't protect you. But don't mail it to him."

CHAPTER 6

Facing the Past

Hunched over the oak dinette Monday morning, I found a searing lava of words pouring onto the paper.

ꙩ

Dear Dad,

Remember me? I was born Nobody's Child. My mother was the daughter of Holocaust survivors who lived in that legacy, guilt-ridden over being alive, buried by lingering depression. She could take little joy in me. Nine years after I was born, she died.

My father was all wrapped up in our perfect brick row home on Green Street, the damned manicured postage stamp lawn, the pampered rose bushes that climbed the silver mesh fence around the back patio. He spent the rest of his time working or arguing. Arguing with Babba Aydel about his lack of money. Arguing with Mom when she was alive about his brother's achievements, about Babba's household cleanliness inspections, about whose brisket was the ultimate. I was always invisible to him.

Remember me? Where have you been all my life? I have only one treasured memory; the time you took me to Uncle Morty's country club and taught me how to golf. When Mom died you started doting on Doris. I used to wish that I had been in that car, that I had lost an arm, or a leg. I kept tripping, falling over things, cutting myself 'accidentally'. I thought that would make you love me. But I had no such luck.

You palmed me off on Babba Aydel and she came equipped with her late life accident, Vincent. Baba, the old battle-ax, with her ugly print dusters and babushkas, cleaning our house, crying over her daughter's death, and pining for Warsaw in the old days before the Ghetto and the Holocaust. Babba was as cold as the Polish stetl she came from. Rather than being a source of comfort, she scared me with her paranoia about living in the Jewish enclave of Northeast Philly.

And Vincent, the slim, he hurt me in ways you don't even want to know about. I was only ten years old when he started abusing me. Didn't it ever occur to you to check on us in the basement? That it was odd that a boy who had already graduated from Northeast High was so eager to keep his little niece company? And I never ever felt I could come to you for protection.

I've always tried to make allowances for you. Even though Babba Pearl was as warm as the Miami sunshine and adored me, I know that she preferred Morty to you. I realize that you didn't know how to be a father because your dad died when you were just 12. In a way we're kindred spirits. But in the end I've paid a price, a steep one. I have been lonely and frightened of love my whole life.

Remember me?

Janna

The letter released the pain I had buried for years and years. It worked its way up and out like a splinter from an infected wound. I realized that guilt over my final words to Momma had cut out my tongue. That I believed my very words had killed her off. And I couldn't take that chance with Dad.

"You know him better than I do—do you think it's OK for me to tell Dad that Vincent had sex with me?" I asked Doris as we sat in the cluttered living room of her chichi Manayunk apartment Tuesday evening.

I had just recounted the full truth of the incest and every word of my confrontation with Vincent. It was an urgent spillage that had to come out: I wanted my sister to know.

Doris looked up from the feng shui fountain she was assembling on the floor. "I had no idea it had gone that far. Vincent is repulsive. A cretin." She stood up and wiped her hands on her designer jeans. "Let me make you a cup of espresso, Jan. Baba Pearl sent special Cuban decaf."

Leaning over the antique rocker where I was sitting, she rested her hand briefly on my shoulder. I gave her a weak smile and nodded.

As she limped into her perfectly equipped white hole of a kitchen, I called out, "But what about telling Papa?"

"I thought you dealt with all this in grad school," she called back. I jumped up and joined her in the kitchen.

"Only part of it. I remember you told me that Vincent touched you too."

"Just once. But I told him to get lost," Doris said nonchalantly as she turned on the espresso machine. My eyes anxiously traced the jagged seam that ran from the corner of her left eye all the way down the length of her neck as she began to mindlessly drive nails into me. "It was no biggie, Jan. You were such a nut in graduate school. When you told me about Stokes and the repressed memory syndrome, I thought it was like your other problems—one week anxiety disorder, the next social phobia, depending on what you were reading in your psychopathology class."

Every cell in my body bristled. "Doris, this was real."

"But that crap happened so long ago. So pulleeze, don't burden Papa. That's just what he needs, more guilt."

I threw down a kitchen towel on the counter. "Damn it! Finally telling him might give us a chance for a real relationship."

"That's just like you, to be so self-absorbed."

"Me? You're the selfish one. You've got Dad paying for your third graduate degree, not to mention half the rent on this gentrified dump."

Doris overfilled two Italian rococo espresso cups with muddy liquid and brown stains splattered her hand and spread over the white Formica of her counter. "Damn it," she yelped as she sucked on her index finger. "I got a stipend for that nursing degree."

"And now Urban Planning. Spending more of Papa's money. For what? What have you done with all those degrees? You with your Mensa bullshit. 'I'm too smart for this, I'm bored with that.'"

Doris shook her head violently so that her golden shoulder length hair flew around like so much straw. "Miss High and Mighty, you've always been jealous of my friends, my relationship with Papa."

"And you weren't envious? You never even gave me a gift when I finished my M.S.W. Not so much as a card when I opened my office. Talk about selfish…"

A vein throbbed in her forehead as she shrieked, "I never asked him to do all that for me." She hurled her tiny cup against the wall and burst into sobs. "You had your trauma with Vincent. But I had mine. With Mama."

"I'm sorry, Doris," I said as sharp pains shot through my chest.

"Jan, please, I never asked him to do for me. Been drowning in guilt my whole life…about her, about Papa working himself to death, about you." She broke into sobs and touched her face. "It's not just this scar…"

CHAPTER 7

Of Loss and Love

Raphaela was covered in straw, as she busily cleaned stalls in the magnificent barn behind the Chester county farmhouse. Nevertheless, she managed to look like some Ralph Lauren model. I stood nearby, nervously twisting my father's letter in my hands. She took the letter, put it on a ledge and handed me a heavy apron and a pitchfork. We worked in silence, throwing out manure and freshening up the stalls. When we finished mucking, Raphaela grinned with the joy of a young child and led me out to a corral nestled in the rolling hills behind the barn. A white Arabian mare pranced up to the fence near us. "This is Joan of Arc. Joan, Janna."

"Hey there." I stroked her cheek. Raphaela moved over to the gate and Joan swished her tail and followed. Suddenly, to my astonishment, she flung open the gate and the mare bolted out of the corral. Raphaela urged it to go with a slap on the rear end. The stately horse cantered happily up a hill to her freedom. Worried, I asked, "Are you sure you should let her go…" Raphaela just grinned. Joan made a quick turn, whinnied, eyed my new mentor and galloped right back to her. She kissed the mare on the cheek and the mare seemed to kiss her right back.

Raphaela turned to me. "This is Lesson Two."

I scratched my head.

"*When you face loss, love blossoms.* Lesson Two. Like horses, we are herd animals. Our greatest emotional horror and our most profound teacher is the specter of being separate. Of being abandoned, alone."

"Yeah, yeah." Frowning, I picked at some splinters in the corral fence.

"I know you don't relish the topic of loss. It brings up the lonely heart. The hunger."

A little frog lodged itself in my throat.

"But loss is what you must face. Fear of loss is what you must master. Otherwise you sacrifice yourself and your own needs in the service of holding on to relationships. You deny feelings of disappointment and anger. You walk on eggshells. You lie and muffle your unhappiness."

"I don't…"

"You do." Raphaela pulled my letter out of her pocket. "Think of what you went through to write this to your father."

I sighed.

"You were afraid that if you were real, if you told the truth, he wouldn't approve. Afraid he would withhold the love, the small crumbs of affection he gave you."

My eyes blurred with tears. Raphaela brushed them away tenderly with her fingertips. Joan of Arc nibbled my ear.

Raphaela patted the rail fence. "Sit up here with me." I clambered up. "The fear of loss is hardwired into our being. It requires no learning. It is as instinctual as ducklings following their mother or puppies attaching themselves to their teats. It first appears when we realize we are separate from Mother. At the tender age of six months we are jarred into recognizing we are in the world alone: Mother can leave. When we cry as infants, we have that first wave of separation anxiety, that fear of abandonment. Then, with every separation, the fear of loss can grow stronger. We become frightened of strangers, of being alone, of the dark."

Once again I felt like Raphaela was telling me a bedtime story and I settled internally.

She continued. "Freud said that that single condition of missing someone who is loved is the whole key to understanding anxiety."

"That much I get."

"A tiny pale and listless infant lies dying in a small metal crib. He does not have any known disease. His eyes are dull, the spirit already gone. Why is he dying? Did he have enough milk to drink? Yes. Did he have enough water? Yes. Was he kept warm and protected from the elements? Yes. The only thing he has been deprived of is mother love. He has not been held, stroked, talked to and played with. And without mother love he is dying. This disease, called marasmus, was the discovery made by Rene Spitz, a psychoanalyst, who studied infants raised in foundling homes."

"I get it."

"To thrive, we all need the powerful magic of a nurturing attachment. The fear of abandonment that is hardwired into our nervous systems serves as a survival mechanism. We anticipate losing the loved one and the fear we experience is a signal that our fragile existence is in danger. This signaling system is so strong that remnants of it remain with us to a greater or lesser degree throughout our lives."

I mindlessly rubbed my stomach.

"But by the time we are adults it has become only a knee-jerk reaction." She grabbed at the mare's neck and held her in a vise-like grip for a moment. "A powerful fear that makes us cling to others in negative ways just to keep them with us. And this kills the life-blood of love."

"You mean it keeps us in relationships that are empty or bad for us, kind of on auto-pilot?"

"Exactly. Where we are taken advantage of, ignored, or even abused. Relationships in which we feel we can't be real. Like you with your father."

"But relationships aren't all good or bad."

"There is the potential for love in almost all relationships. But in order for it to flow, Lesson two teaches us that we have to face down fear of loss, take control and not allow it to run us."

I straightened up. "You mean say the words that can't be said? Stand up for what we need even if we risk the loss of approval or worse, being abandoned?"

"Yes. That is the way. Only then, can love blossom.

"But sometimes it doesn't. Sometimes they leave you."

"That's true—it is a gamble. There are no guarantees," Raphaela said. "But do you want to continue relationships where you can't be yourself? Look where that's gotten you."

She had my number. There was dad, and all these men who somehow I never could be real with.

"When you face loss you may lose the person. But the one gift you always receive is respect and love for yourself."

I groaned. "I'll send the letter to my father."

By Wednesday my father's voice, raspy with age, was on my voicemail. "Janna, uh, I got your letter…uh, I don't understand." He cleared his throat, and after a long pause, added, "What's wrong, honey?"

I quickly called and arranged to meet him the next morning at my office, hoping for a home court advantage.

He came in wearing his usual uniform: gray slacks, buttoned-down shirt and a thin outdated tie draped over his concave chest. Like an old bird, he peered at me through the thick frames of his glasses with a puzzled, worried look. Then he handed over a Flakowitz bag with coffee, bagels and cream cheese. I set up paper plates on my coffee table, positioned myself on the therapist chair and motioned for him to sit on the brown tweed couch.

"What happened, Janna, what happened with you?" he asked with the lost expression of a homeless child.

"The letter said it all, Dad. Can't eat the damn bagels…I feel afraid, of what, I don't know."

"You think I didn't love you, is that the point?" He looked pained.

"No, but you barely noticed I was alive."

"I had my hands full, after your mother, after Sophie died. When we were sitting Shiva on Green Street, Babba Aydel went crazy on me. She was parading up and down the street babbling and cursing God, 'Oy, Rebono shel olam, I spit on you.'" He rubbed his forehead.

"I remember," I said, nervously fingering a lock of my hair.

"'My parents, my only sister, you send to de camps, my husband with de cancer you took, now my shayna maydel, Sophie, gone. Oy, take me away from this Gehenim, already, kill me, you Satan.' Babba Pearl stopped her from throwing herself in front of a truck. Doris had just gotten out of the hospital and her face was destroyed, she couldn't eat. Vincent got drunk and threw up on Doris's bed…" He teared up.

"But, Dad, do you remember where I was when we were sitting Shiva? No, I know you don't. I was under my bed, scared to death, full of guilt, and alone. Nobody held me, cradled me. Except Babba Pearl. I was hiding from the world then. And still am."

His lined face contorted as the tears forced their way out. "Remember you made those holes in the dining room wall?"

"You didn't even punish me," I half-chuckled as I smoothed the front of my houndstooth jacket. "But the truth is you didn't have time for me even before Mama died."

He saddened. "I never meant for my family to turn out that way. Two girls, I didn't know…" His raspy voice trailed off.

"How to relate to us?" I finished his sentence.

My dad let out muffled sobs. Without knowing how, my voice spit out, "Vincent sexually abused me…had intercourse with me when I was 13."

"What? Your Uncle Vincent, he was such a good boy, helping out…" He closed his eyes and held his head. "I can't believe you didn't tell me."

"I was just a scared 10-year old when he started with me."

"Did he, did he hurt…Doris?" He choked out.

Doris, Doris, I screamed inwardly. "Can you forget Doris for a minute?" Speak up, Janna. My mind went to the lesson: *Fear lights the way to mastery.* Speak the truth you have always been afraid to say, I thought. "This is about me. Vincent destroyed my childhood."

"Gott in Himmel. You should have come to me and I would have thrown him out, believe me."

"I don't believe you. Three long years he molested me. I came to hate him, worse, to hate myself…I came to resent and be ashamed of being a woman."

"No, Janna, no. No, honey."

"Yes, I'm telling you, yes."

"Gott in Himmel, I'm so very very sorry."

My dad cried real tears.

It's done, I thought. He reached in his pocket, retrieved a white handkerchief, mopped up the rivulets on his face and blew his nose. Slowly, my father looked up. "Do you want me to speak to Vincent?"

"No, I've already handled Vincent." Sitting back in the clammy leather chair, I continued. "Dad, I don't want to be the girl outside the window anymore."

He pushed his slight frame up from the couch, came over and gave me an awkward hug. I peered up at my father as if seeing him for the first time. I could see the love in his tear-stained eyes.

After he left, I called Raphaela and euphorically reported what happened.

She responded, "Good. When you face loss courageously, love can flow. Come next Sunday."

The rest of the week was quiet until early Saturday evening, when I took messages off the office line. Rhoda's hurried anxious voice said, "Jim confronted Tony, and, God forgive me, I almost ran over him with the Jeep in the parking lot."

"Janna, it's me, Jim, please call me at the office immediately. We have to hospitalize Rhoda." I called and scheduled them for a session early the next morning.

That night, I took Valerian root extract and hopped into bed at eight, hoping for the embrace of Nod. But strange and frightening dream images swam past in succession: a toddler crying tears that turned into rain and a raging squall; a starving baby withering in my arms; a man shattering the bay windows of my house with a claw hammer.

❦   ❦   ❦

The next morning I carefully parked between two Mercedes at the King of Prussia mall parking lot. I had a ten o'clock appointment with Raphaela. At Bloomies. I'm definitely nuts, I thought as I hurried into the shoe department to meet her. She was standing there holding a pair of Jimmy Choo's, looking like a well-kept suburban housewife. Except for the way she lighted up when she saw me. Like sunshine.

As she tried on shoes, she began to teach me, once again answering my questions before I asked them. "Remember Lesson Two: *When you face loss, love blossoms.* It is the ultimate grail that will crown your work. In couples, facing the fear of loss is a powerful crucible for transformation. Without it partners take each other for granted, act like infants, and then abuse each other unmercifully."

"I have this couple that's in serious trouble. They need to confront that fear?" I asked as I sat down on the chair next to her.

"Yes. Think about Maslow's works. Once our basic needs for food, shelter and safety are met, the drive for belonging and being loved is primary."

I nodded. "And the fear of being alone comes with it."

"That fear is a gift that gives birth to love, once we acknowledge it. Healthy couples accept that they are separate beings and could be alone at any moment, through bad luck, ill health, death, or their own cruel behavior. Each day together becomes a blessing."

"But couples who are out of control…"

"Janna, when a couple is in crisis, they have a golden opportunity to master the fear of loss. Their suffering has often grown to the point where they consider leaving the relationship. Then the possibility of real change emerges."

She walked around carefully in a pair of stiletto heels.

"How?"

"Loss seeps into their relationship. It can happen in many ways. One partner may refuse to speak to the other, sleep in another room, or leave the home. By breaking their addiction to each other, the partners can become honestly self-reflective and take responsibility for their own heartless acts. A new dance of love can then be co-created."

"But couples are always threatening to leave and it means nothing."

"These are idle threats. When they become real, when a couple realizes they can truly lose their relationship, everything changes. They can find personal responsibility. Joy, delight and appreciation for each other can blossom."

"But how do I apply this to my case?" I asked as she took off the heels, put them carefully in their box and added them to the ten boxes of shoes she was taking.

"Be still, perfectly still," she answered.

CHAPTER 8

The Lonely-Hearts Club

Rhoda and Jim came in with the hopeless gloom of prison camp inmates. She hadn't even bothered to apply makeup to her ghostly face and he was marked with sunken black circles under his eyes. As Rhoda tearfully explained how the Jeep incident was totally Jim's fault, my mind went blank. Suddenly, a voice in my head spoke: *be still*. Without knowing why, I focused full attention on a spot just above Rhoda's thinly tweezed eyebrows. As her image blurred, she turned to Jim and wailed, "I hate you." Then she dissolved in tears. "And I hate what I've become…" she choked out, "Got to get out."

Nervously I opened my mouth without the faintest idea of what was going to emerge. I was surprised to hear myself agreeing with Rhoda. "I think you ought to. The next time there's a blow up you can pack your bags and go to a hotel for a few nights. After all, you guys are moving in the direction of destroying the relationship." The scent of fear wafted through the air and settled all around the room.

Jim argued. "Don't give up on us, Janna. We want to be together, but…"

Now what do I say? I wondered. *Be still.* "But what?" I heard myself challenge. "Let's face what's so. The marriage is nowhere. Rhoda, you'll probably wind up with custody of the kids. Jim, you'll only see them on weekends. You'll have to sell the colonial in Villanova that you both worked so hard to buy…"

Jim looked like he had just received a diagnosis of terminal lung cancer, but I continued. "It'll take a few years, but each of you will eventually recover, start on the dating scene, the singles bars."

Rhoda blurted out, "No."

I interrupted her. "The economic setback will be pretty severe…"

Veins throbbed in Rhoda's forehead. "You're not saying there's no hope, are you?"

What if I break them up with this harebrained strategy? I fretted. Be still. "The children may be scarred, but you can put them into therapy." Anxiety stormed in my gut, but I pressed on. "Experience the loss that you are both unconsciously creating."

"I don't really want out," Rhoda said.

"Then stop carrying on with Tony. End the affair."

"He makes me come alive, I mean…."

"Exactly. So let's set up a formal separation so you can have Tony without any remorse." My stomach flip-flopped and Jim started weeping.

Jim pleaded. "But she's the only woman I've ever loved."

My inner guide urged; don't let up. Help them face loss. I shook my head. "Love is not enough to bring this couple together."

"Rhoda, please. I want you," Jim sobbed.

Rhoda stared at Jim. "That's all I ever wanted you to say." She turned to me. "Tell me what to do."

"Stop the affair. If you want Jim, the first step is to stop the affair."

Rhoda buried her face in her hands. Seconds ticked away like eons.

Finally she announced with eyes closed. "I'll end it with Tony."

The room seemed to open up. But my internal voice interrupted; *there must be reparation and forgiveness*. I heard myself say, "Rhoda acknowledge to Jim that you have broken trust—that there's been a wrong-doing."

Rhoda bowed her head. "It's true. I've felt like a shit sneaking around, lying."

"Apologize," I instructed.

Rhoda peered up at him. "I'm sorry."

He stared at her in sadness. "You broke me."

"I screwed up big time. I'm so sorry." They held each other's eyes.

After a few moments, I interjected. "Jim, decide on a path of reparation that Rhoda can take so that, in time, you can truly forgive her. Then both of you can let go of the affair."

"For starters, quit the damn job and swear on your mother's grave you'll never talk to Tony again."

Rhoda rubbed her forehead and stared into space. "I'm willing to do it. But what about us? I can't go back to an empty marriage."

Jim sighed and lowered his head.

Again the internal voice coached me; the reparation must challenge both parties. I was surprised to hear myself say to Rhoda, "If you want to save the marriage, you must look at your role. You helped create a passionless relationship and now you must make it up to Jim."

Turning to Jim I challenged, "Don't let her off the hook so easily. Ask her to make amends in the area where she betrayed you. Something sexual, maybe?"

Jim laughed sheepishly. "I don't know..."

Rhoda joined the fray. "I'll do whatever you ask. Besides, it might be fun."

"I'm embarrassed to say what I want. You'll both think I'm perverted."

As if moved by an unseen hand, I leaned forward and said, "Jim, whisper your secret fantasy to your wife." He cupped his hands and murmured into Rhoda's ear.

Rhoda blushed. "If that's what you really want."

"Jim," I continued, "make sure Rhoda quits the job and fulfills her sexual promise to you."

"Done," he answered sitting a little taller.

Appreciation, my internal voice urged. I turned to my clients. "Today you have faced loss head-on and opened new possibilities in your lives together. These possibilities spring from one thing and one thing only: appreciation of the other. If you don't want your family to dissolve, I recommend that you have ten-minute listening sessions with each other every day. These are appreciation exercises where you take the other in fully and listen from the heart with no comments or judgments."

"Sounds hard." Jim played with his wedding ring.

I leaned toward him. "It is, and I'm holding you responsible for seeing that the work gets done daily. Listen attentively to Rhoda and when you want to talk, make sure you either validate or rephrase what she has said. Clarifying, non-judgmental questions are OK too." Then I looked at Rhoda. "When you've finished your ten minutes, switch roles. It's a tough exercise. But taking each other for granted will lead to much harder consequences in the long run, I promise you."

"After we put the girls to bed we could do it," Rhoda said.

I looked at Jim. "And when are you going to start, in a month? I've seen faster construction from state road crews than I've seen from you two. All the progress you've made today could go to hell in a steamshovel."

"Tomorrow," Jim said.

I wanted to jump up and congratulate them, but I remembered to be still. All that came out was a cautionary, "We'll see."

The couple left my office hand in hand. I sat down at the desk mindlessly doodling circles on a pad, unable to integrate the bizarre events of the last hour. Then, remembering Herb had patients on Saturday I scurried down to his office, hoping he was free. The door was open and he was resting in his ergonomic therapist's chair, lost in *The Utne Reader*. Herb put down the magazine and motioned for me to come in.

I jumped into the rocker next to him. Blushing, I announced, "Herb, I just channeled my teacher, Raphaela Love."

Herb guffawed. "What's come over you?"

"Seriously, I just finished a breakthrough session. The techniques were transmitted to me by this strange woman." I told him about the second lesson, how facing fear of loss can generate love.

He fingered his beard as he listened. "Genius," he said as I gave him a blow by blow of the therapy hour. "That's a miracle. No offense, you couldn't conduct a session like that on your own. And neither could I."

"I know. It's extraordinary." Chills broke out on my arms and legs. "You know I don't believe in any paranormal stuff and yet it's happening to me. I'm scared, exhilarated. Not myself."

"I bet. This is not your usual cup of Joe." Herb twinkled.

"I want to laugh and cry at the same time. Am I going off the deep end?"

He clapped gleefully. "Congratulations, you're finally getting that rational stick out of your ass and opening to the wonder of what is. Did you know that a meta-analysis of studies on psi phenomena like ESP, telekinesis and remote viewing conclusively showed these abilities do exist? The statistics were so good that the article was published in *Psych Bulletin*." He looked back at a crammed-to-overflowing metal bookcase behind his chair.

"But what if she tries to take me over like Rajneesh?"

"She has a beard and speaks Hindi?" Herb joked. "Seriously, if any of that starts to happen, you just walk. But she doesn't sound like a cult leader. She may be the real thing. There are such beings; like the Indian guru, Sri Aurobindo."

Herb grinned.

"What did he do?"

"Few people know this, but during World War II when it looked like Hitler would take over the world, Winston Churchill asked the saint for help. He responded by practicing a special meditation and you know the rest. Aurobindo also provided the inspiration for Churchill's galvanizing speeches."

"Amazing. An enlightened being."

Maybe that's what Raphaela is, I thought. Herb's craziness was contagious.

"Haven't you longed to meet such a person, in spite of believing so firmly that it was utterly impossible? Most of us do."

"Yeah," I admitted. "But I can't imagine that if there are saints, one would take a special interest in me. She's hinted that my training involves seven lessons. Lessons that open doors to love." I laughed. "Whatever that means."

"Well, guess what," Herb took my arm. "It looks like you're receiving Shaktipata from a master. You're in a state of grace. Look."

He took me over to the rectangular mirror that hung on the wall of his office. I stared at my face; it was innocent and filled with light.

"You look more alive, more beautiful than I've ever seen you. Just go with the process and see what happens. I'll be your sanity check." Herb wrapped me in a big hug. "It's a blessed adventure."

I drove home with a silly smile but by the time bedtime rolled around, doubts etched themselves into the Mt. Rushmore of my face. Sleep was long in coming. Milo must have picked up on my upset, because he got sick and threw up a puddle of brown goo on my bed sheets in the middle of the night. I quickly changed the sheets while questions continued to plague me. Who is she? What is she? What does she want with me, of all people? I wanted to believe, no, to surrender, but a strange anxiety took hold of me.

Mercifully, my session with Raphaela took place early the next morning. She flung open the beveled glass front door and announced, "Janna!" as if I was the star of a Broadway play. She was in her diamond-encrusted manifestation, with Cleopatra makeup and a low cut yellow silk sundress that was backless. She doesn't fit the image of any saint I've ever heard of, I thought. If I saw her on the street I'd think 'Margate Maven.'

After we moved into the living room, I started nervously. "Raphaela, I just had the most amazing session with my clients. I felt like you were guiding me. Were you?"

She laughed from the belly and said, "You got a crash course on Lesson Two in action: *When you face loss, love blossoms.*" In response, my hands started sweating and chills prickled along my spine.

"You painted a picture of the dismal future that the spouses were creating for themselves. The vision mobilized them to take action."

I fiddled with the hair at the nape of my neck. "But, I don't understand."

"You will," Raphaela said as she disappeared into the kitchen. She reemerged with steaming mugs of jasmine tea.

"Raphaela, the session worked but it made me very uncomfortable."

"That's because of the hole in your heart caused by the loss of your mother that you have carefully covered over." She cupped her bejeweled hand to her chest.

I grimaced and took a long drink of the hot tea. "But aren't therapists supposed to bring people together whenever we can? There's enough divorce in the world already. And here I was pushing them apart."

"What would have happened to this couple if you had continued your old way of no blame, of neutrality?"

"Things were getting worse and worse, closer to divorce court," I admitted.

"Exactly. Instead you held up the mirror so they could see their loss coming and you helped bring them together."

"But spouses are always saying, 'I'm out of here."

Raphaela held up her forefinger. "Are those real threats? Or are they power plays to punish the other and gain control of the relationship?"

"They're manipulative," I agreed.

"And both partners know that. Everything changes when one party has resolved to leave if things don't change. And holds to the commitment. It's in their eyes; in the air around the couple. The real specter of loss hangs over them like the sword of Damocles."

I drained my cup. "And how do reparation and forgiveness fit with facing the fear of loss?"

Raphaela raised her arm and the diamond bracelets sparkled.

"What if I was in a skiing accident and woke up to find that I had lost my right arm?" She wiggled her fingers. "This hand which I have taken for granted for so many years. And then let's say a genius surgeon came along and, yes, he could sew it back on, reattach it. How I would appreciate my arm, my hand." She kissed her own hand.

"It's the same for partners." I nodded.

"Seeing our partners as separate beings and not extensions of ourselves, we appreciate what's right with our partners; those lovable qualities that drew us to them at the outset. We are suddenly on the other side and realize that the grass is not greener. We examine ourselves and come to understand how we have failed our partners, wronged them. Out of this process we naturally want to repair the wounds we have inflicted and at the same time we want to forgive those that have been inflicted upon us. It is nature's healing dance that gives birth to new love."

I clucked. "Even with this couple?"

Raphaela refilled my cup and nodded. "None other than the Bard wrote in the Sonnets,

"*And ruined love when it is built anew, Grows fairer than at first, more strong, far greater.*"

Raphaela continued. "In couples this dance does not always work. But when it does, like a miracle, the greater love appears."

"When doesn't it work?"

"When one spouse or the other refuses the challenge, refuses to grow up. He or she chooses to live in the fantasy that the next partner will be better; the next relationship will be more exciting. That spouse refuses to understand the basic truth."

Scratching my head, I asked. "Which is?"

"We create our own realities, including our relationships."

"To a certain degree…but…"

"The most powerful stance with oneself is to say one hundred per cent; I create it one hundred percent. Taking that position means you can change it."

"But not abused women!"

"You can be hurt once or twice. But you can't be abused if you get out. There are safe houses, after all."

Raphaela poured herself more tea. "As you witnessed with your father, Lesson Two also applies between parent and child, siblings, close friends." I was afraid to look up; afraid she would read my thoughts.

But she did. "I want you to face the loss, the ruined love with your mother." Raphaela said as she went out of the room.

Not that, I thought.

She returned carrying her crystal ball. My heart sank. "Look into the ball and witness."

Feeling like I was going to puke, I forced myself to stare into the quartz. Murky images swirled and then became me at age nine, a fat rag doll, watching my mother and Doris get into the '72 Buick. I turned my head away.

"Face the loss," Raphaela commanded.

I forced myself to look back.

And there I was, jumping up and down, ranting, screaming, "Take me! Take me with you! I hate you!" Waves of guilt-nausea and fear enveloped me.

Then the scene played over again. I saw her leaving me again. And again. Mercifully, the river of pain, the aching, the bursting tears that had been raging, pent up in me for so many years were released. I sobbed freely and without self-consciousness, for the first time since that day when I had dammed off the corridors of my heart. I heaved and shook as I cried it all out. Until time stopped and the numbness left my body.

Raphaela put her arms around me, dabbing at my face with a tissue. She beamed at me. "You have broken the moratorium of your heart. That's what happens when you face loss. It opens you to the possibilities of each and every moment."

I smiled at her. "But what else do I do to heal?"

"Make reparation and forgive yourself," she whispered.

"How?"

"Bring your mother back into your life." She raised her eyebrows.

"I have no pictures of her in my house. I could put them up."

"A good reparation. She loved you. More than you know." Raphaela pointed to the crystal ball. "And what about forgiving yourself?"

I looked intently at the magical quartz.

Raphaela hugged me and whispered, "Forgive that hurt child. Mother yourself gently, and with compassion."

I closed my eyes and nodded, feeling blessed. Shyly I looked up at her. "Raphaela, how in the world did you do that, that channeling?"

She looked away. "It's unimportant."

"You have such compassion, like you know what it means to suffer."

She nodded.

"I want to know about you, what happened in your life."

She smiled wryly. "I have known fear intimately. And loss. But now is not the time to talk about me."

"Were you the spirit in my nightmares, who caught me when I was falling?" My forehead was feverish. "Were you teaching me Lesson One in my dream, when you threw me back towards Bob?"

Raphaela flashed her Mona Lisa smile.

Bits and pieces were coming together for me, in a sea of realization. I remembered the lavender mist and card, the lilacs, the feather, the crystal ball. Had Raphaela choreographed the whole drama, first my dream life and then my waking reality? Or was I just getting lost in a sea of positive transference? I studied Raphaela carefully. Her green eyes became portals to another world.

"Who are you?" I asked.

"Do you really want to know?" She gazed into me, checking to see if I could handle the answer.

"Yes."

"I am that I for which there is no you." Raphaela pronounced each word as if she were reciting sacred verse.

"What in the world does that mean?"

"I am not this body. I am the one Mother behind the many." When I heard the words a feeling of lightning pierced my heart. I fell to my knees weeping and held onto Raphaela's feet.

"Thank you, Raphaela. For Bob, for Rhoda and Jim, for me. I don't know who you are or what you are doing, but it's miraculous."

She beamed at me as she held my face in her hands. "Sometimes there are random blessings. Especially when you're ready to receive them."

For the briefest of moments I was hopeful that my own dreams could come true.

CHAPTER 9

Land Of Enchantment

It was Him, laying close to me, a sylph me, all soft flowing lines. A diaphanous robe billowed about me, fashioning itself into translucent clouds around my legs. At my waist a large oval metal clasp anchored a belt of colorfully beaded jute. We were in a Maxfield Parrish fantasy, on a balustrade perched on a cliff surrounded by blue, purple and orange iridescence. The shimmering mountain light colored the marble floor and glistened as it bounced off the terraced hills and valleys of his sculpted chest. I could hear the coo-ree, coo-ree call of strange mountain birds in the distance.

We lay facing each other on sisal padding between two massive alabaster columns. He was kissing my hands with the tiniest of movements that sent tingling energy through my arms and into my body. It was impossible to make out the features of his face. All I could see was a head of thick shiny brown hair. He stopped kissing me and picked up a two-sided hand mirror in an elaborate rococo brass frame. With a quick movement he held it up to my face and I saw the sylph, beaming a radiant smile, eyes alight with fire. Then he swiveled the looking glass to the reverse side and this time it showed the wan face, the grim soldier who was the woman I was used to seeing in the mirror each day. Before I could even react, he turned the magic glass again and my radiance reappeared. He kept turning the mirror back and forth rapidly, so that I would see the old me and the new me over and over. Finally He put it down and tenderly held my hands.

He began softly kissing each of my fingers in a slow, deliberate way that sent the tingles streaming into me once again. The tingles stayed with me even after I left it all behind in dreamland.

❦   ❦   ❦

Belting out a very off-key but hearty version of *Freeway of Love*, I drove to town to see Raphaela the next morning. The Philly summer was in overdrive that Sunday, stifling humidity that was unrelenting and abusive. At its peak, summer in the city was equal parts bad air and bad vibes. And here I was driving to see Raphaela at 18 West Lehigh Street, in the heart of North Philadelphia.

It was a rundown mélange of tiny houses stuck together with sagging porches, peeling paint, graffiti-covered walls. Drug-dealing teenagers owned the streets and 14-year old black girls pushed their babies in strollers. I parked my car carefully in front of the house so I could watch it, feeling like a soft white peach, ripe for the plucking. Anxiously, I fingered the mace I carried in my pocket as I ran up the three cracked cement steps onto a dilapidated porch, stepped around the splintered hole in the red wood floor and knocked at number 18.

A woman opened the sagging screen door to greet me and it literally fell off its hinges, narrowly missing my feet. For a second, I didn't recognize her, and then I realized it was Raphaela. She had no makeup or jewelry on and her face was strangely nondescript—like a nun's. A faded red bandana was tied around her head. Grinning, she asked, "How is your case?"

"Back and forth. But better. Rhoda ended the affair. Raphaela, what in the world are you doing here?" I asked incredulously.

"Scout work for the Minyan. So we'll be meeting here for a while."

She invited me into a cramped, dingy box of a living room with bilious green walls. Raphaela motioned for me to sit on a ratty green-and-yellow-striped sofa that should have been sent to the dump years ago. She alighted on an old wooden chair.

"What is the Minyan?" I asked.

"A group I belong to. I do the advance work. In the opening phase, there's no substitute for being on site to get a sense of the suffering that people face."

"You do humanitarian projects?"

She nodded. "With Maharishi Sidha, the guru from Calcutta; John Lath, the head of Microware; and Bill Boros. I think you bumped into him a couple of times."

I wiped the sweat off my brow with the back of my hand. "Why are you wasting time on me?"

"You have an important mission in the world." I jumped as a baby mouse streaked across the old linoleum floor and crashed headlong into the wall. Very apropos, I thought.

"You've got to be kidding."

"We'll see about that." Raphaela bent over, scooped up the baby mouse with her bare hands, walked quickly to the front door and let him free. Dusting off her hands on her jeans, she sat back down and studied me.

"Tell me about your project," I asked.

"We have a team leader co-creating a vision of unity and abundance with clergy, business people and educators in the North Philly community. Social workers and psychologists mentoring adults and children who never had any-one to nurture them, to set goals with them."

"Can mentoring really make a difference in this place?"

"Studies show that mentoring kids in urban areas eliminates violence and boosts school success."

"Wow."

"The team also focuses on environmental cleanup and beautification as well as creating more businesses and jobs. That sums up the approach on the outer level."

"The outer level?" I was so fascinated I had forgotten the stifling heat.

"There has to be transformation of both outer and inner domains. To create harmony in the transcendent field we have four teachers that lead daily classes on meditation and we've assembled a group of advanced meditators to practice Yogic flying."

"Flying? In the air? My friend, Herb, said something about yogis being able to levitate."

Raphaela picked up a voluptuous pink peony that sat in a grimy drinking glass on a rickety table by her side. She held it to her nose. "It's no big deal. The real miracle is what happens to the neighborhoods where the yogis practice. In Washington D.C., for example, there was a dramatic fall in homicides and vio-lent crimes when a group of siddhas levitated together for a month."

I shook my head. "How could that be true?"

"They create from a place of pure consciousness. But in order to understand, you're going to have to master Lesson Three." Raphaela's jade green eyes bored into mine. "*The Divine awaits your daily invitation.*"

"What does that mean?"

"At every single moment, no matter what is happening, the Divine is all around you, ready to fill you with connection, with contentment, with beauty, with bliss."

"What is the Divine?" I asked with a mask of politeness.

"The Divine is what underlies the material universe, the universe of perception."

"In physics I remember something like electromagnetism or gravity."

"Yes, plus the weak and strong forces; the four cornerstones of the material universe. But what underlies those?" Raphaela chuckled.

"I just saw a movie called *What the Bleep Do We Know?* The scientists talked about looking for a, uh, unified field."

"Yes, the Superstring. But what underlies that?" She laughed full out.

"It's not God, if you're trying to get me to say that." Raphaela fell silent. Annoyed, I pulled at my sweaty ringlets and admitted, "I have no idea."

"The great void that is simultaneously everything and nothing." Her face was impassive.

"Sounds like a Zen riddle. I hate those—they don't make sense."

"The Divine, the void, is consciousness, or pure awareness. It manifests as distinct objects of matter to create the universe. Take this peony, for example." She took the huge blossom in her hand. For one moment it blinked off like a light bulb. I rubbed my eyes. When I looked again the flower was back. Trick of the mind, I thought, but the hair on the back of my neck stood up.

Raphaela continued to look at the flower. "Any physicist will tell you there is more emptiness than substance in this peony. Things are not in reality as they appear to our limited senses. The gurus even have a term for this misperception—Maya. Maya is our on-going belief that this illusion that we call the solid material world is the only reality. It keeps us caged in a dull and uninteresting world."

"OK, I remember college physics. Solidity is an illusion. But there must be real atoms and subatomic particles, right?"

"Of course," Raphaela replied, "But they are linked to pure consciousness. You can't separate them."

I gestured around the room. "But how do I know that pure awareness underlies all this?"

"Only by losing the bondage of self, the ego, through spiritual practice can you truly 'see'."

A catch-22, just like other religions: you've got to believe in order to believe, I thought.

Raphaela continued. "Runners talk about the runners' high. Non-runners only see the sweating and the grunting. You've got to live it to know it."

I felt inexplicably teary. "I've always been jealous of people happily tucked away in the hallucinated arms of God."

"By inviting the Divine into your daily life you will experience deep serenity."

"But do I have to believe in God to get the benefits?" I asked in exasperation.

"No you don't, though many people simply tune into a Higher Power as they understand it. Bottom line, through spiritual practice you can be cradled in the bliss of pure consciousness."

"Bliss?"

Raphaela went back to sitting on her chair and tenderly studied me. "You've suffered because of feeling so separate, so removed from all that is. When we identify only with the ego, the self, we create misery. When we free ourselves, experiencing self in the other, in the flower, in the rock, in the void, we are happy."

"Show me how," I begged.

"I am giving you three gifts that bring serenity: being-in-the-moment, pranayama and meditation."

"What's being-in-the-moment?" I asked as sweat meandered down my temple.

"It is an outwardly-focused meditation. Think Japanese tea ceremony, the placing of the teapot and the cups, the pouring of the tea, each act performed peacefully, deliberately, gracefully."

"It would be a real stretch for me to be graceful," I said, wistfully thinking of the sylph.

"Nonsense. You can create yourself as you choose in each moment." Raphaela stared at me. "Practicing the being-in-the-moment exercise will help you create the sylph."

She looked at me and winked as a shudder went down my back. How does she know my dreams, I wondered.

"For 15 minutes each morning, I want you to take a being-in-the-moment walk. You are to walk slowly and with care. Place your attention fully on an object near you and once you pass it, choose another."

I mopped up more beads of sweat on my forehead with a tissue from my jeans.

"Focusing attention gets easier with practice and it will take you to a world beautiful beyond measure." Raphaela pulled the old red bandana off her head and slowly shook her jet-black hair loose. As she moved her head from side to side I was mesmerized, as if in a hypnotic trance. I sat staring, shocked and motionless as her face began to shift and change. Slowly it transformed into a rosy golden figure with a young, innocent face, hazel eyes hooded, looking downward.

"Griselda," I blurted out.

As soon as I said the name, Raphaela morphed back to her striking pearly skin and jade green eyes.

"For a minute there you looked like Griselda from the Maxfield Parrish painting," I said, laughing nervously. "Sooze and I just saw the exhibit. You know I had a dream where I was in those otherworldly cliffs, all gold and lavender."

"Janna, my darling, you live in a Parrish world. You just don't see it." Raphaela beamed at me. "You, like most other people, live in a taped version of reality that the human brain made up. The real world is even more luminous than the paintings you are so taken with. Lesson three is designed to free you from the auto-hypnotic trance that blinds your eyes, closes your ears, and deadens your feelings. It will open you to a state of riotous enchantment." Raphaela leaned back in her chair and gazed at me.

"Tell me about the being-in-the-moment exercise. Do I have to walk outdoors?"

"No. You can practice indoors as well, although it's easier when you are in Nature. Try at first to put all your attention on the things you don't usually notice, like a drain pipe, the asphalt of the roadway, blades of grass, or a crawling insect. Sense the object so completely you become one with it. Over time graduate to things you usually do notice, like people." Raphaela chuckled. "Eventually you will realize you never really saw them either."

"Hope I can do this," I said as I fiddled with a curl.

"Of course you can. Come." Raphaela got up and motioned me into the grimy kitchen at the back of the house.

"Here?" My heart pounded.

She winked and put her arm around my back, shepherding me out the rickety door to the junkyard behind the house. We sat on the crumbling cement steps and I looked out over the 12 by 12 foot patch of dry dusty ground that housed a few struggling patches of grass and dandelions, piles of rotting wood slats, and a rusted black steel drum lying in the corner. The area was completely enclosed by a green, chain-link fence sagging off its supports, so much so that the left side had a man-sized hole.

"The world is full of magical things patiently waiting for our senses to grow sharper. Walk around." Raphaela shooed me off like a mother sending a toddler to play in the sandbox. Reluctantly I walked down the steps almost tripping on the last one, which was just an unsecured concrete block that rocked.

"Slowly, slowly," she cautioned with a maternal smile as she disappeared into the house.

I began by focusing on a dandelion. There was one fully formed yellow flower that caught my eye as I walked by. This is so stupid, I thought, especially here. But I put my attention on the bloom and kept walking until I found myself stopping about two feet away from it. A weed, I thought. Doesn't anybody ever take care of this place? It's awful…

"Focus your attention." I heard Raphaela's voice in my head. "Attention is the gateway to Heaven."

I forced myself to study the whole plant carefully. I examined its sturdy gray-green stem, the shape of the spiky green dandelion leaves, the round head of golden color crowning its top. I looked and looked. All of a sudden the flower seemed to swallow me up; it was the only thing that existed. There was no scale of size, no background, no me watching it. Just one magnificent blossom with the richest explosion of tiny petals fanned out in perfect symmetry.

"I burst forth with new seed," it said in its beingness.

Raphaela appeared briefly at the back door and grinned like an excited schoolgirl.

As I turned my attention to her, the expanded awareness left me. "What about the fence?" she said.

"A flower is one thing, but…"

"The fence." She pointed to the back of the yard. I dutifully walked toward the sagging chain link. I let the green lines fall on my eyes, took them in, noticed how round each piece of metal was, how tightly the pieces held together, how the intention in that fence was to mark, to protect. I noticed the regularity of the diamond shape openings between the green metal. Walking up to within a few inches of the fence, I studied it fully, letting it in. For one brief moment I saw a beautifully organized energy pattern without mass. The grid drew me in yet frightened me, and I turned away, hoping the solidity of the chain link would return.

At that moment the hole in the fence swam into view and I gasped in terror. A squat, bald man with arms covered by tattoo graffiti was loitering just outside the yard, staring at me.

Barely able to breathe, much less shout for help, I glared at the intruder. He had the look of a rottweiler on patrol and I expected him to growl before the attack. Tattoos of daggers, crosses and thorns colored the parts of his body not covered by a Harley Davidson muscle shirt, ripped jeans and mud-stained army boots. Sweat poured from me as I calculated how quickly I could make it to the back door.

The tank of a man continued staring, expressionless eyes locked into mine. "This is what I get for inviting the Divine into my life," I fumed. Deciding to make a run for it, I turned and started toward the back door. But I felt like I could only move in an agonizingly slow jog in the sweltering heat. Finally I crashed through the screen door to safety and fell into Raphaela's arms. "A Hell's Angel, he's chasing me…"

She grabbed hold of me and burst out in laughter.

"I see you have met Gilbert." Her chuckles were annoying and my face colored. "Gilbert, come in please."

He promptly joined us, nodding deferentially to Raphaela and disappearing up a narrow stairwell off the living room. She sat on the ratty couch with me and patted my knee.

"He is a devotee-bodyguard of Maharishi Siddha and a fourth degree black belt in Tae Kwon Do."

My cheeks burned red. "I'm sorry."

"Consider those you fear as teachers." Raphaela hit me lightly on the arm.

I was startled to see sandaled feet and folds of material drift down the steps, bringing a figure slowly into view. It was Gilbert, this time covered by a white linen vestment finely embroidered with gold threads.

"He is a spiritual adept who will help with your initiation," Raphaela announced.

I hung my head as Gilbert descended into the room in slow motion, with his eyes half-closed. Wanting to apologize to him, yet afraid to break his trance, I sat silently. He sat on a blanket in lotus position and began emitting guttural, nonhuman sounds that reverberated through my body.

Raphaela sat next to him, also in the lotus. She closed her eyes dreamily and began slowly breathing in through one nostril and out through the other, using her forefinger and thumb to rhythmically close each nostril. Raphaela pressed her forefinger on the left nostril and inhaled through the right and then, releasing that finger, she pressed her thumb on the right nostril and exhaled through the left. With each intake/outflow she would reverse the direction. I followed her in clumsy imitation. She opened her eyes, took my hand and guided me. "Slowly, slowly. You'll get it." After what seemed like an eternity, I had crudely managed the process. My embarrassment faded as I closed my eyes and concentrated on the practice. Gilbert's deep rolling sounds took over the room. I breathed along and tingles spread throughout my body. Gradually, all the knots in my upper back released. The room seemed to breathe with me and I became intoxicated with air.

The chanting stopped and Raphaela's resonant voice caught me. "This is pranayama. Do it for five minutes each day." I blinked open my eyes to a room that had become an oasis of peace. Raphaela and Gilbert sat with their eyes closed like two statues of Buddha.

She broke the deep silence. "Don't be discouraged if you forget how to do it. It will come back to you. As you do the practice the mind will rebel and want to process other thoughts, important tasks, the laundry, grocery-shopping, getting floss…" I giggled. "When that happens, just let the intrusive thoughts go."

"Hope I can do this."

Raphaela opened her eyes.

"No hoping. Just do it."

❧   ❧   ❧

"What in the world are you doing with your nose?" Sooze asked as she stared at me. I was sitting on her couch clumsily practicing my breathing.

"Raphaela's pranayama.technique. It makes breathing more regular, while soothing your nervous system. Supposedly, the more you practice, the more coordinated the left and right hemispheres of the brain become."

"Looks like it'll keep your sinuses clear and save tissue expenses big-time," Sooze quipped as she gathered her purse, keys and a sweater. "Come on. I want to get some Amish gummie bears at the Farmers Market."

I rubbed my nemesis upper back. "Raphaela said that it would strengthen the weaker side of my body and release my mind from what she called the 'yoke of tensions'.

"I'll just take a stiff Cosmopolitan, thank you very much." Sooze insisted.

I continued the rhythmic single nostril breathing. She flopped on the couch next to me. "I just read this awful book, *He's Just Not That Into You.* And I really started to worry about Fred. All his excuses, his total lack of sex drive…"

I kept breathing and mellowing out while watching her obsess about Fred.

Finally, I broke the silence. "C'mon Sooze. Try this."

"I can pick up some vodka at the market," Sooze prattled on.

"Come on, Sooze."

Sooze shook her head like a stubborn child. "No, dammit. He is into me but he just can't get away from that witchy witch."

"Raphaela's gonna teach me meditation. We could learn together."

"And here Swami Sooze has told you for years to learn it. You forget that I've put all my sex abuse survivors into relaxation training and it really helps their anxiety, depression, hyper-vigilance and even insomnia. Guess you like her better than me!"

"This is going to be formal meditation, sitting with eyes closed and silently repeating a Sanskrit mantra for 20 minutes twice a day."

Sooze popped a piece of gum in her mouth. "You think you'll be able to do it?"

"I know, I know. My follow through in self-care taking sucks. Raphaela says I'm fundamentally undisciplined." My New Years' resolutions, diets, deals with Sooze, and other false promises, only served to strengthen, not weaken my bad habits. I shifted uncomfortably, not knowing what else to say.

"And do you need to borrow any more money to pay for this abuse?"

"Actually, no. I was complaining about the HMOs nixing a bunch of my bills and she told me she wasn't charging me anymore."

"That really makes me suspicious," Sooze worried.

"It is kind of weird. She's charging me a bunch of flowers, a few fruits and a white handkerchief to learn meditation."

"She is certifiable."

"I did make one financial deal with her though."

"When are you supposed to sign over the deed to your house?"

"Each time I miss a being-in-the-moment, pranayama or meditation, I put $25 in a jar. At the end of each week, I send the money to charity."

❦   ❦   ❦

The meditation training sessions ate up all my free time for the next week. But the experience was good and ironically I started looking forward to going to each meeting, to searching for peace in the sweltering ghetto.

Late Thursday afternoon I met with Rhoda and Jim. A couple of fights had erupted. I simply brought up the notion that Rhoda should take the kids and go to her mother's for a few days. They left my office holding hands and I sat down pleased but wistfully alone at my desk.

That night in North Philly I asked Raphaela about the fear of loss strategy.

"Part of me feels manipulative. I've been taught that type of behavior was pathological."

Raphaela pulled her hair back into a makeshift ponytail and studied me.

"Most therapists see it that way. And they miss a great opportunity to help troubled couples make quantum leaps in their ability to love. The greatest gift you can give Rhoda and Jim is to go with their fear of loss."

"It's working, no question," I answered from my usual post on the green and yellow striped sofa.

Raphaela managed to look regal perched on the broken wicker stool. "You are seeing Lesson Two in action. *When you face loss, love blossoms.* And what else has transpired from your work on Lesson One?"

"I'm coming to value fear as a great ally. By overcoming my anxiety about being honest with my father, I opened doors for both of us. He shared and I understood him as a real person for the first time. You know, he was the one who discovered my grandfather's body. A 12 year old that had just finished his deliveries of *The Daily News.* He walked into the living room with his milk and rugelach and saw his father lying in his favorite armchair. Grandpa's eyes were wide open, staring." My voice cracked. "I could relate…"

Raphaela nodded knowingly.

"Uncle Morty quit school at 16 to collect money at the parking lot that carried the family. It was Morty who put my father through college so he could be an accountant. He leveraged that lot to build a real estate empire spread all over the Delaware Valley. He invited Dad in, but my mother resented Morty and his wife. So my father turned down the gravy train. He confessed to me how much he's regretted that decision. To hear him speak like that was amazing."

"When you reclaim personal power, good spreads out like ripples from a stone in water." Then she announced, "Vincent called me."

"No way!"

"He told his wife and she threatened to leave him. I spoke to the couple, calmed them down and they agreed to see a therapist."

"So now he lives happily ever after?" I grumbled.

"Don't worry. He has to go through Hell before he hits Nirvana." She half-smiled. "Back to your training."

She left the room briefly and came back with a white tablecloth and a thick white candle. Gilbert suddenly came down the stairwell in his robes and posted himself near a smoke-stained fireplace that I hadn't even noticed before. He began emitting a low rumbling sound, a sweeping noise that brightened up the whole grimy room.

"During meditation, the cerebral cortex quiets down, but in that process, thoughts surface. This dynamic is called the outward stroke or progression. As you let thoughts float through your mind and go quietly back to the mantra, you get an inward stroke, a profound peacefulness. This phase is akin to regression. All growth is rhythmic in this way, outward and inward. Thoughts are good and necessary. Allow them to float past, release your stress and eventually peace will follow."

Raphaela stood up and announced solemnly, "Are you ready to receive the mantra?"

I nodded nervously.

She spread the elaborately crocheted tablecloth over the peeling paint on the fireplace mantle. I brought over the bouquet of white carnations, mums and baby's breath, one of Baba Aydel's old cotton hankies, a bunch of grapes, a peach and a ripe plum. Gilbert lit the candle and sang verses in the melodious, Hawaiian sounding words of the Sanskrit language. Then Raphaela turned to me and whispered a lovely vowel-laden sound in my ear. I sat back down on the couch with my hands in my lap and repeated the mantra in my mind. At first, all I had were thoughts and more thoughts. Remembering my instruction, I just let them be and came back to the mantra. After an uncomfortable eternity, I entered a soft dream state where I was lost in gentle, peaceful flowing sensations. I had vague memories of lying on the beach at Babba Pearl's, the sweet ocean air, the endless azure sky, the timeless sun warming my body.

"Stop the mantra." I heard Raphaela's voice from what seemed a far distance. I was disappointed to be brought back to mundane reality.

"It was good?" she asked, as I dreamily opened my eyes.

I worked my newly mellowed face into a half-smile.

"You are ready to invite the Divine into your life each day. Being-in-the-moment helps focus the mind so the process of thinking slows down. It also frees stuck emotions that may be blocking your ability to be in the present. Pranayama softens the breathing, brings in the subtle energies and further calms the mind. Meditation withdraws the awareness from the senses and allows you to fully drink in all the richness of the transcendent." She and Gilbert bowed to me and I instinctively bowed back. Then she ushered me out the door.

When I got home I was drawn to sit down on the wooden rocker in my living room and meditate while Milo rested his silky tan and brown mop-top head on my loafer. This time I went straight into deep peace. I was bathing in waters of nourishment that straightened out all the kinks from each muscle. Then I heard a strange, pleasurable, and enchanted coo-ree, coo-ree. He was calling.

CHAPTER 10

Altered States

Raphaela left town for the month of July on a clandestine Minyan project. Feeling abandoned, I decided to throw myself into projects I had neglected. My 'early eclectic garage-sale décor' was beyond stale. I found two fabulous brass candelabras at the King of Prussia mall and put them on my mantle. As I stood admiring the elegant character they added to the room, I remembered more of Lesson Three. Raphaela had taught me to perform ordinary acts with my full attention—to mentally focus while I scrubbed the kitchen floor, washed the dishes, weeded the garden, put on Milo's leash. To help that process, I was to repeat over and over to myself a mantra that said just what I was doing in the now.

I am creating beauty, I am creating beauty, I am creating beauty, I said in my mind. As I kept the focus I let go of my normal tangle of worries and thoughts and entered the light of the now. The redecorating became effortless, like an act of communion with the divine as I lugged the stuffed brown corduroy sofa to the wall facing the box fireplace, and set up a new blue, gold and brown Klimt print of a couple kissing in the middle. Then I threw gold brocade material over the two stuffed green chairs Aunt Irma had given me as a housewarming gift. I crowned it off with a purple wandering Jew plant for the sill of the front bay window. Milo woofed his approval at our new digs.

Each day I practiced being-in-the-moment, pranayama and meditation. Jewel moments kept emerging from the labyrinth of my cluttered mind chatter, moments of being one with the ancient oak trees that lifted their arms in happy embrace of the sun in Valley Green, and with the placid water that rested in reflection in the Wissahickon stream. During meditation, idyllic scenes from my childhood before the Accident returned with nostalgic sights, sounds, smells and tastes. Doris and I gobbling up pink and green salt water taffy while we teased the waves at Margate down the Jersey shore; catching the magic fireflies in jars by the tiny wooden bungalow we rented up in the Poconos; or twirling around with our arms spread wide until we dizzily fell into the tall grass of our backyard in fits of giggles.

The meditative practice soothed me until Raphaela returned to the Chadds Ford farmhouse in August. When I arrived to see her again, she was in her ostentatious manifestation, wearing a yellow silk fitted couture suit finished off with an orange and gold chain Hermes scarf and Elsa Perreti diamonds by the mile. Flinging the ornate front door open, she greeted me with a strong inflection, "Yes. There you are. Things have progressed well with your daily invitations to the Divine."

I was unsettled once again by her mind-reading as well as by her changed appearance. She waved me into the living room and I sat on the sofa while she seated herself on the blue velvet throne. Nervously I rooted through my tote bag and handed her a bag of Flakowitz bagels.

"Thank you," Raphaela said. "Now tell me what you have noticed in your meditations."

"I have a lot of thoughts. Depressing thoughts. Nervous thoughts. Silly thoughts."

Raphaela smiled. "It's only a venting."

"But I've also had blissful moments."

Raphaela came over to the sofa. "Close your eyes."

As I did, she put her forefinger on a point in the middle of my eyebrows. A delightful streaming sensation cascaded down from her finger and radiated throughout my body.

In a very soft voice, Raphaela said, "Observe that there are three things occurring at all times. There is the knower, that which is being known, and the process of knowing. When we meditate we learn that we are distinct from our thoughts, that the knower is not her thoughts, feelings, moods, perceptions, ideas or beliefs. This realization is the first step toward transcending the self. Do you understand?" I nodded.

"In the being-in-the-moment exercises and meditations we also come to realize that not only are we separate from our thoughts and feelings but we create them. We recognize that these states of consciousness are not simply happening to us, rather that we generate them."

I opened my eyes. Puzzled, I asked, "I kind of get that, but, what's the point?"

Raphaela smiled and tapped my forehead. "Keep your eyes closed. In your normal state of consciousness you confuse your reactions, your fears, your disappointments, with your essence. In the transcendent state, you come to know that these phenomena are not you. And that they are everchanging and ephemeral. What this means is you can alter them at any time. Just imagine. You now possess the owner's manual to run your own mind and its reactions to events as you choose. You can create tranquility, happiness, and even joy. Whenever you want."

I opened my eyes. "But can I really alter my moods when I'm not with you?"

"That and much more. You're altering your moods right now. Not me. Even now you could make yourself sad or worried."

I shook my head. "Sounds like self-hypnosis."

Raphaela laughed. "Self-hypnosis can be effective precisely because the knower recognizes that she is different than the behavior she is trying to alter. I'm teaching you the deeper principles that allow auto-suggestion to work."

"How do I get out of a rotten mood? It seems impossible."

"Continue your daily practice of being-in-the-moment, pranayama and meditation. Allow the detachment that occurs naturally to ground you in the knowledge that you are the creator of your feelings. A mood is like a show on TV and you have the remote that changes the channels."

I had struggled to gain control of my moodiness my whole life. I was almost afraid to hope that this would really work.

"First you experience the mood fully. Then imagine that it is outside of you, as if it was playing on the TV screen. The important thing is to experience your bad mood while recognizing that it is just that: your bad mood."

"In other words, I have chosen to generate a bad mood."

"Yes. By detaching from it you can lessen its strength over you. This is why the Buddha emphasized detachment as the royal road to enlightenment."

I opened my mouth to ask a question when I saw a circle of light playing around Raphaela's head. She continued, "Once you have gone into the unwanted moods and watched them from a distance, they will dissipate. Then from that clear place you can consciously generate new thoughts and feelings. Like, 'I am blessed.'"

I was struck by the simplicity of the idea. "Would I say that aloud or silently?"

"Either way. Just have a clear intention. You might call it an affirmation."
Raphaela laughed. "But with the clarity of mind you will achieve through your
spiritual practices, you will manifest the mood you want."

"How does pranayama fit in?"

Raphaela grinned. "I call it the oxygen cocktail."

"I've noticed that I'm sharper afterwards."

"Breathing and cleansing help us achieve higher states of consciousness.
That's why I want you to receive panchakarma."

"Pancha-who?'

"It's an ancient Ayurvedic treatment that used to be reserved for royalty in
India. It removes physical impurities and prepares your body, the temple, for
deep spiritual breakthroughs." Raphaela polished her diamond necklace with a
tissue and it danced with light.

"Like this," she held it out to me. "Go to Maharishi Siddha's Ayurvedic
Health Center for a few days."

*   *   *

Warm sesame oil languorously dripped onto my body as two angelic techni-
cians dressed in white cotton sweats massaged each side of my body in syn-
chrony. Silently I repeated my mantra as my body quit fighting and melted into
the massage table. After two and a half hours, I was floating. The chirp of spar-
rows outside the Center window sounded like nectar on air. When they were
done, the masseuses had to help me off the table. As they swathed me in a cozy
white terry robe I stared out the window. Rays of sunlight played on the clouds
like God descending from above. Pure bliss.

That evening, wearing the requisite white turban over my sesame-oiled hair,
I walked in delicious silence down to the dining room. The center occupied an
old Main Line mansion that a wealthy follower had donated to Maharishi Siddha. It was a well-kept Philadelphia edifice, with expansive stone façade, a
stately columned porch and polished mahogany mantels that made me feel
secure, like I was wrapped in old world stability and charm. The eight other
panchakarma recipients sat at a long antique table in mellow communion.
They smiled warmly at me as we were served the first course of a vegetarian
feast. We ate the pink lentil soup quietly. Then I managed somehow to spill a
spoonful of soup onto the fellow next to me. He was quite gracious as he
mopped up his plaid pants. "Quite OK. By the way, I'm Hugh," he said.

Hugh Douglas had warm cafe au lait skin, a strong forehead squared off by a tightly clipped Afro, and sad chocolate eyes. He sported a preppy look, complete with a light pink pullover tied over his shoulders. He was a 39-year-old plaintiff's attorney who worked at a Norristown firm in the black community. On a mission from God, he protected folks disabled in accidents or through corporate negligence.

As Hugh sipped his soup, he kept eyeing me. Finally he asked, "Shirodhara. Have you had it?" He pronounced each word as if he were giving a speech in a diction class. "They slowly drip warm sesame oil on your forehead."

"Sounds great," I said politely.

"It relaxes both hemispheres of the brain," he continued. Then he blushed and clammed up like a love-struck seventh grader. It made me nervous. After dinner Hugh asked me to take a walk. I politely declined and wandered around the manicured estate alone like a happy child just let out for recess.

The second day I received the shirodhara. As they dripped the warm oil on my forehead, I saw bright streaming waves of energy, cascading through the universe. It was like living out my dreams of Him: expanded beyond all limits of time and space.

That day at dinner, everything looked radiant and lovely as if some lens-maker in the cosmic sky had given me new glasses. Even Hugh looked good to me. As we ate our rice and dahl we exchanged sweet glances. His eyes were large, inquiring and so clearly smitten with me. Then he gave me a boring lecture on the importance of having sweet, sour, salty, bitter, pungent and astringent foods at each meal. I immediately tossed him back into the nerd bin.

CHAPTER 11

Out of the Chrysalis

"After three days of panchakarma I'm calmer, clearer. And my meditations have fewer random thoughts," I said to Raphaela as she sat in the Chester county farmhouse living room. "I brought you a thank you batch of my favorite pretzels from the Farmers Market on Bethlehem Pike."

Raphaela chuckled as she took the bag. She bit into a pretzel and closed her eyes, savoring the flavor as if it were a Belgian truffle. Gazing at me, she nodded. "You're doing well on your inner work. Now we turn to the outer. Let's talk about men."

I found myself in a coughing fit. Finally it subsided.

"Real love is a healing gift that rips open portals of intimacy with another and more importantly with your self," she said as she plastered mustard on her pretzel and once again bit into it with relish. Her long fake nails were painted with esoteric red-orange Sanskrit designs. Is she referring to Him? I wondered.

"Raphaela, did you send me dreams about…"

"Him." Grinning, she completed my sentence. Raphaela studied my face. "You needed help to come alive. Don't be afraid of the dream world. It is there as a gift for you." Her words settled me. "Tell me about the dreams."

"It's perfect with Him. Sexy, yet I feel pure and innocent. You know I associate sex with being dirty or shameful but not with Him."

Raphaela dug into her pretzel feast.

"Yes, it's the way it was meant to be with Him, a healing cosmic connection to your soul." She carefully wiped mustard from her marquise diamond ring and spoke again, "You could get in that ballpark with a real man."

"Right. The other night I was watching a re-run of Ally McBeal. She was reduced to dancing and singing with a pillow and a fantasized Al Green. That's me."

"Nonsense," Raphaela scowled.

"Anyway, there are no good men out there. Maybe for my clients but not for me. The nice ones are boring and the sexy ones screw me over."

"Ridiculous." More mustard fell on her white silk poncho. She totally ignored it.

"I'm not exactly a Ph.D. on the subject, but still!"

I had only three passionate relationships in my life—Jake, Stokes, and Larry Needlebaum, a Boston psychologist. Every one was crushing. I was 19 when I met Jake at State College. A brawny Irishman with wild hair, freckles, and an infectious giggle, he was the first person who I opened up to.

At first with Jake I was shy, bottled up. But he was patient. He tickled me with a peacock feather, fed me grapes one by one in bed and looked into my eyes while he rubbed me with almond oil. I was mostly able to be present with him during lovemaking, although I always jumped in the shower afterwards, which annoyed him. Jake gave me a claddagh ring and proposed that we elope to Elkton, Maryland after graduation.

Three weeks later he called me, yes, called me to break off the engagement. I threw the cheap piece of shit ring into the Schuylkill River. It was all I could do to not throw me in with it. After that I started to study psychology. To save my own life.

Raphaela put a huge dollop of mustard on a pretzel. As she bit into it, the yellow dropped on her chin. I took a napkin and started to wipe it off, but she just waved at me with a laugh and kept enjoying her pretzel. By now her white poncho was a ruinous yellow. And I'm supposed to be the klutz, I thought. Then I realized what she was doing.

Raphaela studied me. "So the only reliable male in your life has been your dog."

"You could say that." I took a pretzel, squirted the mustard on big time and took a huge bite. "I haven't been in a relationship with anyone since Larry."

"When was that?"

"About six years ago." Even I couldn't help but laugh. She rested her ankle on a little leather footrest near her chair. She was wearing a gold anklet with dangling hearts that caught the light.

"He was a psychologist who I dated off and on for a year. We met at a convention in Florida where he was presenting on sexual abuse and I was in the audience. Larry was a horn-rimmed brainiac, but I got into the meeting of the minds. Fantasized about moving to Boston." I glanced down at my mustard-stained fingers. "Then I found out about the Barbie doll psychoanalyst who worked with him at McLeans. He finally sent me a Dear Jane letter after being offered a tenured position at UC Santa Barbara. Guess I was geographically undesirable."

Raphaela totally ignored my story. "Do you want real love in your life?"

"I guess." She had knocked me off guard once again.

"Do you?" she pressed.

Anxiously I picked up a faded horse figurine that was lying on the spindly, antique coffee table in front of me and began to stroke its back with my thumb. Suddenly the horse opened his eyes and stared at me with a fierce look. I squawked an "I do," and dropped the statue on the table.

"You set yourself up to fail by choosing men who are distant like your father was…"

"Or slimeballs like Vincent."

"Then after being hurt a number of times you simply sealed yourself off, Rapunzel in the tower. Now it's time to let your hair down."

"For who? There are no knights, no warriors, only fools and jesters."

"Stop that defensive crap," Raphaela said curtly.

"OK," I blurted out. "I do want love in my life, but the truth is…the truth is…that all that work on the incest and my father was great, but I believe that, that it was not a matter of losing my mother, or being molested, or even being the grandchild of survivors."

Her eyes drilled into me. "So what is it?"

Tears streamed down my cheek and fell onto my t-shirt. "It's just me. I was born unlovable and nothing will ever change that."

Raphaela came over to the sofa, sat down beside me and held my chin so I had to look at her.

"Even you can't raise the dead."

"How do you know what's possible?" Suddenly she pointed out the window overlooking the rolling green hillside. A fawn stood right outside, perched on impossibly long knobby legs in the dappled sunlight. "Focus all your attention on that pure being." Raphaela insisted. "So much so that you become one with it."

I cradled against her as I stared out the window at the young deer. A memory of being held by my mother came to me. I must have been about seven or so, a little cherub with a head full of chocolate curls. I had just fallen off my bike. After soothing my gashed knee with a cool ice bag, Mother had rocked me in her arms while she hummed softly to me. The image opened a honeyed feeling in my heart. All at once the fawn bounded away. I sat up and looked at Raphaela, love welling from my eyes.

"Sweet being, you are not defective. You were never prized so that you could find the special beauty in yourself. Did you ever see parents looking at their first-born? They are completely entranced, crazy about this new being. They see only perfection. That's what you need so desperately in order to complete yourself."

She petted my hair with her fingertips.

"Inner mirrors outer. The infant takes in the parenting that was given and she also feels causative in that process. You had a tremendous void: a distant father and a mother who was in love with your sister. You decided at an early age you were unlovable. Then piled on top of that was the incest with all the shame and self hate. No wonder you feel so damaged."

She smiled beneficently at me. "The Fourth Lesson is: *Falling in love with yourself is the first step to finding the love you seek.* All of my teachings are aimed at helping you fall in love with yourself, that you may experience the innocence and beauty of your true essence. My presence in your life is aimed at this goal."

"How do I do that?"

"Say loving words to yourself every day. Tell yourself what a good person you are, how talented and special you are. Compliment yourself when you do something right."

"Usually I do just the opposite, calling myself klutz, constantly criticizing my body…"

Raphaela nodded. "You know what most of your body is made of?"

"Fat?" I asked.

Raphaela smacked my arm. "Water. You are about 60% water." And do you know how water responds to thought?"

"No."

A Japanese scientist, Dr. Masaru Emoto, studied newly-forming crystals of frozen water. When they were bombarded with positive words and intentions, they formed bright beautiful snowflake patterns. When they were given negative suggestions, they formed chaotic patterns that were dull or even ugly."

"I bet that's why people who feel good about themselves have a glow…"

"Yes. Charisma."

Raphaela continued. "I want you to take out several pictures of yourself when you were a beaming little girl, before you were wounded. Put them up all around the house. Everyday, tell that little girl, Janna, how great she is. Love her up."

I nodded.

"As for the adult Janna, I want you to give to yourself, be gracious and generous to yourself, bring out and accent all your skills, talents and beauty. And then love will appear in your life."

"Sounds good," I said, stifling a yawn.

"It's time to adorn the temple of your being and to come out of your shell."

"What does that mean?"

She jangled several heavy gold bracelets on her right arm and laughed. "I want you to take ownership of your womanly power and beauty."

"That stuff is superficial," I complained.

"Like many other survivors you have lived under layers of silence and shame, afraid to attract the attention of men. You have disowned the great feminine, the goddess within." She jangled her trinkets again. "This is what you judge negatively in me and others."

"My mother and Babba Aydel constantly made derogatory remarks about 'society' women. They loved to vilify my Aunt Irma, who was the wealthiest and most attractive woman…"

I nervously glanced down and noticed a mustard stain on my shirt.

"They felt they couldn't compete. After my mom died my aunt tried to take me under her wing. We worshiped at Har Zion, the synagogue that Frank Lloyd Wright designed, went to Broadway shows, and attended openings at the Philadelphia Museum of Art."

"Go on."

"It's funny, I could name every artist in the Dorrance Gallery and yet…"

"You always felt like an outsider."

"Exactly."

"As if identifying with Irma would be a betrayal of your mother, a mother you never had."

A buried part of me, rife with unfilled longing and raw wounds opened. I stared out into space. "She belonged to my sister, the goyish blonde, not to the chubby plain klutz."

"It's time to change all that." Raphaela took my face in her hands and studied my head as if I was a thoroughbred for sale. "You have marvelous cheekbones, luscious full lips, and liquid brown eyes. Your beauty is simply hidden, not highlighted."

Her touch started a new ache my heart. She pushed my hair back from my face and stared at me. For an instant her face glowed with an otherworldly light, as she appeared to see a hidden quality in me, a kind of loveliness that lit up her countenance. In return, I offered up a weak smile.

"I want you to go and see Sebastian. His beauty salon is in Warminster, but he studies in Europe each year and wins the New York hair shows. He's a hair sculptor who releases a great piece of art in the rock. Surrender to him and you will find yourself being more of yourself than you've ever been."

"That's shallow," I protested, expecting to be Sebastian's first failure. I worried that Raphaela was trying to turn me into a clone of her ostentatious self. Next she would insist that I wear fake red nails.

Raphaela continued. "Grooming, clothes and jewelry are props that help us stage our role in the play of life. On this plane they can help bring us attention or success." She wouldn't get off it.

"To a degree, I suppose." You meet a saint, a living, breathing saint, and she tells you to get your hair done.

Raphaela answered. "I work progressively and regressively, in the tradition of Tagore, the Indian poet and mystic—the goal is to be fully empowered in the material world while you cultivate a deep spiritual discipline. Get over your fear of being attractive and desirable. Remember, 'The fear is the wish.' You would love to have money, to be eye-catching and charismatic."

"I really don't care..." I protested, while an inner voice screamed, liar, liar, liar.

Raphaela closed her eyes and recited, her voice rich and full, "One day when She was amorous, Nature created them, Amor as Lord and the heart as his great house, Within that house, the Lord lies there sleeping; Perhaps he sleeps briefly, perhaps for years. Dante."

I stared at her, speechless.

She continued, "True beauty shows itself then in a fine woman. Her beauty so delights the eyes, that the heart conceives at last a desire for this sweet thing."

"That's sexist. I don't need a man to feel attractive."

"You missed the point. The poet said, 'the heart.' That includes your own heart, self-love." Raphaela shot me a knowing look

I nibbled. "How much does it cost?"

"Make an appointment and go. You'll survive."

"OK," I begrudgingly agreed. But Raphaela wasn't done with me.

"What's more, I want you to develop yourself as a person. Enlarge your world. Take acting lessons, play golf, paint. Find out what really turns you on. You need to ignite yourself, find your passion and others who share it with you."

"I have nothing besides my work that excites me."

"Bullshit. What did you dream about doing when you were a child?"

"I wanted to be a ballerina, thin and graceful. I cried watching Margot Fonteyn. She was the opposite of me, the anti-klutz."

"How about ballet lessons? You can't just sit around eating with Sooze."

I turned red. "Ballet is too demanding. But I can work on developing a graceful golf swing."

"Let's agree on these new assignments."

"I'll definitely start on the golf. But, Sebastian's...I just got my hair done," I waffled.

"Not good enough," Raphaela said, ushering me out.

*   *   *

"My hormones are wacky. Haven't been myself lately," Sooze said between bites of lemon tilapia, asparagus and couscous. She sat at my dinette, her forehead lined with wet ringlets. "And you," she pointed her fork at me. "You're never around."

Sooze dabbed at her forehead. "I just can't get into what you're doing...that woman scares me."

"You'll never believe the latest. She's sent me to some trendy salon."

"For what?"

I looked down and brushed couscous from my lap. "A makeover."

"Oh, please. Next you'll go on The Swan."

"Well, Raphaela is giving me exactly what I missed out on—the guidance of a mother figure..."

"She's a mother, all right. Clara would approve," Sooze said, referring to the diva.

I took a long swig of Chardonnay and put another piece of fish on Sooze's plate. "She wants me to nurture myself as a stepping stone to being in a loving relationship with a man."

"What do fake nails and mascara have to do with love?"

"Men go for looks."

Sooze scowled. "You probably think I should go."

Bacchus took hold of my tongue. "Well, our eggs are sulfuring up fast."

"Speak for yourself. I've got a picture of Dorian Gray."

"Aunt Irm used to say…"

Sooze's face contorted. "Now you're quoting that overdone, pretentious old bag!"

"It's time we…I accept…"

"Next you'll tell me what a pretty face I would have…" She shoved her chair back from the table and cried into her hand.

"Sooze, stop being so damn sensitive," I spit out.

"And you're a Moonie. Next she'll select a husband for you and marry you off with 1200 people in a mass ceremony at Madison Square Garden."

"Thanks a lot for the support."

I can't stand what you're turning into."

Sooze lurched up, grabbed her purse and lumbered out the front door.

I sat there for a few stunned minutes. Then I angrily picked up the phone and called for the appointment with Sebastian. Luckily, or unluckily, he had a cancellation the next day. The salon was filled with model types, each with carved hairstyles, perfect makeup, miniskirts, long legs and, supreme self-confidence. And these were the hairdressers. I was a nondescript mongrel among AKC show dogs at Westminster.

Sebastian was a handsome fifty-something who wore his scissors in a gun holster, gangster style. I was sure the 'wise guy' would carve me up good.

He studied my head the same way as Raphaela, only his evaluation stretched on and on. Finally, he snapped his fingers and said, "Color, color, she needs color—a bronzed chestnut." He fingered my shaggy eyebrows, and clucked. "Kim, come over here. Can you see the arches? Yes, beautiful. See where her eyes deepen, I want the arch right there and tangerine rouge to bring out her cheekbones. Bronze tones especially on that full lower lip and a hint of gray-green liner for those almond eyes. They're great but you can't see them."

As he started to cut my hair, I closed my eyes and silently said my mantra. The meditation proved to be an antidote to my paranoid frazzle.

Hours later, when it was all over, I was in shock. The lady in the mirror was sophisticated, put together, yes, beautiful. They had cut her hair spiky and short so that it exposed the shape of her head and neck, which looked elegant, almost swan-like. Her mouth was a coppery pout and her eyes and brows were straight out of L'Oreal.

Sebastian sent me right over to a friend at Nordstrom's to buy clothes that complemented the new look. The salesperson conjured up a magic trick: wearing short A-line skirts to hide the lumpy bulges in my upper thighs and show off the leaner lines in my calves. Presto—I looked ten years younger. I bought four skirts and a shiny brown A-line slip dress.

That night I put on the dress and carefully studied myself in the full-length mirror behind my bedroom door. A stranger stared back at me.

CHAPTER 12

Journey to Mars

"Raphaela said to go out of my comfort zone with men. She wants me to date ones that are boring or nerdy, date a whole bunch of men, actually three at one time," I said to Sooze as we sat in her cozy nest at 191 between clients. We had white-flagged it a few weeks after our blow-up. And despite or maybe because of Sooze's hesitations, she wanted to gossip about every step of my work with Raphaela.

"I said, 'Three! I can't get a date with one.'" I wiped sweat off my brow. "Then she pointed out I had met that guy, Hugh, at panchakarma."

Sooze spooned some Cherry Garcia into her mouth.

"That stiff?"

"Raphaela calls it 'the program of three'. You date three men so you don't get into that passionate moth-to-a-flame over-involvement."

Sooze offered me ice cream and I shook my head. "Oh yeah, I know it well. It was in the last *Star. Woman, Found Dead, Glued to a Cellphone that Never Rang*," she chortled.

"The aim of the program is to stay emotionally balanced while you're dating. So if one guy doesn't call, another will. You learn to come from abundance."

"Theoretically, yeah. But we're talking men here," Sooze said.

I took a half-spoon of the B & J and continued. "You want theoretical, get this. She wants me to be Margaret Mead in the Land of Men: to study the way they listen, nurture me, self-disclose, get along with their families, how and when they turn me on. She wants me to find out what I really want and need in a partner."

"Yummy. Slutsville, here we come," Sooze teased.

"No. In the program of three you're not supposed to have sex with any of them, at least for many months. Raphaela said that having sex and coming releases the bonding hormone, oxytocin. It hormonally sews you into attachment whether you want it or not!"

"That makes sense."

"Sex can plunge you into the over-involvement trap. You need to hang firm and tell them you're not ready, that you're dating several people for a while."

"Just say no? Guys will really go for that," Sooze said as she got up to get a new pint.

"So I said to her, 'How do you keep the good ones interested if there's no sex?' and you know what she said?"

Sooze spooned more ice cream into her mouth and shook her head.

"That's how you know they're good."

Sooze laughed. "In your dreams! So you told her fuggedaboutit?"

"Not exactly. I'm starting with Hugh."

❧   ❧   ❧

Our first date opened most auspiciously in the Meadowood Country Club pro shop: the klutz knocked over a whole basket of golf balls. I was trying to bend down and corral them in my micro A-line skirt without my rear end making a grand appearance. But Hugh half-smiled, quickly picked up the balls and went on as if nothing had happened. Hmm, I thought.

Turned out his mother was an Askenasi Jew.

"My mother would have liked that," I chuckled.

But when I picked up a driver, visions of new catastrophes began dancing in my head. What if I broke the club or conked the guy who ran around collecting balls? I was considering walking out right then. Instead I did being-in-the-moment exercises on the towering cedars that sheltered us and felt myself relax. Hugh's quiet presence was also soothing. And when he showed me how to hit with an iron, curling himself behind me to shape the proper grip, I felt a delicious tickle run up my spine.

After a few hours play on a hot sticky day we drove to A&W and he bought me a root beer float. It was the nectar of the gods my father had given me after our golf date so many years ago. As I nursed the libation with measured sips, Hugh grinned and handed me napkins to dab at my foamy mustache.

Hugh drove me home in his shiny spotless Saab and suggested we meditate together. There was a new line. We sat in the shaded space of my living room, lit only by a tiny Tiffany table lamp. I worried that Hugh was trying to bed me and how awkward that could be or, worse, that he would find me unattractive and reject me.

After ten minutes of this nonsense, I returned to my mantra and found myself soaring. There were no thoughts, only an empty expansive silence that imbued my consciousness. The rolling chirp, chirp song of crickets that lived in the backyard punctuated the profound quiet. I drifted along until Hugh whispered, "Stop the mantra."

Softly I said, "I'm floating."

"Meditating with someone else is deeper because the brain waves harmonically converge and synchronize," Hugh began to lecture. Oh, no, I thought.

Another strike against him was that, aside from teaching me how to swing, Hugh never made any physical contact; he didn't take my arm or try to hold my hand. After he left I recycled him back into the nerd bin.

A motley crew of guys came out of the woodwork after my visit to Sebastian's. I met my neighbor Ray at the grocery store. Not the most attractive, but he sported a mile-wide smile and an infectious laugh. Ray was Irish, in the tradition of Jake but goofy. He took me to see *Bombay Dreams* and then did a *Saturday Night Live* parody in a fountain in Fairmont Park with a dishtowel wrapped around his head. Then there was Steve, a neighbor I met while walking Milo. He told me he had just lost 100 pounds and that the highlight was looking down and seeing his 'friend' for the first time.

Even Doris called to set me up with a guy. "He's loaded," she proclaimed with a wink. Ralph, a retired rag dealer from the Main Line, was so old his skin looked like wax paper. He reminded me of the mummified aspect of Philadelphia living—that certain staid, stultified part that used to get on my nerves when I was my more conservative self. Ralph didn't make the cut either.

I continued to date Hugh and Ray, mainly because of Raphaela. But they were running way behind the man of my dreams. Hugh was smitten; I reminded him of his mother. He was all roses and schmaltzy cards. But I couldn't stand the way he sat at dinner carefully cutting his food into bite-sized pieces.

Ray made me laugh, but there wasn't much else. He was a movie buff and we wound up endlessly going to Loews together, or watching videos at home spiced with rounds of necking. He wasn't even a good kisser. But I was hungry and hung in, fantasizing that Ray was Him. And there were a few languorous back rubs both given and received.

Raphaela insisted that I needed to meet more men to do my research, so I kept looking. She wanted me to pay careful attention to each one and even rank-order them. That was easy. Hugh was running a poor first—at least we could golf and meditate together.

She also wanted me to construct myself as the star of my own reality. I was to pick out the most appealing outfit in my closet each day and add jewelry and makeup until I saw beauty in the mirror. That was hard enough, but the worst assignment was to then look at myself and focus on what was right with my body instead of on the bulges, pimples, pockmarks, varicose veins, and other assorted imperfections. At first an ugly and familiar-looking klutz kept staring back. Then I pretended I was Raphaela studying me. In an instant I became bright, beautiful, the way I always wanted to be. But strangely enough it made me feel despondent and empty.

🍁   🍁   🍁

As Hugh came closer, Sooze faded out of my life. But one Philly boiler day all our distance and fights vanished with one phone call.

"Janna," Sooze's voice quaked. "Please come. I need you."

A dreadful feeling took me over as I jumped into the Volvo and frantically sped over to 191. I hoped it was just a trick of the eyes, but Sooze seemed larger than ever. She was wearing a turquoise duster that ballooned over her stomach as she slowly settled on the living room couch. Her wavy red-brown hair wasn't brushed and spiked out this way and that. Two enormous rings of sweat sat under her ample arms. She burped up nervous air.

"I called Morgenstern to get a prescription for Prozac and I was complaining about how bloated and gassy I've been lately. Long story short, he insisted I go to Lankenau for a physical and the pelvic exam showed a mass on the right side. Then they ran a CA 125 and I just got the results. They're high."

"Oh, honey," I whispered, trembling as I sank into an armchair.

She bit her lip. "But the nurse told me the reading could be false, I mean, my mother had a benign epithelial tumor on her ovary. I'm scared." Teardrops lined her cheeks.

"It'll be fine, I'm sure," I lied.

"They've scheduled a transvaginal ultrasound tomorrow. I don't want to go." Sooze took a tissue and mopped up her eyes.

"Sooze, you have to."

"It's just, I remember my mother. I hated those doctors, that antiseptic smell, the cheery nurses. And it all happened so fast…they botched the operation…she bled so much, she almost died."

Visions of parasitic growths in her uterus stalked my mind. "I'll take you. Please, Sooze."

I got up from my chair, walked over and tenderly brushed a wisp of hair out of her eyes. She smiled weakly.

The ultrasound confirmed the mass. In an unsettling whirlwind the gynecologist scheduled a biopsy downtown at the Hospital of the University of Pennsylvania. The cells were malignant. During the grueling three hour procedure that followed, the surgeon removed a Stage II tumor along with both ovaries and Sooze's uterus. The gynecologic oncologist told us that the cancer had not yet spread to the lining of the abdomen or lymph nodes and that with chemotherapy her chances for survival were good.

But my gallant Sooze wept bitterly. It was a crushing loss for her, a mutilation. And the absolute death of all her dreams of having a child

I watched Sooze age 20 years, watched her lose her memory, watched her shed her lovely mane of reddish-brown hair. I called her daily, cried with her, reassured her and took her to the hellish first cycle of chemo appointments. Each time the taxol and carboplatin cocktail would sink her into a pale whirl of nausea so palpable that I became sick myself.

I clung desperately to the life raft of meditation to carry me through the storm. That, plus Hugh's support.

The autumn splendor soothed me as I practiced my being-in-the-moment exercises while driving the winding hills to see Raphaela. It was early October and the leaves on the pin oaks, maples and copper beeches were turning to magnificent Pennsylvania hues of burnt orange, red and gold. Raphaela was outside the farmhouse puttering amidst eggshell and burgundy chrysanthemums that were putting on a show in the beds along the driveway. We hugged each other before retiring to the living room.

Raphaela said knowingly, "Sooze is doing well."

"She finished the first round of chemo. What a load off," I sighed.

"Good. It is a blessing for her to have you." She studied me. "Now about Janna."

I dangled my keychain in front of her. A tiny photo of me as a cherub three-year-old dangled from it. "See, I've been keeping my sweet little self with me all the time."

Raphaela smiled. "Adorable! Any dreams lately?"

"It was just a fragment; I was watching a surreal ballet on the cardboard puppet stage that Babba Pearl gave me when we lived on Green Street. The ballerina, a huntress in a tunic, pink tights and a feathered cap was leaping like a gazelle. She finished with her hands fluttering like a bird in the air. Then these little gnarly gray men came out and covered her with cloaks, hundreds of cloaks until she collapsed under the weight." I tugged at the hem of the short black skirt that was riding up my thighs. Looking at Raphaela, I realized that she looked 16 years old, dressed in a pair of stretch white hip-huggers and a red and white-checkered halter-top that showcased her ample bosom.

She caught me checking her out. "I'm youthing," she said. "As are you." Gesturing toward the picture on the key ring, she continued, "Keep focusing on her as the real you. You'll get younger every day."

"Sign me up now!"

Raphaela sized me up. "You are progressing well on Lesson Four, coming to know that you are a goddess, a woman of striking beauty and uncommon valor—Artemis."

I pinked up. "I know what the dream means. I've been cloaking myself as punishment. For Mom, the incest, for Doris, for being a survivor's granddaughter, you name it."

"You must discipline yourself to allow your true self to emerge. You must cherish yourself in fullness as I cherish you." Her face became a radiant mass of light. "You know what 'Janna' means?"

"Not really. I don't pay attention to numerology or whatever."

"God's precious gift. And the letter of your first name, which speaks of what you came here to learn, is a 'J'. This stands for spirituality. 'A', the letter of your last name, indicates that in this lifetime you will be center stage, a star."

"I don't believe..."

Raphaela cut me off. "You are as lovely as the most glorious foliage. Show it like the trees lift their leaves to the sun."

She pointed out the front window at the dazzling fall display.

"Then you will attract, and be willing to give yourself, a full measure of a man." Raphaela laughed and waved her hand in the air in a slow lazy circle. My eyes followed her hand involuntarily.

"I guess it's impossible to love someone else when you don't love yourself."

"Exactly."

"Otherwise you would always feel less than, needy, like you were going to be left," I said knowingly.

"You are the ballerina. Uncloak and create the pas de deux." She stretched gracefully.

"But where do I find a man who remotely approaches Him?"

"The partner you seek will not manifest as the complete person you imagine. But together with you he'll grow and develop."

"You're telling me that I've got to meet a broken guy and repair him. All I have at this point is Hugh and Ray." I rolled my eyes. I felt safe enough to show Raphaela my contrariness instead of suppressing it or seeking her approval.

"Stop your fantasies about the perfect man. Stop thinking about Him. If you're married to Him, you'll never find a man in real life." Raphaela got up abruptly and went into the kitchen. She returned with two ceramic mugs of mulled apple cider. Settling back in her carved wood and velvet seat, she took a long sip from her mug. "There are two main questions to ask yourself about your friend Hugh: Is he crazy about you? Is he willing to grow?"

"He calls, sends flowers, and plans romantic dinners when he can. And he did finally get around to kissing me. I was stunned—his kiss was sensual, hot, so not Hugh. When he's physical he drops the plastic veneer and there is chemistry," I admitted reluctantly. "But I want more."

Raphaela looked at me expectantly. I couldn't believe the complete focus and attention she centered on me. I wondered whether I gave my clients anywhere close to the same level of concentration.

"Hugh and I meditate together and that has connected us." I took a sip of my cider and savored the Macintosh taste. "And we went clothes shopping. He ditched the prep look and switched to jeans. Actually he looks good in tight jeans."

"Good. What about Ray?"

"He's not really a candidate at all. We just laugh together."

"Well, I want you to continue with these two and add a third." Raphaela's nonchalance irritated me. She talked about picking up another guy like getting another helping at an all-you-can-eat buffet table.

"I'll try."

"You'll do it." Raphaela shot me a stern look and sent me out the door.

Since it was Friday, I went right to my office to attack the endless HMO paperwork. But Raphaela's instructions about ending my fantasies of Him were having just the opposite effect—like trying not to think about a box of Godiva chocolate that's sitting in your cupboard. I would look at a form and see His eyes looking into my soul, searing me, branding me. I jotted down codes and played with my hair, imagining His honeyed touch. After a long hour I quieted my mind, finished the last treatment summary and dropped the pesky forms in the mail-slot.

My building had this wretched parking lot with narrow stalls on hilly asphalt—it took the skill of an Indy 500 driver to maneuver in and out. On that fateful day, as I awkwardly backed the car out, I heard this awful bang-crunch and felt the impact of metal against metal. My victim was a black BMW sedan. Covering my face with my hand, I emerged to survey the damage. The BMW's driver side was dented but the real problem was the left front wheel housing. The fender had crumpled the chrome and silver rim and the spokes had impaled the tire. The classic car was a crippled beast unable to run.

Artemis? Hardly, I thought.

"It's just metal and rubber. You're not hurt, are you?" he said.

I was so chagrined it took me a full two minutes to take in his Brad Pitt face. At 6'2", he was thin and wiry, with dirty blonde hair, electric eyes, and a baritone voice that sang when he talked. Way, way out of my league.

"I, uh, I, uh," I stammered, hoping a chasm would open in the earth to swallow me up.

He looked at me with a little self conscious grin.

"Stephan Weisgart. We need to exchange information."

"J, Janna Abel."

My eyes met his for a second before I ducked into my car to search for my insurance card. When I finally emerged, he was ready with a Waterman pen and paper. Rich, but needs to prove it, I thought. As he leaned over the hood of my car to write I surreptitiously studied his racehorse lines, the thick mane of his hair, the perfect maleness of his squared off jaw.

Stephan called the local BMW dealer to have the car towed there. The service manager told him the shop was about to close, but he would wait for the tow truck to bring the car in. However, all the loaner cars were out. Wracked with guilt, I immediately offered to drive Stephan home.

He lived in Rittenhouse Square. I started the expedition in a cloud of self-consciousness, clutching the Volvo steering wheel and trying hard not to get in another accident. At first I thought I was just imagining it but when we stopped moving in the rush hour traffic, he cocked his head towards me and looked directly into my eyes.

Stephan broke the silence of the drive. "If you had $10 million in the bank and could create anything you wanted with your life, what would you do?"

"Open women's centers all over the world," I answered as cavalierly as I could. I wasn't about to reveal my struggles around wealth to this man. "A lot of hunger and poverty comes from the way women are treated; especially in third world countries."

With a hearty laugh he said, "That's totally on the money."

By the time we arrived at Stephan's glass and steel high-rise, I wished he lived on the other side of the Walt Whitman Bridge in New Jersey. Better yet, San Francisco. When he got out of the car, he bent down and gave me a peck on the cheek, said thanks and the infamous, "I'll call you."

I was utterly charmed and sure I would never, ever see him again.

Stephan entered my fantasy life big time. I kept thinking about the way he tilted his head, the tender way his lips glazed my skin. One night I dreamt he brought me tiny Faberge eggs, pink, aqua and lime green, each ornate, delicate and exotic. That dream was mind fodder for days.

Then, a week after the accident, I was checking my office phone messages and there was that baritone asking me, yes, me, to call him back. I saved the message to play it for Sooze. Even she could barely hide her surprise, but we figured it had to be related to the insurance claim. My hands shook as I called.

"Could you meet me at Suzanna Foo's for dinner next Thursday?" he asked.

"Uh…" My throat closed.

"You must be busy…"

"No, yes," I practically shouted.

The next morning I couldn't wait to see Raphaela. She greeted me at the farmhouse door wearing a flowing Indian print sari covered with orange and purple Sanskrit symbols. Even though I had seen it before, the mammoth star ruby ring on her index finger immediately struck me. The blood red gem had a perfect, blazing white star off to one side. I had noticed the ring on the back of a Tiffany's catalogue and the $45,000 price was so outrageous it unleashed a string of critical judgments about jaded values and babies starving in India.

Again she read me.

"There's a very old tradition among the Jyotish, the great Hindu astrologers, that rubies are magical, luck-bearing amulets. Worn close to a woman's skin, they bring great fortune. Would you like to borrow it?" she asked in an amused tone.

"No, um, it's sweet of you to offer," I stammered.

Was she serious? I'd owe her too much, besides I might lose it! Raphaela lifted her hand and the star ruby pulsated in an otherworldly way. I looked away and changed the topic.

"You wanted me to stretch, to date different kinds of guys. I've met a new one who is definitely different, not to mention one of the most successful men I've ever met."

"Give me your hand," Raphaela replied, ignoring what I was saying completely. I was annoyed, but I put out my hand. Suddenly she grabbed my index finger and put the star ruby on it.

"Perfect," she exclaimed with a hearty laugh.

I squirmed.

"You want to run out the door." She laughed with abandon. "Do you understand the healing purpose of jewelry?"

"No," I responded while being slowly seduced into admiring the gem's gorgeous energy.

"The Jyotish believe through reading your natal horoscope, they can tell your personality, and the specific challenges you are about to face in your life. Based on an understanding of your destiny they recommend different gemstones to help you overcome obstacles to what you want to create. These little stones are valued in our culture as outward manifestations of love or power, yet their real worth lies in their ability to create inner harmony or to ward off misfortune."

"Oh, I always thought of them as symbols of excess. Vanity." A warm flush took over my face.

"Take the trinket and wear it for a while. The gemstone complements you."

In spite of myself I was touched. I teared up.

"Really, no, I can't take the ring," I croaked.

Raphaela patted the ring on my hand. "It's hard but somebody's gotta wear it," she said with a gleeful chuckle. "Get over your ambivalence about having money and fine things."

Having composed myself somewhat, I looked over at Raphaela. She was playing with her marquise diamond ring, twirling it around her perfectly manicured ring finger. Concerned about running out of time, I begged her to coach me about Stephan.

"If he's as successful as you say, we need to complete our work on wealth," she pressed.

"According to my mother you couldn't be a good person and have money."

"Like Irma?"

"Mama called my aunt 'her highness' and yet ridiculed my father for not measuring up to Morty. Dad always put down their parking lot business and Aunt Irm's furs and diamonds. 'Can't buy health or happiness,' he used to say. Uncle Morty was crippled with arthritic psoriasis. I think my father thought it was a curse that came with success. My parents fought like mad about it. The whole thing made me crazy."

"So you've got your parents' confusing programs about money embedded in you. That's why you haven't created wealth and power for yourself."

"I guess so." I looked at the ring and bit my lip. "We only have a few minutes left. Please coach me about what to do with this new guy."

"First, get rid of your approval-seeking, the façade of making yourself look good. Instead, be real and truthful with him. Second, continue working on Lesson Four by creating the passionate person you want him to fall in love with."

She chortled annoyingly.

"Right," I said sarcastically and then immediately felt guilty as I glanced at the ring.

Raphaela stood up, arranged the folds of her sari and said, "I will be going to India for the next two months. Wear the ring to keep me with you."

I was alarmed. "But…"

"Can't discuss it with you now," she said as she came over and hugged me. Raphaela gave me a kiss on the forehead, looked into my eyes. "Don't worry, sweet being."

As soon as I walked out the door I started missing her.

❦   ❦   ❦

Sooze was back in Auschwitz again at HUP, but this round of chemo was kinder to her system. She even had enough energy to give Fred a fear of loss ultimatum. "He's been so distant since the cancer," Sooze said. "And last week when you couldn't take me to treatment, I asked him and he said no. I lost it and swore I wouldn't see him until he started divorce proceedings. He was always 'on the verge of filing', the bastard." Sooze's face was a death mask once again. Moving slowly, she retrieved comfort junk food from the kitchen and dumped it onto the coffee table in our living room bunker overlooking the autumnal forest.

"No thanks," I said to the Chipwich cookies and Cherry Garcia, thinking of being thin for Stephan.

"Fred's wife fell on her knees, owning what a bitch she was, swearing she would go into therapy." Sooze ignored the treats, laid her head down on the arm of the sofa and stared out into space.

"Oh my God, she responded to his fear of loss maneuver," I practically shouted.

"Right," Sooze spat out. "And he's such a weak butthead! Instead of breaking it off with her, he broke it off with me, so he could 'give it one last shot.' They're in marital therapy now."

"While you're in chemo. That's sweet of him." I leaned over to embrace her and she collapsed sobbing in my arms. "I'm proud of you for challenging him."

Sooze jumped up, ran into the bathroom and retched loudly for several minutes. She emerged drawn and weepy.

"He's such a schmuck, missing out on someone as incredible as you." I pointed at her and the star ruby on my index finger shot a ray of white light towards her heart.

"Janna, what in the world?"

I was totally shaken. "I don't know…"

"My nausea is gone. You've got voodoo magic there." Sooze gave a puzzled chuckle. "Or we're both going off the deep end."

"You've pinked up. Amazing."

She touched my face tenderly and said, "I've been so self-absorbed. What's happening with you?"

"Just when I need Raphaela's help with Stephan, she's leaving town again. And, believe it or not, she lent me this damn $45,000 ring as a good luck charm in her absence."

Sooze grabbed my hand, stared at the star ruby. "She is definitely one strange bird. I hope it's insured."

I glanced down. "I think it is. I hope it is. Anyway, I decided I'm not gonna lose it."

"Talisman has Supernatural Powers," Sooze intoned with the nasal twang of a swami.

I kissed her forehead. "And in other strange but true news, Rhoda and Jim are in a truce and touring Turkey. Plus do you remember that accountant my sister met at a Mensa mixer?"

"The one with the squeaky voice?"

"She's marrying him," I said without enthusiasm.

"Things will work out for you. Raphaela may be from a voodoo world, but she has helped you. You look 'mahvalous.'" She patted my thigh, adding, "And you're dating Brad Pitt."

"Speaking of which, I'll ask Hugh if he has a friend and then we can double."

"Great. If I live long enough."

❈   ❈   ❈

Thursday, the night of the Date, I anxiously ushered out my last client, put on fresh makeup a la Sebastian and changed into a black skirt and silky pantyhose that showcased my legs. I finished the look with a cream blouse that set off an ebony and gold fitted jacket. The whole process was agonizingly difficult; a slow-motion nightmare where I couldn't get the pieces to fit right. Finally the construction was complete and I studied myself in the office mirror. Artemis stared back.

Late, I sped downtown, left the Volvo with the valet, and walked into the restaurant. Stephan saw me and immediately came over and put his arm around my waist. He was wearing a perfectly tailored Armani jacket and a silk turtleneck setting off his blondish waves. Very European royalty. He knew it too. As I kept stealing not too obvious glances at him, he told the hostess we were ready to be seated. I was drooling, along with every other woman in the restaurant.

He showed asked about my work and how I'd like to expand it.

"Maybe I'd like to start a center for homeless women and their children," I said, thinking of Raphaela.

Stephan lit up. "You might be interested in my work. My partners and I have a nutritional business and give 10% of the profits to feed poor children in third world countries."

"Tell me more."

"My friend, Brenda Kalter, is a biochemist. About five years ago she developed a superfood that makes you younger and healthier. We've had miracles happen with the product—MS clearing up, learning disabilities in children vanishing, cancer going into remission."

"My best friend has ovarian cancer."

"I'm sorry." He touched my hand.

"Then she should definitely try it; she has nothing to lose. The product is ten times more potent in supporting the immune system than any other edible substance on earth."

"Wow," I said, hopeful.

"These skinny little kids in our African feeding program start to run, laugh, play again—they come alive. One little guy had a skin tumor the size of a grapefruit on his thigh. Each day we could see the mass shrink." I was mesmerized. The man was dreamy, successful, and philanthropic. Best of all, he might be able to help Sooze.

Stephan continued. "It's hydroponically-grown in vats in Florida."

"What is it exactly?"

"A genetically-altered strain of algae called Chlorophyx."

Just then the waiter brought the Peking duck that Stephan had ordered. Stephan quickly fashioned little crepe sandwiches filled with sweet brown sauce; bits of scallion, crispy duck skin and moist meat for each of us. Could this really be Him? I wondered. The doubts descended like harpies: he wouldn't want me...he's too good to be true...this won't lead anywhere...he's probably involved with this Brenda. But I kept my smiling face in the game.

Then he relieved one of my worries. "Brenda's husband, Ed, is a marketing genius and the three of us formed Greenway to distribute the algae. I'm the sales trainer." He dabbed at the corners of his mouth with the white linen napkin. "It's a network marketing company. Do you know what that is?"

Sounds sleazy, I thought. "I've had clients who tried Amway. None of them made money though."

"You have to get in at the beginning, when the company is in momentum phase. That's what Greenway is doing right now. We are able to give money to save the rainforest in the Amazon and to support organic farming in Central America. The most fulfilling part of all, of course, is feeding the Chlorophyx to starving children around the world." Sensing my discomfort, he had seamlessly moved back to the philanthropy.

I resisted scratching the raging itch under my chin and mused out loud, "Is it legitimate?" See, I'm being real, I thought.

"Totally. No one is ripped off, like in those old pyramid schemes. You do your job, you earn money." I listened, trying to give him a break. He went on, "It's the future. In Japan it's the fastest growing form of business there it."

"I could use a little extra income."

"You use the products, see what a difference they make for you and then tell your friends about them. It's just like sharing a great book or movie. Except that you get a commission every time they order. And your friends start their friends. Pretty soon there are hundreds, even thousands of people eating the Chlorophyx, getting healthier and making money, in a chain all started by you."

"It sounds easy." It can't be that easy, I thought.

"Network marketing gives you time freedom. And you get to help your friends." Stephan glowed.

"I would like to try the Chlorophyx."

Well, I would, I insisted to my internal critic.

"Great, we'll set you up with sample products and a distributor start-up kit."

Stephan held my hand as I floated out of the restaurant. When the valet brought my car, Stephan kissed me gently, no intrusive tongue, just a romantic, light brush of the lips.

"The night was perfect. He's perfect!" I reported to Sooze's voicemail that night.

Raphaela's lesson, *Falling in love with yourself is the first step in finding the love you seek,* played over and over like a song as I took off my clothes and got into my flannel nightgown. Lying down in my bed, I held up my left hand and smiled at the star ruby. The gem winked right back at me.

CHAPTER 13

Charting Progress

Network marketing and me? Just as a hobby, I reassured myself as I sent out 200 marketing tapes. And keeping busy helped ease the pangs of missing Raphaela. Not to mention being able to call Stephan every day…

Sooze completed six courses of chemo and the last CA 125 tests showed her cancer was in remission. She was sure the Chlorophyx had helped her bounce back from the once every three-week ordeal and started to refer clients with various ailments to me for the products. Placebo or not, I had three people report 'miraculous' healings—reduced Parkinson's tremors, fewer aches and pains from fibromyalgia, and the disappearance of chronic fatigue syndrome. Even Doris tried the Chlorophyx—not for the macular degeneration, but because she wanted to lose weight before the wedding.

Stephan and I went out for dinner once a week, usually on Saturday. It was mostly the work that joined us. But he was a great coach with a sexy vibe. He called me his 'Juno' and the whole relationship made me happy yet strangely anxious and miserable.

Three weeks before Christmas Stephan invited me to the Jersey shore for the weekend. One of his Diamond distributors had a beachfront condo in Stone Harbor and he wanted Stephan to give an opportunity meeting. I wanted it to be my opportunity too.

At the meeting, Stephan had the self-assurance of an Olympic gymnast stepping out on the mat. He talked passionately about the current epidemic of cancer, cardiovascular and other chronic diseases, tying it into the SAD, the

Standard American Diet. Then, taking the whole group right along with his passion and excitement, he presented Greenway as the ultimate solution.

He illustrated the model on an easel with colored magic markers. "This circle is Sally, my secretary."

He gestured toward the twenty-something pixie who was putting together distributor kits at the back of the room.

"She's been working the business part-time for six months and has reached Emerald status."

Stephan drew a pyramid of circles on the easel. "As you can see, Sally's income for the month was $1000, which, on an annualized basis is $12,000. That's the equivalent of a $400,000 CD at three percent. Think about that." A ripple of murmurs spread through the prospects. I elbowed Sheila, my chiropractor, who had come down for the meeting.

By the triumphant close, six of the seven attendees had fallen under his spell and signed up, including Sheila, who started in my downline.

After the meeting, Stephan and I settled down alone on a blue tufted sofa in front of the picture window in the sparsely furnished 6th floor unit. I couldn't help bringing up Sally. "How come my check last month was $17.25 and hers was so high?" Was he giving her all the plum leads?

He noticed the look in my eyes and shook his head. "Each person's downline is unique." He touched my arm. "Come on. I brought Dom Perignon to celebrate. Don't worry, your business will take off, I'll make sure of it."

A few glasses of champagne later, my worries had dissipated. He held me as we sat on the couch and I took in his earthy smell, inhaled his sweet breath on my cheek. We stared at the endless changing patterns of white foam caps as the rhythms of Mother Ocean took us home.

He tilted my head back and planted the gentlest kiss on my upper lip. I ran my hands down his wiry, well-muscled back and then he kissed me fully, mouth open. His inquiring tongue made its acquaintance with mine while his fingertips softly caressed my cheeks. Then he stroked my stomach and, ever so gently, he moved lower and lower. Streaming sensations of pure pleasure drove me nuts. He unzipped my slacks and put his hand down there, stroking me tenderly. The champagne and the power of his rhythmic touch broke down and shattered my defenses and all thoughts of Raphaela's celibate program of three. I moaned and pressed into his probing fingers.

"Bet you like it deep and hard, baby." His words broke the spell.

What? I wondered. "Come on, fuck me baby," he growled. All my passion melted away, although I kept up my end of the sex play. Stephan was acting like some insecure teenager who had to prove himself. He kept up the jarring sex talk throughout the rest of our lovemaking. It was like some awful porn alter ego had come out in him.

When he entered me I was surprised that I didn't feel much physically. Was it the condom? Did his words turn me off? Will I ever enjoy a man?

I didn't have an orgasm that first time with him. Stephan kept working at it until he finally came. I felt like a schoolgirl who had failed her cheerleader audition.

"Don't worry, Juno. It'll happen," he reassured.

But I worried that I had blown it. That it would never work with us. That Raphaela was wrong about me and men. Then I decided to settle myself and to practice my newfound technique.

Stephan went to the bathroom and turned on the shower while I meditated. Anxiety nibbled at my brain. Let it be, I urged myself. And I kept going back to the mantra. Finally, after ten minutes, my mind settled. I visualized the whole fiasco that had just occurred as if it were part of a Friends episode. I chuckled as images played out complete with a Barry White soundtrack. Afterward, I felt calm, clear.

Now for an affirmation, I thought. I said to myself, love is in my life. I repeated this affirmation like a mantra, until I felt my mood shift. Just then, Stephan emerged and plopped down next to me.

He studied my face. "Janna, you know I've been thinking about us."

The big kiss-off, I thought, alarm bells ringing in my stomach.

Stephan continued, "If you were to come work at my office, we could see each other more and really work this business together. Besides, it'll save you expenses."

I jumped up and hugged him.

"The Shuar are a proud tribe of ex head-hunters who live in the Amazon basin," Herb said, as he sat on my office couch shooting me strange glances. We both had no-shows and Herb had just returned from an Eco tour studying with Ecuadorian shamans. "They diagnose by having you rub a candle all over your body. Then they light it and call their spirit guides. In the jungle, we visited this half naked shaman who picked up my colitis, without me saying a word to anyone in the group about it." He stared at me and shook his head.

"Even more amazing is the way you look, Janna. Your hair, it's like copper, your face, radiant…"

Herb's face broke out in a leering grin.

"Gee, thanks," I shot him a mock scowl and pulled my brown tweed A-line skirt over my thighs. "So what happened in the rainforest?"

"The shaman picked a bunch of rare plants, straggly gray sticks really, to steep as a tea for my GI troubles. Since the trip my symptoms have been cut in half."

"Say, I have a natural product that might help your stomach," I said, feeling sleazy.

"Thanks, but right now I just want to work with the Shuar herbs. Can't get over how great you look." He twinkled at me.

"I think I'm in love. It's wonderful but I feel like shit," I confessed. "It's weird."

"What's goin' on girl?"

I shook my head. "Love and other difficulties."

He studied my face. "Go on."

"Strange to feel blue when my life's completely turned around. It's almost like I can't tolerate happiness. And, by the way, you played an important role."

Herb's eyes widened. "I ruined your happiness?"

I slapped his arm. "No. You supported my relationship with Raphaela, the one who brought me to the Ball. She's given me lessons. In living."

I gave him a heartfelt thank you kiss on the cheek.

He put his hands behind his head and his Birkenstocks up on my coffee table. The chemical smells from colorants and perms at the salon next door were oppressive.

"Damn, it stinks in here," Herb complained. I went over and opened a window. He mockingly clutched at his chest. "Yea, I have survived the warrior's trial, the poison fumes of Mordor. Now you must reveal these mysterious lessons to me."

"So far she's given me four lessons. First she had me face my fears, take a stand for myself and for what's right. Remember when that client was stalking me?"

"Sure do."

"Raphaela had me call him, take charge and get him to see Ron. She also insisted that I confront the incest trauma that plagued me for over twenty years. Facing my uncle, the perpetrator, the biggest demon from my past, changed me. I'm sturdier inside."

Herb twinkled at me.

"I went through a rite of passage with Raphaela guiding me," I reflected.

Herb rubbed his beard and gazed out the window. "You own your power instead of projecting it onto other people and living in fear."

"I'm definitely beginning to feel brave." Admitting my personal truths, even if they were embarrassingly positive, was liberating. "I told you about the second lesson she taught me—when you face the fear of loss, love blossoms. Totally changed my couples work. My toughest marital case has completely turned around. I just kept painting the picture of their miserable future if they divorced. Now, they're more in love than they were 20 years ago."

Herb nodded admiringly.

"It's like a near-death experience bringing forth a richer life. Helping people confront loss allows them to experience real appreciation for each other. The love that's buried or forgotten can surface. Then they can act out of compassion and caring toward each other."

I clasped my hands together and opened my palms as if a dove was flying out.

"That's deep." He sniffed the foul air, went to open another window and came back to the couch. "What else did Raphaela teach you?"

"She taught me a waking meditation, a way to look deeply into the nature of things, an eyes closed meditation, and a weird breathing technique. I've been doing them daily and I feel more grounded a lot of the time. Not all the time, but…"

Herb's face was a mass of light as he looked at me.

"She's opening your eyes." He recited: "*You are not enclosed within your bodies, nor confined to houses or fields. That which is you dwells above the mountain and roves with the wind.*"

We sat together in a mellow state for a few moments.

"The final lesson was that I was to love myself, give to myself and make myself more attractive."

I blushed.

"I can see that." He leaned over and kissed me. Startled, I pushed him away.

"Herb, I'm involved with someone. I love you as…"

"A friend," he finished. "I know but I had to try."

I rose from the couch and changed the subject.

"Say, do you know anything about the Roman goddess, Juno?"

"Yeah, she was one of the vulnerable goddesses who married her own brother." Herb crossed his arms over his chest.

"Zeus was her brother?" All of a sudden the smells in the room became oppressively strong.

"She was humiliated by Zeus' constant philandering and became jealous, and given to vindictive rage."

"Great," I said as I nervously rubbed the star ruby on my finger. All at once the white star blazed like a camera flash. Herb and I jumped. A moment later the disgusting smell from next door had completely vanished.

❦   ❦   ❦

It was mid-December when I saw Raphaela again in the North Philly row home. She had asked me to park a couple of blocks away because of 'a happening' on Lehigh Street. As I hurried along the cracked sidewalk towards Raphaela's I was startled to see a yellow gem of a rowhouse, spruced up with lemon-colored paint on the shutters and door. Slowly it dawned on me that it wasn't the only one. Home after home was restored to its original brick façade, each with a porch painted in mustard, ivory or colonial red. It was like taking a trip to a kinder gentler past. When I came to Raphaela's street I saw a boisterous crowd of children surrounding the green and red mascot, Philly Phanatic, who was happily signing autographs. They were gathered in front of what used to be a decrepit corner grocery store. The building sported a fresh coat of robin's egg blue and a hand-painted sign announcing the, "West Lehigh Community Center."

Chuckling with delight, I walked right past Raphaela's home, which was reborn with white painted brick and maroon shutters. When I bounded back and ran up the refurbished cement steps Raphaela opened a new screen door with her usual dose of high energy, scooping me up in her arms in a bear hug of hello.

Old stonewashed Levi's and a plain black t-shirt could not disguise her beauty as she settled herself with the regality of Cleopatra, on a newly slip-covered armchair. I perched on the matching sofa, feeling blessings all around.

"I don't even recognize the neighborhood. What happened?"

Glowing, she said. "The Minyan and the City of Philadelphia worked out a deal where homeowners and landlords got tax rebates for rehabing the neighborhood. The community center is being supported by the Minyan and a local minority-owned construction company. I can show you around. We have twelve computers and a basketball court on the lot across the street." Raphaela pointed her brightly manicured finger out the front window.

"Amazing," was all I could muster.

"In the past six months, we've trained teachers, clergy, and child welfare workers to use bonding, nurturing and limit setting with adolescents and we taught the kids to meditate for ten minutes each day. Juvenile violence is down 20%, while school attendance is up 23%." She flashed a satisfied grin. "We've also used coaching with the adults and unemployment is dropping."

I shook my head in admiration. "And how was India?"

"A most auspicious trip. Maharishi Siddha came out of six months of silence with potential solutions for Mother India. Population there is already over one billion people and it's exploding at a rate of almost 2 percent per year. This can only lead to more suffering and pain. Maharishi said that we are at the dawning of the enlightened age yet starvation is on the rise. So he and the Prime Minister, with the Minyan's backing, are going to roll out a spiritually-based sex education and voluntary contraception program."

"I feel petty wanting you to focus on my measly problems."

"Nonsense," she said studying me like I was a racing filly. Nervously I straightened the wrinkles out of my denim skirt, smiled my appreciation and leaned toward her.

"Raphaela, I found Him. He's smart, cultured, and he's crazy about me…"

Raphaela interrupted me. "What do you mean? I instructed you to date three men."

"I have," I protested. "Ray, Hugh, and now, Stephan."

"And you think you're in love with Stephan. You had sex prematurely with him. I wanted you to have a wide variety of experiences, to not get caught up too quickly with one person," she scowled.

I continued to babble. "But I know you'll love him—he's got an incredible business that feeds starving children…"

Her eyes flashed steel, stopping me in mid-sentence. "And so you're doing your usual pattern of clinging to one man."

I fingered the hair at the back of my neck. "No, I mean, yes…I don't know."

She held me with her gaze. "By now you probably feel pretty shitty."

I bowed my head sadly. "It's crazy. I'm so happy with my life and yet I do feel depressed. Sometimes I'm sure I'm losing it." I stared out the window. A light December snowfall was starting to cover the cracked sidewalk and patches of grass out front. Raphaela abruptly left the room, which startled me. I got up and ran after her. She was fixing mint tea on the new electric stove in the freshly painted kitchen.

"Please help me make it with this guy. He could be the one," I pleaded.

Raphaela poured the tea into two brown plastic mugs. Then she marched back into the living room with me trailing behind.

Once back in the armchair she turned to me and said, "Now is the time for Lesson Five: *Your path is a dance of two steps forward, one step back.*"

"Which means?"

She settled back and took a sip of tea. "The path of growth is always strewn with rocks and obstacles, many of them internal. As we take two steps forward, as we dance into new arenas and tackle fresh challenges in our search for mastery, we often experience a sudden sense of chaos, fear, confusion or sadness. Those feelings are signals that we need to take one step back."

I began to relax as I shifted into a familiar role. "How do you 'take a step back'?

"Ironically, each thrust forward in personal development, each gain in self-empowerment is accompanied by a resurgence of the old self, the old way of being. You've courageously entered new arenas by confronting Bob, Vincent, your Dad, by inviting the Divine into your daily life and by creating yourself as a beautiful and empowered woman. That's bound to take you backwards, to left-over feelings and beliefs from the past."

"So I'm not crazy."

Raphaela laughed. "We all go through a kind of dislocation, a regression as we progress. The new identity resurrects the old one, the identity formed in childhood. It also surfaces our closely-held beliefs about how the world operates, our role in it and how we should behave, so that we can confront and alter them."

I nodded. "I do feel like a stranger in an alien land."

"Robert Frost said it best: *I felt my standpoint shaken in the universal crisis. But with one step backward taken I saved myself from going.*"

I sipped my minty balm.

"You're being hit with old feelings of self-doubt, and sadness. It's your wounded inner child that's come to the fore."

"Even the meditation hasn't made these feelings go away."

"Without it, your pain would be much greater. Now let's examine those feelings." Raphaela looked compassionately.

"I don't know. I feel like I'm 13 all over again."

"What exactly was happening then?"

"I remember it so clearly: 'Come, Bubie. They're auctioning off a party with Andre Robert from WMMR at the Art Museum fundraiser,' Aunt Irm said. Doris couldn't go—she had her junior prom."

"But Irm continued. 'Not to worry, you'll come with Melanie. But first we'll go to Lord and Taylor's for a dress. The way your father lets you walk around, it's a *shanda*. Such a pretty face, too.' She gave her imperial no-nonsense look and I had to go."

"That night I joined Melanie, Aunt Irm's 16-year-old niece, she of the overdone nose job and flaxen highlights. The black velvet dress my aunt found after a hasty and frustrating shopping trip was swimming on me despite my chubby midriff. Covered with a plaid vest and bows, the gown created an authentic Harpo Marx effect. Melanie wore a fitted pink lace number, a la Grace Kelly."

Raphaela nodded her understanding. "Go on."

"Aunt Irm shepherded us into a clutch of girls with impossibly clean poker straight hair, half-carat studs, and short sheaths. Melanie was immediately swept away while I sat and studied my hands at a linen-covered table in the cocktail area near the bar. Peeking out from the mass of brown cocoons that hid my face, I studied Melanie's neighbor, Scott, a lanky sixteen year old as he asked for a seven and seven for his mother. I remember his hair moussed back in a seamless black wave and his face speckled with acne. I was shocked when he sat at my table and talked to me. We downed the contraband when the bartender wasn't looking."

"Scott and I wound up sitting under a table hidden by the damask linen folds, giggling at our own private BYOB picnic. That is, until he reached down the blousy top of my dress and fondled my breasts. With that I upchucked—vomited right on the lapels of his navy suit."

Raphaela touched my knee and encouraged me to continue.

"Well, I cried and retched as the entire assemblage gathered round to view the spectacle. 'It's her fault,' Scott told my aunt, as she wiped my dress and ushered me into the safety of the ladies room. I ran and hid in a stall. Soon a few girls came in, snickering away. Melanie hissed, 'Scott said she's just a cheap slut from the Northeast. She doesn't even belong here.'"

Blushing, I looked down at my hands. "Her words branded me. When Aunt Irm finally came in, I refused to leave the stall. She had to ask one of the museum guards to get a screwdriver to jimmy the lock."

Raphaela looked at me. "Through these experiences you created an identity in which you did not belong and needed to be hidden away. Now that you have broken away from these restrictions in your current manifestation, the old self is coming to the fore."

I nodded. "Even though I'm acting differently my core beliefs have stayed the same."

Raphaela nodded. "There's a real disconnect for you. You look beautiful and are becoming an empowered woman but you still feel like a fat little girl who doesn't fit in."

"That's me."

Raphaela touched my hand tenderly. "The regressive pull to the old feelings of self-hate almost always follows progressive movements through the glass ceiling. We've got to learn to expect it, welcome its appearance as an opportunity to study and understand ourselves."

"Something wonderful happens and it's OK to feel like shit!" I laughed. "It doesn't have to mean you're crazy. Or that something's wrong with our new accomplishments."

"You've got it." Raphaela grinned. "Think of it as a tag sale for the mind."

I chuckled. "A garage sale?"

"Yes. You know, whenever you move to a better place, you go through all your things to see what you want to keep and what you want to get rid of. In this regressive process you go through your old identities and beliefs the same way."

"OK, then. The fat ugly urchin goes!"

I gestured like an umpire calling a third strike.

"Can we talk about Stephan now?" I asked hopefully.

Raphaela looked at her watch and shook her head. "Next week."

❦   ❦   ❦

I was dreaming of Him again. This time we were on a deserted beach in the Caribbean. He came out of the crystal clear waves and teased me to run after Him. We played along the shoreline, darting after each other, giggling and splashing water. Then He lifted me into His sinewy arms and kissed me with a thousand colors. He held me to His magic mouth, nuzzling my bare breasts.

Without warning He bit me. I smacked His face and He dropped me on the sand. When I looked up, He was running away from me, towards a woman in a billowy white silk dress who was beckoning to him with open arms. I doubled over, a spear of pain in the gut. I woke in a sweat, glad I was to see Raphaela that very day.

It was just before Christmas, on a cloudy blustery morning, that she ushered me into the refurbished living room in North Philly. I immediately told Raphaela about the dream.

"You were acting out your old pattern—of clinging and then running away. Lesson Five's main message is to not let the moods and fears of the inner child dictate your behavior. Otherwise, you'll act in the old ways that have undermined your success in the past." I frowned. "So in your case, you must not repeat your old patterns with this Stephan."

I looked down.

Raphaela continued. "Like in the dream, you set up a bad triangle with a man and another woman and then get bitchy because you feel you can't compete. And then you drive away the object of your love; constantly repeating that loss, just like when your mother died."

I flashed back to a recent fight with Stephan about Sally's check. "But I mean I don't have to…"

"And in that self-defeating pattern, you act out of empty desperation, waiting on his calls, resenting it when he doesn't."

"Yeah, but…"

"And la piece de resistance, dumping other men."

"But…" I argued vainly.

Raphaela shook her head and looked at me. "No dumping of other men. Instead you need to deepen your understanding and be a fair witness to your internal process.

"What's a fair witness?"

"That's the part of us that simply watches our actions without judgment or commentary. You must cultivate the quality of detachment to strengthen the witness." She rubbed the area between my eyebrows with one perfectly manicured finger. A rain of tingles spread through my skin. "When you are overwhelmed with emotions you need to stand outside yourself in your mind's eye. And then observe the thoughts and feelings you've created and allow them to be fully present so that they can pass through you and dissipate like storm clouds clearing on a sunny day."

"But what about people that cry or that break down all the time? How come they never seem to pull out of the muck?"

"They never cultivate detachment. In other words, they never come to realize that they are not their feelings. They are not their thoughts. They are something much larger."

"What is that?"

"A fragment of the infinite."

I frowned. "I don't understand."

"You will."

"But how do you get the self love, the discipline it takes to not let your old baggage run you?"

Raphaela gave her Mona Lisa look. "Practice daily. And from a place of serenity continue to work on altering your moods so you can easily and effortlessly use the remote control for the TV that is your mind."

As I took in her words my neck muscles relaxed.

She beamed at me and continued on the theme of detachment.

"Frost's poem is really a celebration of the fair witness." She recited, *"But with one step backward taken I saved myself from going, a world torn loose went by me. Then the rain stopped and the blowing and the sun came out to dry me."*

Raphaela's eyes bore into me.

"Now in order to be in the sun here, you need to be on the program of three so that you are balanced internally and can manage the old wounds when they rear their hideous heads."

"But I don't feel attracted to other men," I whined. The smell of the freshly-painted living room was closing in on me.

"That's part of the unconscious reenactment. Instead of examining and letting go of your old identity, you're letting it run your dating life. Like you did with Jake, Stokes and Larry."

"Yes, but Stephan is different. Anyway, I'm still getting love letters from Hugh."

Raphaela rolled her eyes, infuriating me. "If you don't actively date two other men, the whole thing with Stephan will backfire and you will be retraumatized. I can promise you that. I don't even want to discuss him."

CHAPTER 14

A Side Order of Pain

The morning brought a new letter from Hugh. I had been putting them in a drawer. But this time I forced myself to open and read it.

Dear Janna,

I am restless, being so because I've been inside all day, so being because I've not seen you for what seems so long a time…restless because of things on my mind and things yet to surface from me. Thinking. How to explain to you what I have trouble explaining to myself? We were together such a short time, yet I miss you today. I miss your eyes, your hands, your endearing clumsiness. My want is to be with you…not even to kiss and hold you, but just to feel you in my presence and place myself in yours.

For me there was this most special place, a place where we met and I became more fully me. When I was with you the words came and seemed to be right. You pleased me not with a sense of security, but with making me feel alive. You stimulated me and made me think. I found myself wanting to draw all that is good within me to present to you.

You bring poetry to my soul.

Standing among the multitudes
I find myself alone…
Before my eyes
Stands an emptiness,

A void
Where only minutes before
You stood as a prism
Dispersing the colors of the universe.

I had distanced from Hugh, but he had obviously not distanced from me. He was so very great on paper. He opened me on paper. But feeling these feelings upset me—I wanted Stephan. Only Stephan. I decided to take a stand. Carefully I wrote and rewrote Hugh a Dear John letter.

❦   ❦   ❦

"Raphaela, we need to talk. It's about Stephan and yet it's not. It's really about you and me." I teared up against my will.

We stood at the door of the Chester farmhouse that was wrapped in fresh blankets of snow. Raphaela carefully tied her raven hair back with a blue print bandanna and beckoned me into the living room. For some reason I avoided my old perch on the sofa and fretfully sat down on a Queen Anne sidechair. She rolled up the sleeves of the paint-splattered coverall she was wearing and calmly sat on the sofa.

"Stephan's the most wonderful man I've ever met and you're not supporting our relationship. I want; no I need you, to really coach me."

Raphaela smiled. "I am."

I threw up my hands. "'The program of three, the program of three. Don't let your inner child run you.' That's all you say. The whole situation is making me crazy because I could never be with a man like him without having you in my life." I choked back throat-stabbing sadness.

"Go on." Raphaela was still and her jewelry-covered manicured hands looked garish, folded in her lap.

"I thought you wanted me to be happy…This man makes me happy. Mostly, anyway." I studied her face. "Well, will you discuss Stephan with me?"

"I have." We sat in stony silence as the snow came down and darkened the window.

"Well I'm working in Greenway with Stephan, making a relationship with him, maybe even a life with him." I spat out the words, like a dare.

"Working with him too? It's just a ploy because you don't feel good enough. Ignoring your real calling is a prescription for disaster." Her tone was arctic.

"He's the most important person in my life. If we can't discuss him, maybe we don't have anything else to talk about." I was horrified to hear the words come out of my mouth.

Raphaela was deathly still for an eon. Then she said, "Janna, do what you need to do."

As if possessed, I blurted, "Here's your ring back. I don't need it anymore." I tossed her the star ruby and it vanished with a garnet-red flash in mid-air.

❦   ❦   ❦

I ran blindly from Raphaela, like a *Guernica* refugee who had lost hearth and home. Barreling through two red lights on the way home, I kept an iron grip on the steering wheel and a lead foot on the gas. Once in my front door I dragged myself to the phone and willed my lifeless fingers to dial Stephan. He wasn't home. In desperation, I arranged to meet Sooze at 191.

I didn't shed a tear until safely ensconced on her couch. Sooze just kept handing me tissues.

"You got what you could from her. Then you bumped up against her rigidity. And you did the smart thing; you cut bait." Sooze dabbed at her forehead with a tissue.

"You're feeling OK, right," I asked uneasily.

"Got a clean bill of health. Don't worry—you're still stuck with me." Sooze fetched me an Appleton and coke. "And you've got Stephan. Who cares about Raphaela?"

"I'm in shock," I whispered. "Another mother who's abandoned me."

I drank the medicine down.

"How is Hugh?" Sooze asked.

"He took the Landmark Forum last month and his whole face is awake, like he's taking the world in whole instead of in small chunks," I said.

"No shit."

The rum was working its magic. "After three days of confronting his own stories about being a victim at the hands of his alcoholic father, he wound up taking responsibility for his role in their lousy relationship. Hugh flew out to Florida and reconciled with his dad."

"He got his father back after one short weekend?"

I praised the Appleton Estate for its Nepenthe. "That seminar could put us out of business."

"So how do you feel about the new and improved Hugh?"

"I'm sending him a Dear John."

❋   ❋   ❋

Leaving Raphaela reawakened the nine-year-old waif flash-frozen inside of me; that child's stoic cynicism that colored everything gray. As I sat in my therapist's chair day after day I struggled to put on a mask of hope for the clients.

Nightmares made my sleep disjointed, fleeting. Sometimes I found myself alone in a desert, wandering, circling endlessly, parched and hungry, my head encircled by a cloud of flies I couldn't shake off. In one dream, an ephemeral lake, a shimmering body of water just beyond the next dune, lured me, but I was too weak, too tired to make it to the oasis. Death's embrace slowly turned me from burning hot to icy cold and I startled awake into the wintry night.

But there was Stephan. Having him in my life buoyed me as I faced the karma of being endlessly in mourning for a parent. He never opened up much on a personal level and the sex was lousy. But I loved to be with him, to look at him. And I really loved working with him. He was a genius. I threw myself into Greenway, cold-calling chiropractors and holistic MDs, naturopaths and dentists from at his apartment two days a week.

Two weeks passed. Late one night I was sitting at the kitchen dinette journaling instead of writing the marketing letter I was supposed to send to my downline. My hand moved quickly and seemed to take on a life of its own as it wrote:

Think about Lesson Five. Think about the rhythm of your growth, the waves of progression and regression and ride them like waves on the ocean beach. Go with the swelling water to meet the shore of your dreams. Then paddle your way against the turbulent eddies on your way back out. Act on the progressive urge, the vision of what you wish to create, but not on the regressive urge that comes from the old scars and pains. What do you wish to create?

I want love in my life. Real love, I wrote.

You have discarded real love in discarding Raphaela.

But she wouldn't help me.

All of your pain is your own creation. You have acted on the beliefs and feelings of your past identity instead of merely observing them. In so doing you generated a reality in which your mother-hunger is ripped open once again. This is why you feel so empty inside.

The words went right through me. My hand dropped on the paper. I was left sitting in a cold sweat, trying to stop the trembling in my legs and wondering if I had another visitation from Raphaela.

"The pattern of two steps forward, one step back, fits with finding Raphaela and then losing her." I exclaimed to Sooze as we strolled along the woodsy path behind 191.

"But according to the teaching you didn't have to create losing her."

I put my hand over my eyes. "I should have just processed my feelings and not acted on them. Instead I pushed her away and clung to Stephan."

To my immense satisfaction, her face was ruddy with health. She had even put a few pounds back on, which I enjoyed as a good omen. We sat down on a wooden park bench surrounded by gnarled oaks pointing their leafless arms to the sky. Sooze threw a gray pebble into the stream and we studied the circles rippling out.

"Stephan's phobic about intimacy. Makes me feel so lonely," I said.

I buttoned up the crimson mohair Anne Klein overcoat that Stephan bought as a Valentine's Day surprise.

Sooze studied me. "I hate to say this, but I think you have to call Raphaela. Talk it all out with her."

I nodded. "I was such a baby with her."

When I got home, I picked up the phone. My heart leapt when I heard her voice. But it was only a tape recording. "I am currently out of the country and will return in the late spring." I sighed and clutched the receiver to my heart.

Doris' wedding came on a late April Saturday. The small affair was held at the Morris Arboretum, a historic Chestnut Hill estate nestled among ancient specimen trees and sculptured hedges. Doris posed for photos among the budding lime green leaves and bright yellow forsythia bushes in her simple off-white silk chiffon gown. And her pearled crown headpiece that we had picked out together. With curly hair wafting around her head like fine spun gold and happiness radiating from her face, she looked more than good, she looked perfect, whole. It was as if her limp was gone and the scar on her face had disappeared.

Stephan was impeccably groomed with his head of thick perfect hair and yards of the finest Italian wool tailored to his lean torso. I floated around introducing him, feeling like a bride myself. In the past several months, Stephan had hinted at marriage. And except for some major blow-ups about a business trip he took with his secretary, Sally, we felt more real as a couple. Even the sex was improving although I rarely felt relaxed enough to climax with him.

We watched my father, dapper in a Calvin Klein tuxedo, dance with Doris. He was so happy I hardly recognized him. It was the first time since the accident that the family was complete. I felt so different, without any jealousy. Silently I thanked Raphaela. And Stephan.

Aunt Irm, a silver fox draped in a flowing Susan Unger gown, was surrounded by a coterie of sycophants and true admirers. "Look at my Bubie," she exclaimed to them when she saw me. "Mort, come over here. My Janna is a movie star."

Sebastian had coifed an asymmetrical copper swirl that worked perfectly with my fitted halter dress—purple velvet—and with my mother's crystal jewelry.

"Melanie," my aunt sung out, "you remember Janna."

Oh, no, I thought, but sure enough, it was my museum bathroom stall nemesis. She had grown up to be as large as a cow! I smiled compassionately at her and triumphantly called over Stephan for the introductions.

Afterward Babba Pearl led the Hava Nagila. At 80 years, she was younger than most of us, resplendent in her blue sequins and pearls, the life of the party. She placed me, her *shayna,* in the front of the line. After we exhausted ourselves she interviewed Stephan.

"Nu, your father vat does he do?"

"Mechanic for BMW in Fort Washington. Retired now."

Babba half-closed her eyes. "And in Germany in de var?"

"He worked in the maintenance corps on jeeps and trucks."

Scowling, she pursed her lips.

"Could you excuse me?" Stephan bowed his head and hurried to the men's room.

Tightening her lips again, she turned to me. "Maybe it's your alte Babba's *narishkeit*; I tink dis man is not so gut." I bit my cheek. Just then Doris squirreled her off for a photo and I went to look for Stephan.

I found him at the entrance, talking on his cell. He covered the phone with his hand, but not before I heard Sally's voice on the other end. It was a saber in my heart.

"I'm sorry, Luv, stomach trouble," he coughed and scratched at the five o'clock stubble on his cheek. "Gotta go."

Without looking back, he ran out the door.

When I got into bed that night, Milo planted consolation doggie kisses on my hands. I tossed and turned in upset and finally at 3 AM passed into a dream state. I was completely lost, walking and running in circles in a murky haze. I heard Raphaela's distinctive voice calling me. Running after the sound, I tried and tried to find her, knowing I couldn't.

❦   ❦   ❦

I took a cool swig of Evian and watched the fiery sun flash off my trophy ring.

"We have a non-engagement engagement," I mused as I waved my left hand and made more sparkles. "Big rock si, date no."

We chortled as we lazed in wood rockers on the porch of a log cabin nestled in the spring tapestry of the Morris Arboretum. Gawky adolescent swans and ducks honked and squawked on a glassy pond nearby.

Sooze was back to being pleasingly zaftig with a full crop of red-brown curls. She mopped the back of her neck.

"After Stephan abandoned me at the wedding, we had the biggest fight ever. I thought it was over. And he gets me this." I waved my prize.

"That's the fear of loss that Raphaela taught you about. Even works for Peter Pan Weisgart," she said.

"It really seemed over. Maybe he'll wise up all the way and create the reality he really wants instead of repeating his empty past."

Sooze waved her hands like Janet Jackson and belted out, "Two steps forward, one step back, because opposites attract." After we finished giggling, Sooze continued. "Too bad, Stephan fights the process."

I picked up a stone and skipped it onto the glassy surface of the pond.

"What about couples work?" Sooze asked as she took a pack of Doritos out of her purse and offered me the chips.

I declined, drumming my nails on the arm of the rocker. Sooze stuffed a handful of Doritos in her mouth.

"I would love that. We don't talk enough. And we need some serious help in the bedroom. He still tries to hard and I'm pretty dead down there. But he won't go. I tried."

"He probably believes intimacy and marriage lead to suffocation. Or worse," she said.

"First he's got to get into that core baggage. Then he can create a new identity. After that maybe some couples work," I said as much to myself as to Sooze.

Sooze held my arm. "If he doesn't go into therapy, you should give him back the ring."

Just then a huge black and gold bumblebee buzzed around my head. I cried out as the marauder proceeded to land right on my engagement ring. I sat still as a frightened rabbit. Sooze bravely waved her hand over the intruder but he just sat on his gem throne.

"Maybe it's a sign from Raphaela," I wondered.

Much as Sooze waved, the bee sat, holding me captive.

"OK, already, I get the message. I could get stung," I jokingly said to the armed creature. At that moment he flew off.

"Stephan has his priorities mixed up," Sooze said, shoveling in the chips.

"We've got to get through the Greenway conference before we can even think about setting a date. I've been planning breakouts and plenary sessions instead of flowers and dinner menus," I groaned.

"Well, at least that excuse will be over in a couple of weeks."

Just then my cell phone rang. It was Sheila, the chiropractor in my downline.

"Janna, I've been hospitalized and Dr. Schmidt says it's toxic fulminant hepatitis…I need a liver transplant."

Her voice quivered.

My belly did flip-flops.

"I'm so sorry."

"I think it's the Chlorophyx. Remember I accidentally took three times the recommended dose."

"Stephan has taken much more that that. Is there anything…"

"Dr. Schmidt feels that it's the most likely explanation," she interrupted. The line went dead.

"Janna, what the heck was that?" Sooze put her hand on my shoulder.

"Sheila's very sick. Maybe dying," I choked out.

✦   ✦   ✦

By the end of the welcoming presentation in the Orlando Sheraton grand ballroom, fifteen hundred exuberant Greenway distributors were roaring with excitement. Their shiny faces came in all ages, shapes and sizes, ages 18 to 80, business types and professionals mixed in with housewives, Gen X-ers and aging ex-hippies in tie-dyed shirts.

Stephan, the master of ceremonies, took the stage like Ponce de Leon coming to claim the New World. He opened the show with a slick video featuring an animated algae cell, Mr. G.W. Mighty. G.W., who looked like a green Mighty Mouse, flew in upward spirals to illustrate the explosive growth of company sales—10% increase each month!

Stephan announced, "This is the golden moment. This is the time and this is the place to be. You are being swept up in a great tidal wave of success!"

Next Stephan showed videos of the newest Red Diamond distributors, with their dazzling new homes, cars and jewelry. It was amazing—there were retired executives and doctors, as you'd expect, but then a hairdresser from Idaho appeared, and a high school dropout from Duluth. We got the message: if they could do it, so could we. We were saving the world from disease and malnutrition. We were all going to be stinking rich! Stephan ended his presentation and we went crazy, stomping, roaring and clapping out our approval.

And I was going to be married to this giant of a man.

Then a riveting documentary started on the screen at the front of the room. It was three-year-old Teo Dar. His small sad face was projected into our hearts and souls all the way from Ethiopia. Teo was a tiny street urchin, living among mounds of garbage, crumbling makeshift houses and muddy squalor. Since he had been on the Greenway Foundation program, he had gained 10 pounds and the mysterious sores on his legs and arms had healed completely. Behind him other children played happily in the garbage dump that was his village. They too had dramatic recoveries. Stephan left the podium with tears in his eyes.

Brenda Kalter came onto the stage in a red floor-length sequin gown. She must have had professional coaching, because even though she was a midwestern farm girl, Brenda exuded the radiant authority of a celebrity. She was also feeding off the missionary zeal and adoration of the distributors in the ballroom, who continued to scream and cheer.

"Our vision is to create health and wealth for every child, every man, every woman in the world." Brenda beamed at the audience as they roared in response. "You all, yes, I mean each and every one of you. You're saving Teo's life. By supporting Greenway, you are contributing to our feeding programs in third world countries. There are 10 million children like Teo in Ethiopia and a staggering 120 million around the world. We need to build wealth, share wealth, to create hope for all of them."

Her husband, Ed, dressed in a tux, came up and held her hand in a winner's high. The audience gave them a standing ovation.

After the session Stephan met up with me in our room. Sally was staying with us in our two-bedroom suite—we had one room while she had the other. Stephan had explained that he had a lot of work for her to do and this would make it easier. It still left a knot in my stomach the size of Texas. I swallowed my misgivings as usual.

Stephan sensed my upset and was very focused on me. After I bestowed the kisses of congratulations on Senor de Leon, he presented me with a scarf-sized Hawaiian print sundress.

As I modeled it for him I asked, "Honey, are you sure the Chlorophyx has nothing to do with Sheila's problem?" I searched his face.

"Completely. If anything, the Chlorophyx helped stave off the hepatic failure. We have a lot of testimonials about the product helping with hepatitis and other liver diseases."

I put my head on his shoulder and nuzzled his neck.

The next day Stephan rushed off for a private meeting with the new Red Diamonds while I visited with Brenda. We sat in the Florida sun on a stone bench overlooking a redolent flowerbed brimming with bougainvillea, birds of paradise and salmon hibiscus. I noticed a woman sunbathing in the grass who was a ringer for my poor Sheila. Sadly I turned to Brenda and said, "Remember Sheila, the chiropractor in my downline. She claims the Chlorophyx made her so ill she needs a liver transplant."

"What a shame," Brenda touched my arm.

"Her doctor thinks there are toxins in the product."

"Y'know we test every batch we harvest for bacteria, heavy metals, and other contaminants."

"How big is a batch?'

"It's a day's harvest." Brenda looked at her watch. "Sorry, got to run and meet Ed."

She picked up her lecture notes and began to walk rapidly.

Wow, that's several tons I thought, as I ran after her.

"Brenda, would you take a look at Sheila's tests and tell me what you think?"

"Sure," Brenda called over her shoulder as she scurried into the hall. I went back to our room and was delighted to find Stephan resting on our bed. He looked exhausted, but completely pleased with himself.

"You're terrific, honey!" I beamed at him. "How about a Grey Goose and tonic?" I asked while I quickly changed out of the blue A-line shift I was wearing and into a sexy floral robe.

He unbuttoned his shirt in reply. We hadn't made love in a week since he was so busy with the conference prep. I quickly took ice, vodka and tonic out of the mini-bar and fixed the drink. When I sat down on the bed near him, he pulled me down to kiss him. His lips sensuously explored mine while his hands moved slowly over my breasts. I opened my mouth to his and our tongues met eagerly. Our souls were coming together and I hoped that with much of the stress of the conference out of the way we could move forward. I kissed the sculpted six-pack of his chest as he lay back enjoying. Inching my way slowly down, my tongue flickered over his sculpted abs. He moaned and arched his back, his member swelling. I unzipped his pants and followed the path of pleasure all the way to its home.

After I paid full homage to Stephan's masculinity and he was gloriously spent on the bed, I took a shower. Fantasies of his repaying me in kind boogied lasciviously in my head.

When I came back into the room I gasped.

Sally was sitting on the bed wearing only a black lace thong. Stephan, still nude, was snorting white powder on the nightstand with a rolled up $100 bill. He rubbed powder on his gums and said, "Hey, baby, do a line with us."

I almost vomited. Stephan's ravishing blue eyes had turned to ugly narrow slits. His perfect face was a grotesque mask. With rapid-fire speech, he said, "You've such trouble coming with a man, maybe a woman like Sally could…"

The bitch grinned, licked her fingers and inserted them into Stephan's mouth while she leered at me.

"Fuck you both!" I shrieked. Blind with humiliation and rage, I tore through the living room weeping. I realized the sleeping arrangement in the two-bedroom suite had been a set-up. How weak I was. What I dope I had been. Ripping my cell phone out of my bag I frantically dialed Sooze. Nothing. Even my phone had failed me. "Fuck everything!" I screamed as I bashed it into a coffee table.

Holding my robe closed, I ran to the lobby pay phone and called Sooze. She sounded hoarse and sickly.

"How are you?" I asked nervously.

"Don't worry. I just have a chest cold."

"Thank God. Sooze, Stephan got coked up with that Sally and tried to make me have a threesome."

"Shit! But it's worse than that," Sooze's voice was hollow. "I've been trying and trying to reach you."

"What do you mean?'

"I just got off the phone with Corinne, Sheila's assistant. Janna…Sheila died of liver failure yesterday morning." My stomach churned violently and I could taste the bile in my mouth. "And I'm certain it was the Chlorophyx. Corinne got sick too, no jaundice, but swelling, nausea and vomiting."

"No, no," I croaked. "It can't be. I've heard so many testimonials…"

"Placebo effect."

"I've got to get out." Hanging up the phone, I frantically belted up the front of my robe and stormed back to the suite. Stephan and Sally were still in the bedroom, laughing as if nothing had happened.

"Sheila died!" I blurted out as if Stephan had killed her.

"That's a downer," he said as he offered me a rolled up bill.

I hit it out of his hand on to the floor. "And someone else is sick in her downline with the same symptoms."

"Oh lighten up," Sally interrupted me.

"Janna, don't be hysterical. Chill," he urged.

"I'll show you hysterical," I screeched, as I pulled out the drawers, went through the closet, packing my stuff and dumping all of his on the floor.

"God damn it! Don't do this to me!" Stephan raged as he wildly punched a hole in the wall.

How could I have been so blind and stupid? I bolted out of the bedroom, dragging my suitcase behind me, spitting out, "I'm leaving." He pulled at my arms, but I shook him off violently and hurried to the door. Slamming it behind me, I could hear his siren voice calling.

"Juno, Luv, don't…"

CHAPTER 15

Homeward Bound

A week after the Orlando debacle I sat glumly in the kitchen slowly shredding a poster of Mr. G.W. Mighty into tiny green pieces. Milo stood among the green debris with his ears pinned back in worry. I picked him up and held his head to my cheek so he could give me soft licks of comfort. Tears flowed, as scenes from Sheila's funeral flashed in my mind. Sentinels of white roses stood bearing witness to her passing in the prime of life; a colleague's tribute to her soft strong healing hands; and, her five-year-old niece unknowingly saying a final goodbye as she placed carnations on the coffin. I grabbed the phone and dialed Raphaela.

The outgoing message announced she was still in India.

Impulsively I picked up my keys, jumped in the Volvo and drove in a mad dash to the Chester County farmhouse. No one was there. Crying softly, I sped to the North Philly project. As I parked in front of the Community Center, I noticed Gilbert sitting on a Harley counseling two strung out brothers. Wiping up my face, I waited quietly until he was done. Then I rushed over to him. He took one look at me and shook his head. "She's not here."

I grabbed his massive forearm. "But I have to see her."

"I don't think so. You get only one chance at being Raphaela's apprentice."

Horrified, I stared at him. "But, you don't mean..."

"Sorry."

A familiar wave of nausea washed through my gut as I sank against the cycle. No, I said to myself, damn it, no. I drew myself back up and raised my voice. "Gilbert, you have to tell me. Where exactly is Raphaela? Tell me now."

He shrugged. "Ballygunge Circular Road. In Calcutta."

❧   ❧   ❧

Packed sardine-style in Air India coach, I stared at the red-orange-green sunset spreading over the cloud-strewn horizon, reassuring myself I was not crazy. "After all, I have nothing to lose but a couple of weeks and a plane ticket," I said out loud. The elderly Indian woman sitting next to me snorted in her sleep and patted my arm. "Shanti, Shanti," she mumbled. Settling back, I closed my eyes, enfolded myself in my mantra and passed into a strange hypnogogic state that carried me all the way to the Calcutta airport.

The stench of diesel fuel and burning cow dung greeted me as I wandered out into the sprawling ugly city. Coughing wildly, I hailed a three-wheeled auto-rickshaw and dug my fingernails into my palms as we careened down the pot-holed chaos of traffic. Two cars coming from opposite directions nearly ran us off the road.

My stomach flip-flopped the whole time I was India. "Delhi belly," the locals all said. But I knew better.

After several false turns I made it to the address Gilbert had given me. It was an ancient temple packed with about 100 devotees, seated on the floor beneath colorful temple deities. From what little reading I had done, I recognized Lord Shiva and his consort Parvati, along with Krishna and his consort Radha. At the front of the group sat a gnarled old man swathed in white, his eyes closed in deep meditation. Sitting next to him there was a woman wearing an orange sari, her face shrouded with a gold embroidered scarf. My heart jumped—although I could not see her face, I knew it was Raphaela. A bolt of adrenaline surged through me. One by one the devotees came up and touched their feet.

Sweet silence permeated the room. Not knowing what else to do, I settled cross-legged on the floor and began to meditate. After the darshan ended and the last person was blessed, I walked to the front. Hesitantly I went to Raphaela, hoping she would throw off her veil and embrace me. I touched the hem of her sari, then her toes. Nothing. No response. I backed away, softly sobbing. Quietly I settled in a corner of the room. They stayed in deep meditation all night while I sat stubbornly until bone-aching fatigue forced me down to sleep. When I awoke the next morning they were gone.

Maybe I hallucinated that it was Raphaela. But for some reason I remained rooted to the spot. When I refused to leave the ashram they gave me a closet of a room with a sleeping mat. For several hot sweaty days and nights I tried to meditate while I held my belly, slept fitfully, tossing and turning on the hard floor, and taking many unpleasant trips to the outdoor latrine. I finally could eat the thin dahl and rice offered to me by a slight goateed boy.

After I was finished he tugged at my sleeve and led me into an oasis of a courtyard lined with coconut trees. There, still veiled, she sat on a blanket. In front of her sat a washbowl and cloth. I stared at her as the boy disappeared. Slowly, tenderly, she bathed my feet.

Then she drew back her veil enough to fix me with her jade eyes.

"You have searched bravely and you shall have what you need."

She opened her arms and I fell into them. Instantly I fell into a dream-like state. Images of fat little Buddha babies laughing, rose petals floating, being cradled in the arms of a great elm tree passed through.

When I opened my eyes, I was lying on a high stiff bed inside the temple. Raphaela came in looking ten years younger than when I had last seen her. She had cut her dark shiny hair short into a curly do that gave her a childlike, innocent look and a simple gauze caftan billowed around her.

She brushed the sweaty ringlets from my forehead. "You have earned Lesson Six," she said. "The boy will help you regain your strength. Then you must fly home and meet me next Wednesday afternoon in front of your old house on Green Street."

❧　　　❧　　　❧

As I stood near the tiny row home of my childhood waiting for Raphaela, I felt like an excited child waiting for her mother. All resentment had vanished when she had welcomed me. Humming nervously, I studied the old brick nest. The latest owners had painted the trim an awful turquoise, but the postage stamp garden in front still held my mother's ancient lilac bush, now in full bloom. As I did a being-in-the-moment meditation I inhaled deeply and the essence of the plant wafted in to soothe the lingering pain of Stephan.

It dawned on me that my surliness with Raphaela grew out of an inner fortress of defense. I allowed myself inside to feel the fears that had plagued me—about being abandoned, left alone and bereft. These demons had given rise to the anger I had felt toward her. As I let myself feel into the swell of emotions, the primitive anxieties, the sadness, passed through me and were replaced by heart-felt gratitude. I love Raphaela, I admitted.

A voice spoke right in my ear and I jumped. It was Raphaela, who had appeared out of nowhere. She held my head against her soft bosom and stroked my hair.

I sighed.

"I'm sorry. I behaved like an idiot with you, a spoiled child. And..." I felt myself turning red. "Much as I hate to admit it, you were right about Stephan."

She showed no emotional reaction. No 'I told you so'. What a relief, I thought.

"But you were awfully rigid in refusing to discuss the situation, don't you think?" I asked defensively, all the while cautioning myself against creating what I feared most: pushing her away again.

"Thank you for saying that. I was too rigid; probably juggling too many projects. I'm sorry too." Raphaela's eyes were weary.

I was shocked by her response.

Her eyes met mine. "I'll be more careful, Janna."

I breathed a deep sigh and Raphaela patted my cheek.

"Now I know we don't have to live in the painful distance when cut-offs happen with loved ones. If we fully own the way we damaged the relationship there can be healing."

"Enough now. Tell me your journey."

As we walked down the street where I had played as a child the little rowhomes that had been a vacant boring backdrop years ago seemed now to be homey and inviting. Raphaela listened quietly as I reviewed the past five months, only stopping me when I started to berate myself.

Then with total compassion, she said, "You have replayed the traumas of your childhood by weaving the spider's web to torment yourself, first with Stephan and me, then with Stephan and Sally. One person was thrown out of the web as the enemy, while the other was spindled into it." Raphaela lifted my chin so our faces were inches apart.

"I want to break the damn patterns once and for all. I'm sick of it. I'm ready to create a different life."

"No matter what the pain. The wounds. No matter what the tragedy you can go home again," she whispered. She shepherded me back down the block towards my old home.

"What?"

She held my arm close. "Lesson Six is: *You can go home again.*"

While I pondered the meaning of the lesson, she prodded me.

"Think about your deepest issues."

Mrs Smith

Bread

Nassay 10pm

35 00

212-206

Forest
N309   11p
Queens Plaza

"Being closed off, afraid of being powerful...and a mother hunger that won't quit."

"Go on."

"Then I met you and I opened. You were different, you got who I am, and I knew I could trust you to help fill the void."

"So you had a sense you could go home again, that there was a new mother figure for you in the world. But then what did you do?"

"I threw it all away—didn't listen to you about dating...thought I knew best...let my arrogant pseudo-independence get in the way of your guidance. And finally I rejected you."

Raphaela nodded. "Think about the legend of Ceres, whose mother, Demeter, was the Goddess of crops and of the earth's mysterious creative powers. Ceres would leave her mother and go to the underworld each winter and all the vegetation would die and go barren. That's what you did."

"I remember. Ceres could come out of the underworld and create springtime by returning to Demeter and the earth would be transformed back into the Garden of Eden."

"All women are Ceres. We have all experienced mother-loss and heart-desolation. But we can find Demeter again and again. And if we choose," she shot me a knowing look, "to surrender to her, we have the new hope and joy of being mothered once again by the great maternal that surrounds us."

Raphaela picked a fragrant lilac and held it up to me. Then she said, "You made me into Demeter."

"It was because you were so strong..."

"Freud used to call it positive transference—the idea of experiencing another person as the good parent. The analysts thought it was neurotic, something to be worked through."

"Therapists always tried to interpret it away."

"They didn't understand that transference also has great Darwinian purpose."

Raphaela twinkled at me.

"Meaning?" I asked.

"That the positive qualities you bestow upon the mentor can ultimately help you evolve into a more effective person."

I took the flower and touched it to my lips.

"Lesson Six teaches us that if we find the right teacher, one who sees the perfection in us, and open ourselves up to their parenting, we can transform our lives completely."

"In other words, by granting them the right to parent us we give ourselves the power to be healed?" I asked.

"Yes, granting them that sacred role."

"But how do you know if you've found the right person?"

"The right one excites and inspires you to be real and generative. She or he holds you to that vision no matter what, helping you set limits so you don't backtrack. No matter how old you are, you can find a true teacher—be it therapist, pastor, sponsor or, most importantly, lover."

"What about your best friend? Women are constantly talking to their girlfriends about matters of the heart."

"Friends who listen with empathy are not change-agents. So you end up acting out from the wounds of the past and endlessly repeating the same self-defeating patterns."

"Tell me about it. Sooze and I always end up reinforcing our worst habits."

We came back to the front of my little row home and sat back down on the curb. Raphaela smiled. "To have a successful emotional garage sale, you need more than just having someone listen to you. More than someone who interprets the past for you."

"That's why my client work could only go so far."

Raphaela nodded. "You need someone who actively parents you—who tells you when you're stepping into the same pile of crap again. One who sees the best in you and pulls out all the stops to help it emerge. We're calling it parenting. But it's more like having a mother, father confessor, envisioner, believer…."

"Or drill sergeant," I added laughing.

"You might call the right teacher a personal trainer of the soul."

I realized, despite my obstinate and childish behavior with Raphaela, her teachings had chained down to my clients. I'd envisioned higher goals, encouraged them to press on despite obstacles and set limits when they needed them. I remembered my client, this perpetual whiner who never followed through on her homework assignments. I told her that she was fired from therapy. The client was so shocked that she finally took on her life instead of just complaining. I smiled and unconsciously picked a particularly fragrant flower from my mother's old bush.

Raphaela continued, "Depending on their childhood, some people need a softer sweeter touch, others tough love, still others an unswerving belief in their potential. Most, though, require a healing posture that combines all three kinds of love."

"You gave me all that," I acknowledged. "And despite fighting and second-guessing you, I still internalized what you taught."

Raphaela stood and pulled me up to face her. "Each of us weaves the love we receive from others into our own unique tapestry of being. *You can go home again.*"

She gestured toward my house. For a moment it was transformed into a stately stone mansion with a wide welcoming porch and a white swing. A mother mallard and six ducklings swam together in a charming pond in front of the house. I gasped and rubbed my eyes. The hallucination still stood in all of its Main Line elegance.

She chuckled. "To your new and improved home."

CHAPTER 16

The Strength Within

Stephan called me regularly. At first I raged, erasing the messages as soon as I heard his voice. But after a few weeks my heart softened. He was pleading for me to talk to him, to see him. He claimed that he was firing Sally; that he wanted to help Corinne; that he loved me.

The rational part of me knew contact would inevitably lead to pain, but I overcame logic by telling myself that for my own personal integrity I needed to speak to Stephan about the illnesses.

"Juno, my luv, I miss you," he courted in his honeyed baritone.

"Just wanted to talk about Sheila and Corinne," I clipped back.

"There's a chance that the Chlorophyx caused cleansing reactions that briefly worsened whatever diseases they had. I'll have Brenda call you and Corinne. But Luv, when can I see you?"

"Let me know when Brenda's available for a three-way call." I hung up with my heart racing. Milo, ever the caretaker, licked my ankles furiously, dancing around my feet in a wet anxious whirl.

That night I tossed and turned and tried to cuddle Milo. But in the middle of the night I had a dream. The comforting presence of my mother came back to me complete with her signature lilac scent. I could see the brown curls framing her face, her deep-set dark chestnut eyes gazing at me. She was trying to tell me something, something important, but I couldn't make out the words. I called out, "Mama, I can't hear you."

To my horror, she glared ominously at me and growled, "Janna, it was you. You killed me."

I woke up with a start and immediately began practicing the pranayama that Raphaela had taught me. As I alternated opening and closing my nostrils, focusing only on breathing in and out, the panicky feelings subsided. I settled into meditation and silently repeated my mantra. Suddenly I saw visions of Raphaela calling me on the telephone, telling me to come to India the next day. On Air India, JFK, Flight number 102. Annoyed I went back to my mantra. The visions intruded. When it happened for a third time, I muttered, "Enough already," and stopped meditating. The shrill jangling of the phone startled me right out of my relaxed space. I picked up the receiver.

Raphaela laughed heartily when I answered. "You got it right," she said. "AI Flight 102."

❧   ❧   ❧

Raphaela sat motionless in a half-lotus in the small antechamber at the back of the ashram on Ballygunge Circular Road. She called her deep meditation 'submersion in all that is.' Glad to be whisked away from questions about Stephan, Corinne and Chlorophyx, I meditated on and off beside her in the blistering heat.

A few days floated by. The goateed boy brought us food and water, although Raphaela took none. Finally Raphaela spoke. "There is a corollary to Lesson Six. As you are reparented on the outer level through gifts of love and guidance from others, you are prepared for the most profound journey. You move back home to the great cosmic mother of all. Then minor and major miracles are possible."

I scratched my head.

"That means as you welcome and take in the love that is all around, your compassion for yourself and for everyone increases. You will see pure God-like consciousness in yourself, in others, in all things. You will be at home, grounded in this awareness. Even when the ebb and flow of human drama plays out and threatens to consume you, you will be able to stop your suffering. You will recognize that your battles in life are merely creations, interesting stage plays but definitely not the Eternal you."

I looked at her Buddha face. "You mean by connecting with a loving mentor the stage is set to connect with the essential Self that is in all of us?"

"The revelation that has come to many mystics and poets can come to you as well. Everyone is being prepared to reach the state of dropping worldly attachments, dropping all obstructions to peace and contentment. When the ego is transcended you won't struggle anymore. Instead you will live in the Eternity that is now. And you will easily perform right action."

Light passed from her eyes into mine, filling me with the serenity of a child floating on a calm sun-dappled lake. She dipped her finger into a clay urn that was beside her and dabbed the center of my forehead with a thick ochre paste.

"You are enfolded in the raptures of the Infinite. She/He/It has been with you from the beginning and is with you now. Blessed Be."

I bowed my head.

"May this deepest flow of love," she chanted, "lead you back to your immortal Self."

❧   ❧   ❧

When I returned home, I rededicated myself to my client work. My last clients were Rhoda and Jim. They sat close together on the couch staring at me.

Rhoda started. "Janna, you look so different, I mean centered.

"It's your eyes," Jim added.

"Thanks," I beamed at them. "But back to you."

"I want more, I don't know how to say it," Jim blushed. Rhoda tiredly rifled through her purse.

"Intimacy? You want more intimacy?" I interjected.

"More like, spontaneity. Everything in our life is pre-arranged, when we go out, when we're alone, when we have sex. Though sex has never been better."

He winked at Rhoda.

I clapped my hands. "Excellent—you've switched roles. You're no longer stuck in your old vaudeville routine of overbearing, long-suffering Rhoda and stoic but dead Jim."

Rhoda giggled. "Now, it's poor dead Rhoda and never satisfied Jim."

Jim leaned forwards. "I guess, honey, I wish you didn't wear yourself out at work. Your new business will still be there in the morning."

Rhoda tenderly touched his cheek.

The phone rang. Normally, I ignore calls during session. But this time I immediately picked up. I knew it was Sooze.

"What's wrong?"

"My CA 125 was elevated so I went in for an ultrasound yesterday. It's metastasized."

Instead of panic, I felt centered and full of love for Sooze. I put down the receiver and turned to my clients.

"My best friend's cancer has spread."

Rhoda and Jim were stricken.

"Don't worry about us. I know what to do," Rhoda said softly.

They stood up and awkwardly hugged me.

Sooze and I revisited the six cycles of Hell. Once a week I drove her to HUP for twenty-four hour drips of cis-platinum and paclitaxel. Once again the napalm ripped out her hair, leveled her life force and left her dry heaving in the toilet. The doctors gave Sooze a whopping 35% chance of responding to the chemotherapy but the latest studies on 'salvage therapy' gave no assurance that it would prolong her life.

My daily practice allowed me to be a steady presence for Sooze, a repository for her pains, fears and worries. Sadness welled through me on and off, but I felt strangely OK. Raphaela was away again, and even that didn't throw me off balance.

After her treatment series, Sooze was buoying and I could turn my attention to other matters. I started through my mail and found a letter from Hugh.

꙰

Sitting in the stillness my soul calls out. It calls forth what is yet unnamed in the universe to sing to you, to draw your soul from within and pour it with mine into the same luminescent fountain of life, at least for one moment.

Could you give me a sign, a few moments to see you, to open our connection again? I'll listen to the wind and see what the fates whisper.

I thought of calling him but I didn't quite know what to say. It had been months since I sent him the goodbye letter. Instead, I called Doris and read her his poetry.

"Marry him," she said.

"Sure. I'll call him right this minute."

"Janna, I've been meaning to ask you…you signed Sheila up, right?"

"Yeah."

"Listen, if her family sues the company, they might be able to go after you too." I had visions of them taking my house and confiscating my meager savings. "Didn't you say that Hugh was a lawyer?"

"Actually, he handles people like Sheila."

"Well, you better call him and see if you're at risk."

We hung up in a hurry and I called Hugh.

Awkwardly I said, "I have a problem."

"I'd love to help." Good old Hugh.

"You know I'm in a network marketing company that sells nutritional products. A woman in my downline just died and the doctor is blaming my product."

"That could be sticky."

"The doctors say it caused her liver to fail."

"Come to my office so we can talk."

Hugh's office was in a brownstone building in the judicial center of Norristown, the county seat. The airy waiting room was graced with comfortable leather furniture and primitive Caribbean paintings. I was ushered into his plant-filled private office by a graying austere African-American woman.

When Hugh came in I was surprised to find myself savoring his new look. He had let his curly dark brown hair grow out and it softened his intelligent cafe au lait face. Hugh walked over and took my hand, and I remembered how warm and alive his touch was. He motioned for me to sit in a red leather chair while he sat stiffly behind his desk. The secretly shared written intimacies hung between us in stark contrast to our face-to-face formality. Hugh anxiously cleared his throat while I poured out the story of Sheila and Corinne. But it was hard for either of us to make eye contact.

"Do you have product liability insurance?" For an instant his eyes seemed to be caressing my breasts.

"No," I answered sharply, attempting to reestablish my boundaries.

His eyes quickly shifted away. "Janna, you could have, um, exposure here. Significant exposure. The executor of the estate or the family can come after the company and after you as well, for willful negligence. You need to retain counsel."

"Oh, no. How much will it cost?"

"Well, my colleague, Ken, is the best one to handle the case. Our fees are reasonable."

"Couldn't you…"

"Under the circumstances, I don't think it's appropriate for me to take the case." He looked awkwardly at me for a split second and fingered the one file folder that marred the sterile orderliness of his desk. I winced.

"Hugh, I really...really appreciated your letters. I mean I've been going through strange times, hard times lately..." I didn't know what to say. I didn't want to lead him on, but my heart was fluttering in an odd way.

Hugh's almond eyes misted over. "I was wondering if you even read them. I never heard back from you...But I'm happy to help you, just as a friend."

"You're a life saver."

"I'll just ring Ken's office and get you two introduced." He seemed remote, wistful, as he picked up the phone. Ken was on a conference call but said he could meet with me in 45 minutes. Hugh went to the kitchen next door to get us coffee, which I proceeded to spill on the beige Berber carpet in front of his desk. He laughed as if I had done something adorable and the sound went right into my heart. We wound up on our hands and knees mopping up the stains with tissues. And then he turned my head and kissed me deep and full, his hungry luscious lips enveloping mine. We kissed for an eternal moment, his big tongue tenderly exploring the secret corners of my mouth.

The intercom buzzed us apart. Ken. I quickly packaged up a mélange of feelings and ran to the bathroom to comb my hair and fix my makeup.

The meeting was short. Ken said, "Toxic hepatitis can be caused by poisons and drug reactions, as well as contaminants in water. Don't worry about it until we get the autopsy report."

I wrote him a retainer check for $2000 and left the meeting in a total state of confusion.

When I got home I pulled myself together to surf the Net and find a Chlorophyx chat room. To my dismay there were numerous complaints about Chlorophyx and other algae products. Three of the cases had symptoms similar to Corinne's. I lost my appetite and couldn't down the chicken and broccoli I had prepared.

Then the phone rang.

"Have you seen the latest edition of *Yoga Journal*?" Hugh asked with concern.

"No. Why?"

"There's an expose on Greenway. Two MDs who've been selling the products in their practices have had six cases of toxicity."

"I need to see the article." Perhaps it wasn't that bad.

"I can bring it over to you tonight," offered the steady knight.

"But, uh, one thing, Hugh. I'm sorry about what happened today...I mean I don't want..."

His voice cracked. "You just want to be friends. I understand. See you at nine."

I grabbed the magazine out of Hugh's hands as soon as he arrived. The article quoted Stephan: *Greenway products could not have caused the purported gastrointestinal and other ailments.*

In disgust I threw the magazine on the floor.

"The bastard is trying to whitewash the whole thing," I exclaimed.

"I'll make some Mint Medley," Hugh offered.

"I'm sorry. I have to be alone now," I said.

I dispatched him with a peck on the cheek and immediately phoned Stephan.

"I'm pissed off you didn't tell me about the *Yoga Journal* article."

"I was afraid, Juno, Luv," he responded, dripping syrup. "Those two quacks quoted in the article have started their own nutritional business. It turns out the people on the Internet who complained about the products were their patients. They're using negative PR to kill the competition, namely us. That's how big business operates. You just don't understand."

I was beginning to think maybe he had a point. My knowledge of the business world was average for a therapist, in other words, less than zero.

The next morning I had the three-way call with Brenda and Corinne. Brenda suggested Corinne's nausea was a cleansing reaction and she should cut back on her daily intake of Chlorophyx. She also prescribed 8 to 10 glasses of spring water a day to speed the process along.

Sure enough, a few days later I checked in with Corinne and the nausea was gone. She said she liked the Chlorophyx because it gave her lots of energy and planned to continue taking it. I started to think maybe I had overreacted because of my ambivalent feelings for Stephan. After all, the Chlorophyx was a strong detoxifier and when toxins were released, they could cause reactions. But in the long run, a good housecleaning was a great boon for your health. What if the product was really fine, but Stephan was not? What if Sheila simply had a fatal liver disease?

CHAPTER 17

The Call

Nightmares about Sheila and my mother lit some kind of fire in me. I needed to know I was not responsible, for Sheila's death, that I was not responsible for anyone's death. *Fear lights the way to mastery,* I repeated to myself over and over, like a mantra, as I raced downtown to Stephan's apartment and used the key he had bestowed on me to let myself in.

As I went down the hall I continued the mantra to give me courage. When I poked my head into the living room, I saw that, mercifully, no one was there. Just then I heard Stephan's voice and realized he was on the phone in the bedroom at the end of the hallway. The door was half-open and I tiptoed over to eavesdrop. They seemed to be talking about a new PR campaign when suddenly Stephan asked, "And how's the latest study coming? What?…Sixty percent of the mice?…No choice, Brenda. Bury it."

Stifling a gasp I scurried back to the front door. I opened and slammed it and called, "Stephan?"

He came sauntering out of the bedroom. "Juno, Luv, what a surprise!"

He embraced me and, thinking quickly on my feet, I kissed him on the mouth. He was so shocked he barely kissed back and then he held my shoulders at arms' length, studying my face. "That was a long lost treat. I've missed you so much."

He went for the full-court French kiss and reluctantly I let him even though it made me gag.

"Stephan, about what happened in Orlando…"

"Luv, I was high out of my mind. It's you I want." He took my hands in his and I studied the plastic boy doll in front of me—perfectly coordinated in charcoal Hugo Boss slacks and a meticulously ironed black polo sports shirt. "I'm in counseling. I've been overwrought about hurting you. It's the last thing I ever intended to do."

His words were perfect. Perfectly hollow.

"Maybe I was just over-reacting."

He stroked the back of my hair. "I remember, about you and triangles."

No wonder he's so lethal; he has a photographic memory. Very useful for making the sticky mucus for luring flies to his Venus trap, I thought.

My hands were wet and trembling, but I wanted to lull him into a false sense of security, in order to uncover the whole truth. Somehow. I decided to make my escape.

"Listen, I'm in a rush, I just needed to pick up a copy of my genealogy." I smiled weakly.

"Can we have dinner, can we talk?" He asked, pleading with perfect eyes.

"Just give me more time, Stephan."

He retrieved my genealogy from the file and handed it to me. I brushed his cheek with my lips and left.

After that galvanizing moment in Stephan's apartment, I knew I had found the smoking gun. But to shut Greenway down would mean getting my hands on any reports that showed the problems they were hiding. My father and sister counseled me to report the company to the FDA anonymously and let it go—they were afraid I might be attacked by Stephan et al. Herb suggested I consult a male witch he knew who could neutralize evil energies. I wanted to beat Stephan at his own seduce and kill game. But I was frightened, not sure I could pull it off. Besides, I told myself, I had too much going on with Sooze.

My luscious peach had become a bald wraith from Auschwitz. I escalated my search for alternative therapies. Via the Internet, I consulted a biochemist in California who generously e-mailed his findings on the miracle of CoQ10. Another chat room buddy, an aromatherapist, suggested I massage her feet and abdomen with frankincense oil, a remedy that the ancients used to heal tumors.

On Herb's recommendation I called Phyllis Hakmin, the psychic healer, who came over and waved her hands over Sooze's shrunken body. She panto-mimed pulling long, goopy poisonous ropes out of the abdomen. And I made a hypnotic tape for Sooze to listen to daily where she visualized the cancer cells being killed by her NK immune cells, like so many casualties on a battlefield.

Miraculously, she rallied enough to resume seeing a few clients.

❦   ❦   ❦

A few weeks later as I lay in bed watching the pink-gold-orange tones of sunlight tint the scattered November clouds Milo suddenly jumped to attention at the foot of the bed and started barking at the doorway. Startled, I looked over and saw a shimmering figure floating in the doorway.

"Raphaela?" I whispered with trembling lips. In answer, light appeared from the top of the being's head and scattered in a haze all around the room. An intoxicating lavender scent filled my chest with warmth.

"Raphaela, I'm so glad you're here. What do I do?" I pleaded. "Other people could be dying!"

She transmitted her thoughts directly to me: *The challenge is there in your life to sharpen you, to hone you like a fine saber.*

"*But how?*" I wondered.

The purpose of your life is to become your own Beloved Warrior. This is Lesson Seven. You are to build a life you are proud of, that is fulfilling to you in all dimensions, a life that leads to self-respect. Build admiration and appreciation for yourself and your actions. You and only you can determine the right path. Choose your own goals and then act with one-pointed intent.

"*I remember Joseph Campbell saying that the hero of the Grail is one who acts out of his own spontaneous nature.*"

Exactly. There is no set way to proceed in the reality drama you have crafted for yourself. As a warrior, you may embrace yin or yang, soft or hard, yielding or unyielding in order to actualize your intentions. You must be open to your deepest intuition, listening carefully for the faint voice in your heart. When you are willing to follow that whisper and be as flexible as the reed without compromising your integrity, all will unfold perfectly.

"*So you mean I have to determine what will help me be stronger?*"

Yes, no matter how difficult it is. And when it is the right choice, the hero's choice, it will help others, make them stronger too. Then you will inspire, become the leader, the strong role model.

"*Part of me wants to take on Greenway, but…*"

Confusion and inertia are smokescreens.

"*But this is big…dangerous.*"

The greater the challenge or threat, the greater is the person who faces it.

The figure vanished as quickly as it had appeared, leaving only perfumed air. I rushed to the doorway, just to be where she had been for a brief moment. A surge of energy trickled up my spine to the crown of my head.

Slowly the energy dissipated and I sat down in my rocker to savor the surprise visit. My stained glass keepsake box sat on the table near me. Mindlessly I stroked the lead beveling that separated the blue and red glass shapes adorning the top of the box. With a will of its own, my hand reached inside, removed a pen and my journal, and began writing a letter to myself:

ᦕ

Janna,

In you are all possibilities. You are sister, mother, friend, companion of visions and dreams. You are pupil and mentor. You are a means of solace and a source of inspiration. You are courage, power and hope. These are possibilities you made real by striving to return to your Self, a being as pure and lyric as possible within the boundaries of each short day and night.

As I read this letter to myself, a surge of purpose, of energy filled me.

My reverie was interrupted by the phone. It was Sooze, but I hardly recognized her voice. "My stomach…the pain is exploding…"

I met her at the ER intake room. Cavernous circles rimmed her eyes and her stomach was nine months distended.

"We'll handle this challenge together," I reassured both of us.

Rise, rise to the occasion, I reminded myself.

By Saturday, Sooze had improved, but they wouldn't let her leave the hospital, which we were all pleased about: the Almighty dollar was not running her care. I hung crystals in her window and streaming rainbows of light surrounded her. As they danced around the sparse, sterile room, she laughed with child-like delight.

"Sooze, I had another visitation from Raphaela and she taught me the purpose of life is to be your own beloved warrior. You Bravesoul are living proof of that lesson."

She smiled shyly. "I wish Raphaela would visit me."

"She said she can come to you only through me." I studied a huge swath of rainbow light that swayed on the wall above her head.

She picked up my hand and kissed it.

"Your steadiness has given me so much strength. Either that or it's the drugs." She giggled. "The heavy duty oxycontin is making me constipated. Whoever said you can't take it with you is wrong." She patted her stomach. "I thing I'll just take all this shit with me."

These veiled references to her dying had started to appear.

I tried to laugh.

She groaned, "Help me go pee."

I pulled her up slowly from the bed. The fresh pink of the skin on my hand against the sallow jaundice of her arm made me feel guilty, guilty for having vitality while she was wasting away.

My sweet daughter/sister inched her way through the pain to the bathroom. I waited, staring out the window at the bare-armed November spread of tree branches that waved slowly in the wind. When she came out, I tucked her back into bed and studied her face to store an image of her in my memory. Sooze's eyes had become saucer-like and her hair was a halo of wispy red-brown ring-lets.

I petted her forehead gently and she closed her eyes in appreciation.

I whispered, "Imagine white healing light streaming into your body from the top of your head, bathing every cell in healing energy."

Sooze followed me as I guided the light throughout her body. She became a peaceful cherub lying among the white sheets.

Suddenly out of nowhere she opened her eyes, grabbed my hand. "I don't want to die, Janna."

As she sobbed tears welled in my eyes.

"Death is the final challenge, my darling. Let go," I soothed as I held her hands.

She said, "But I never got to write my blockbuster, *Taxol Your Way to a Perfect Figure.* If only I could have two more years…And I won't get to see you cut the ribbon at a women's center."

Sooze bargained on as she wept.

"Enough," she chastised herself. "Get my mind off this ugliness."

"Are you sure?"

"I'm ready to hear about the miseries of everyday life. Distractions are good, ma cherie."

"Sheila's autopsy showed she died of liver cancer, which is a relief. My lawyer, Ken, says I'm in the clear. But I suspect the Chlorophyx causes health problems. I don't know what's wrong, but I think I overheard Stephan and Brenda conspiring to squelch a study that showed Chlorophyx hurt lab animals."

"I knew it!" She grimaced.

"I'm calling the FDA," I said half-heartedly.

"You have to for your own self respect. Maybe that's why the lesson about being a heroine came to you."

"Well, Ken thinks I should let it go. And Hugh's been away the last couple of days."

"Lawyers! But Hugh, he's different—he has morals. And he's cute. Stiff, but cute. Discuss it with him when he gets back." Sooze took a long sip of water from the straw in the glass jug on her hospital tray. Just then the crystal hanging in the window dispersed rainbows over the blank white wall.

"See, Janna, it's a sign. He's the one," Sooze smiled. "That man has the soul of a poet."

"You'll be pleased to know then that we smooched."

Sooze sat up. "Yummy. In midday?"

"Yeah. Mr. Slow Hand is a virtuoso. He's 180° from Mr. Pond Scum."

"I need more details. Details I say," she intoned with a mock British accent. She closed her eyes deep in thought. Then she said, "Give me your cell."

Startled, I fished it out of my bag and handed it to her.

"What's Raphaela's number?"

"Hit speed-dial 2. But she's in India."

"I sense not." Sooze pressed the button and handed the phone back to me.

"Oh, Raphaela, you're home. It's Janna," I croaked in wonderment. I looked at Sooze and then at the phone.

"Let's meet on Thursday," Raphaela offered.

"Are you sure? It's Thanksgiving?" I asked.

"Exactly," she said and hung up.

Tenderly, I took Sooze's hands in mine and asked, "How?" Sooze's wizened orange face broke out in a knowing smile. "My brain must have been granted an early crossing to the other side. Anyway, you need her. To get yourself straightened out, so you can take us into uncharted land of love and other impossibilities."

I drove home even more desperate to help her. I phoned Herb and asked him to scour the Internet for healing miracles, breakthroughs, for hope. That night, he called me back with the website of a company that was marketing a substance called lactoferrin, made from bovine colostrum that supposedly had reversed terminal lung cancer in a few cases. I quickly ordered it for Sooze.

I had never dealt with a dying person before, much less my best friend. Rooting through my closet bookcase, I found my Kubler-Ross, *On Death and Dying*. I touched the cover, thinking how the author, herself, had finally crossed the rainbow bridge. It's such a short walk through life. Sooze was deeply into the denial/bargaining part of the path. I needed to help her work through the next couple of stages, through the inevitable anger to peaceful acceptance.

Later that night I lay awake in bed; my mind humming like an engine. After tossing and turning fitfully I arrived at a resolution: To be my own heroine, I had to consciously take charge of all my choices including my love life. I mused about giving Hugh a chance, a real chance. He gave me devotion. He took the Forum and was still working on himself. I deserve love, I insisted to myself. If not now, when?

CHAPTER 18

Right Action

This is it, the moment of death. Mushrooming shock waves of terror circled out from my solar plexus. Gasping for air, I tried to scream but no sound came out. Suddenly there was no breath, no body; I found myself expanded in an infinitely vast amorphous energy field. After floating for an instant/eternity an orange-white light appeared and beckoned me. It radiated at the end of a long purple tunnel like a homing signal that was live with sentient energy. Raphaela was waiting and by mere intention, the quantum of energy that was my being floated down towards her. She licked my face and I woke up. Milo was on the bed, busily slurping my face. My copy of Eadie's *Embraced by the Light* lay on top of my down comforter.

Milo's jewel eyes fixed on me.

"Milo, baby, I hope the dying experience does play out that way for her, for me, for all of us."

"Woof," he answered.

As Milo and I made our Valley Green pilgrimage in the brisk wintry air, butterflies flapped nervously in my stomach. I did being-in-the-moment exercises on the glassy winding stream, on the ancient moss-covered boulders, on the gray-brown squirrels that laughed and darted among the mounds of leaves. The rich presence of the now quieted me. But as soon as we got back in the Volvo, the pesky butterflies returned. Time to see Raphaela.

She was down in Stone Harbor, at the Jersey shore, an eerily beautiful beach town even in the dead of winter. By the time I arrived on the island, two hours of holiday traffic on the Black Horse Pike had agitated me into annoyance and agitation. I laughed at how unprepared I was to be a heroine.

The house, a weathered wood and glass contemporary at the end of a long winding dirt lane, was on a large expanse of beach with commanding views of the gray Atlantic waves pounding on the shore. Despite my inner work my palms were sweaty as I rang the front bell. She opened the metal screen door and embraced me at once. Instantly, I felt like I was home. We walked into an enormous space with vaulted ceilings, decorated in tones of cobalt and tan that complemented the majestic ocean scene. She motioned me into an overstuffed nubby navy sofa while she sat swathed in a white robe like a monolith on the matching armchair. At her feet were five Neiman shopping bags.

"I see you've been busy," I chortled.

"Feed the body and the soul, I always say." She laughed. Somehow her quirkiness had come to comfort me.

I settled back into the pillows on the couch. "Raphaela, about Stephan and Greenway…maybe I should just report them to the FDA and move on."

"But…?" she coaxed.

"I don't think I have it in me to go after them personally, much as I'd love to…"

She laughed and I was immediately offended. Ignoring my reaction as she had so many times in the past, Raphaela said, "You can be a coward if you choose."

Her challenge infuriated me. Red-faced, I stood up and spat out, "Damn it!"

"You can chicken out." She smiled enigmatically. Something, some resolve took me over.

"Damn it! I'm gonna do the right thing, even if it kills me."

Raphaela twinkled. "When dealing with sharks, especially dangerous sharks, you have to play tit for tat. The only winning position in the short term is to act with them as they act with you. By disciplining these creatures you can stop them from hurting others. In fact, it's giving them what they need to wake up."

Raphaela raised her arms and her voluminous white sleeves spread like wings on the angel of justice.

"Of course, you must also keep yourself safe in the process, by being shrewd and gathering strong allies."

I found myself pacing with anxiety and agitated excitement.

Raphaela nodded her approval. "Just by your decision you have started to become your own Beloved Warrior."

Raphaela touched my cheek. "On this path your job is to please your conscience completely, so that you are guilty of no wrongdoing whether it is through inaction or acting destructively."

Then she ritualistically put both of her hands over my head, as if blessing me for the hero's journey.

"May you be powerful and pure as you quest to create Good in the world."

"I need to work directly with the FDA so we can shut down the bastards."

"I'll put you in touch with an official there. And I'll be with you."

I wanted to thank her for believing in me, for encouraging me, but the sadness welled up in me.

"And the worst challenge in my life now is Sooze," I choked out.

Raphaela put her arms around me.

"She is dying. And you don't know if you can bear it, much less take right action."

We sat side by side in silence until I had regrouped.

"We tried CoQ10, lactoferrin, essential oils, and even a psychic surgeon. All for shit. Here I was starting to believe in something spiritual and then I get hit with the cruelest, the most painful experience…"

Raphaela turned her head and stared out at the roiling waves and suddenly her face turned dark. It was like someone had shut down the light that illuminated her from within.

"I know this sounds crazy, but can you heal her?" I pleaded.

Raphaela held her knees and looked off wistfully. Her voice became scratchy, broken. This was not the Raphaela I knew. She looked small, shaken.

"What is it?" I asked.

Silence.

Then she spoke. "It doesn't work to fight loss. I know all about it. Twelve years ago I was married. In love. I had two daughters, Ariel and Maddie, three and five years old. We were going to the shore. And something happened."

I put my arm around her.

"I was driving. And the next thing I knew, I was pinned behind the steering wheel and buried in steel. My husband was dead in the seat next to me." She paused, her eyes glazed over. "Gone."

"And the kids?" I asked, dreading the answer.

"From the back seat…it seemed so so far away…I could hear Ariel crying for me, screaming, gurgling 'Mommy.' I could do nothing. Nothing."

"Oh my God." I pressed her close to me.

"Ariel passed in the ambulance. Maddie in the hospital. I told them I didn't want to see the bodies. I didn't want to see anything."

Tears welled up in my eyes.

"After that I was bed-ridden, guilt-ridden. Couldn't eat, couldn't drive, couldn't leave my house."

"How did you…"

"Bill Boros. He was my husband's friend. Took me to Mother India, to Maharishi Sidha and other gurus in the hills." Raphaela smiled wistfully. "They gave me the lessons. And the lessons gave me my new life: being in service." She kissed my hand and held it to her cheek.

The teardrops streamed down my face and fell onto my blouse.

"Janna, you have been saving me as much as I have been saving you." Raphaela handed me a tissue. I dried my eyes and cleaned the mascara off my face.

"I'm so sorry, I mean…"

She shushed me. "It's OK. Dying has a purpose. Death is a peaceful going back to all that is, the wonderful stuff of god consciousness from which the fabric of Nature is constructed. That's where your precious friend is going. Your purpose is to midwife her passage."

As I pondered what it all meant, Raphaela left the room and returned with an elegant black Japanese teapot. She poured the elixir for both of us and leisurely sat back down on the armchair. "Does Sooze have a mantra?" she asked.

"No, but I could give her my mantra, if that's OK."

"Good. She needs to meditate, as much as possible each day. And teach her the being-in-the moment exercise." Raphaela gazed at me with great care and focus. "These practices will carry her towards the Infinite. And you need to increase your meditation time as well. A quiet mind will allow you to see and perform right action."

The warmth of the tea comforted me.

Raphaela continued. "Get Sooze to talk to you about whatever comes to her mind. Listen carefully and love her. When she's ready, and you will know it, inspire her to be a warrior and face her fears of death head on. Ask her to orchestrate a good dying, a fulfilling series of events that will bring her closure on this plane."

I took a long soothing sip from the delicate cup. "What do you mean?"

"Ask her what interactions she needs to have with the important people in her life, what unfinished business she has to complete in order to be at peace.

What legacies she wants to leave. Ask her how she would like to be remembered, how she would like to say her good-byes."

"At least she doesn't have to worry about her cases. We've transitioned most of them to Herb and Morgenstern, and I took on the four who needed to see a woman."

"Good. You'll know when things are right because her room, even if it's at the hospital, will be a sacred place that calls to people. And she will be an angelic presence who is radiating grace." At that moment, the sun's golden-orange rays on the water were reflecting and filling the whole room. Raphaela's white silk outfit had turned a rich aurum. The overwhelming beauty of the light took me into a haven of prayerful stillness. When the communion ended, I reluctantly hugged Raphaela goodbye.

At home I sat in a long meditation to prepare for the battles ahead. Images of Martin Luther King kept floating through my mind. When I finished my practice I pulled a book of his speeches off my shelf and opened it at random. I felt like he was speaking directly to me:

Whatever you choose as your life work, do it well. Don't be content with sheer mediocrity. Do your job so well that nobody could do it better. Do it so well that all the hosts of Heaven and Earth will have to say, 'Here lived a man who did his job as if God Almighty called him at this particular moment in history to do it...'

❦   ❦   ❦

Within a few days of our meeting, Raphaela put me in touch with a high-ranking FDA official and by Friday I was sitting in a conference room in the Federal Building downtown, trying to calm my palpitations. Across the table from me sat a brawny South Philly Irishman, Special Agent Pat Boyle from the Office of Criminal Investigation, who looked like he would win any Passayunk Avenue brawl.

"We've had a number of complaints about Chlorophyx, but at this point, we have not been able to implicate Greenway in any illegal activity." He rubbed the red stubble on his well-developed jaw.

As I told my story, Boyle grinned like a schoolboy ready to take on the class bully.

"We've been planning a sting operation to gather evidence against them but you're the first source we've met who is close to the top executives in the company." My jitters increased. "May I call you Janna?" I nodded. "Janna, we need an insider to wear a wire and tape the Kalters and Weisgart."

Prickles snaked up my spine.

"I'm just a therapist…" I mumbled.

Agent Boyle gave me a dimpled smile.

"These are not violent people. And I'd be right there in case you needed help."

I desperately wanted to say "I'll do it." Instead I excused myself and went to the ladies' room. There I stared at the mirror.

"The play's afoot. Get on the stage," I said with the same inflection as Raphaela.

❦   ❦   ❦

The planning meeting a few days later was an anxious blur as I listened to Boyle's instructions for the sting. My part was simple. Before every get-together with Stephan, agents would tape my chest with intricate microelectronics that would record our conversations. After I was prepped, a van would park in the vicinity of Stephan's Rittenhouse Square apartment or wherever the meetings took place. Three agents would monitor the conversations, ready to intercede if I were ever in danger.

I had cast myself in a Hollywood B movie as Mata Hari.

Almost a month had passed since my last conversation with Stephan, but, picking up right where I left off, I called and put on an Academy Award performance so that he didn't suspect my intentions. We met that weekend at his apartment. I hugged him, accepted a goblet of Merlot and draped myself on the soft leather couch in his glassy living room.

"I'm just devastated over Sooze."

"Juno, Luv," he gushed from his post on a jet-black leather chair.

"And now the sharks are attacking my business." I crossed my legs so that my velvet mini-skirt unveiled my thighs. "First the *Yoga Journal* smear and now these vicious chat rooms on the Net. And those hack doctors bad-mouthing the products!"

"Infuriating!"

"Speaking of being pissed off, I ran into Sally at the hospital when I was visiting Sooze."

Stephan paled. "Really. She has a bad prescription drug addiction. But, you know, I fired her for you, Janna."

I touched the wineglass to my lips and said nothing.

"Now she's on a lovesick vendetta, blaming the Chlorophyx for her illness."

I shared a little sadistic piece of gossip, "Well she certainly has it in for you. She's hired Bill Pugilista, the toughest pit bull litigator in the city."

"Sally doesn't know who she's dealing with," he replied ominously. "No one fucks with me and gets away with it."

Miss Stupid, how in the world did you ever wind up in this mess? I worried. I quickly began saying my mantra over and over and it served to quiet me enough to get back in role.

"But, Stephan, I heard Pugilista never loses. Against a guy like him, we need ammunition. What about those studies you mentioned during your Orlando speech?"

Stephan looked down at his goblet. "Oh, those. They were never completed."

"Well, were there any partial results that we could use?"

He shifted uncomfortably in his chair.

"Maybe Brenda knows," he shrugged.

"Partial data can be extremely misleading. If Pugilista got his hands on any results that show the product is toxic…" I let the words hang ominously.

Stephan cleared his throat and came over to the couch to hold me. I was repulsed but let him. After a few minutes I sat up out of the embrace and took a sip of wine.

"You know, Stephan, I asked a patient of mine who's with a national PR firm for advice. She suggested that the company hire a spokesperson with impeccable credentials to go on the air and do a testimonial. I've given this a lot of thought and I'm perfect for the job, a licensed social worker, who could testify to all the benefits I've received from the products."

"Say, Luv, that's not a bad idea. I'll run it by the Kalters. Now, how about retiring to the other room?" he purred as he stroked my hair.

I got up and took his hand.

"You ought to spend time with people who are more uplifting than me, what with Sooze being sick and all." I anchored in my sincerity with a few kisses and hugs.

Stephan bought it.

Two days after setting the bait, I called Stephan and invited him to come over for dinner. The agents wired me up and then retired to a Philadelphia

Electric van parked across the street. Milo picked up on the streams of adrenaline pouring through my bloodstream and started yapping and zooming around the kitchen in crazy circles as I tried to steam red peppers and asparagus. Looking down I noticed my hands were shaking uncontrollably. My God, I'm having a full-blown anxiety attack, I realized. I sat at the dinette to observe and control my breath. But scary images of him finding the wire and attacking me bombarded my brain. So I decided to embrace the fear, to make it even stronger. Anxiety came over me like a spinning tornado that sucked the air out of my lungs. Then, mercifully, almost as quickly as it started, the ordeal passed.

After 20 minutes of meditation, I was calm enough to finish the asparagus and baste the pork roast. A porcine dish was most fitting for my 'friend.' After the roast was safely back in the oven, I dressed for my role, slipping on a slinky black A line slip dress with a push up bra to fill out an hourglass figure, black stockings and strappy suede dress sandals. Carefully, I applied a new coat of Red Fire polish on the long acrylic nails I had gotten from the salon next door to my office. Shaking my hands for a quick dry, I studied myself carefully from all angles in the mirror to be sure that Boyle's mini-transmitter did not show. Satisfied, I blew myself a kiss.

"You're a cross between Raphaela and Mata Hari," I announced to the reflection.

He entered bearing a bottle of his favorite California Cabernet, Newton Vineyards, and a single red rose. Milo greeted him with a low growl and nipped his pant leg.

"Milo, no," I yelled and he slunk away.

Stephan just laughed it while his eyes ominously followed Milo's path into the kitchen. Nervously, I scooped my puppy up and locked him in the safe haven of my bedroom.

Putting my trembling hands behind me, I said, "I've just started taking tranquilizers and won't be able to drink tonight."

He sat unsuspecting, at the dinette, which was set up with white linen place mats, blue glass plates, and crystal wine goblets. I poured him a generous glass of Cabernet and filled my goblet with water.

"Here's to Sooze's recovery," he toasted me and downed half the glass.

"She's not going to recover."

My eyes misted over as I quickly served pork, potatoes and asparagus.

"What a loss. I'm so so sorry," he answered smoothly.

"But tonight, we have to focus on us, our coming together again. A toast, to us," I clinked my water glass to his goblet and happily watched him down the rest of the Newton.

Three quarters through the slightly burnt entree, Stephan had emptied the entire bottle of Cabernet and was clearly where I wanted him. Tears came to his eyes.

"Our company's too good—too good for a cutthroat world. So we're attacked. Like Christ, or Gandhi."

What little food I had gotten down came right up and I covered my gagging with a cough.

"We have to pull together now," I said. "Let's talk to the Kalters about my being a spokesperson."

"Are you available this weekend? Brenda and Ed are in town."

"Yes. And those partial studies?" I asked nonchalantly while I stabbed at a piece of potato on my plate.

Stephan held his forehead in his hands. "What a mess."

"What do you mean?" My heart beat double time.

He looked at me beseechingly. "There was a mutation problem."

"Mutations happen all the time in nature…"

"Yeah, it only occurred in two out of the twenty trials."

"And?" I came around the table and hugged him from behind.

He clung to my hands. "Janna, the mice in those trials died."

Bingo. "But only in two trials, right? In science, everything is statistics, you know."

I massaged his neck and back.

"We're trying to fix it. I mean Brenda's looking for the cause of the mutation and we paid our chemist, Elliot, a $100,000 'bonus' so he won't talk any time soon. But Elliot's assistant left and it's not clear if she stole a copy of the data. And then there's Sally. I don't know how much she knows."

The bastard was really only concerned about covering his own precious ass. I turned toward the stove and touched my hidden tape recorder happily.

Then I turned back to him. "Look, you don't have to worry if you understand statistics. I got straight As in statistics in graduate school; in fact, I was exempt from taking the final. A flare for math runs in the family. My father's an accountant, you know." I kneaded his scapula with my fists. "We might even be able to show a positive outcome."

"Great idea, Luv. Now for your reward." He tried to paw at my breasts and I ducked away, my heart racing. Poking my head into the refrigerator, I tried to quiet the tachycardia. A prearranged phone call was supposed to rescue me. Now, I urged. Right on time, Boyle called pretending he was Sooze asking me to come to the hospital. I quickly handed Stephan a cup of Jamaican Mountain Blue, much as I hated to give him the good stuff, sobered him up and ushered him out the door.

Exhausted, I answered the doorbell a few minutes later to debrief with Agent Boyle. "I did it, I did it," I jumped up and hugged him in a manic fit of glee.

"You're a natural, brilliant, actually—you gave us great ammunition," he grinned.

"If I ever consider a career change I know who to call."

CHAPTER 19

On The Path

Hugh helped me smuggle Ben and Jerry's and Godiva into the hospital for Sooze. He ran interference with the nurses, ensuring we could comfort her any time of the day and night, regardless of the posted visiting hours. He held me when I wept. And he cheered on my undercover work with Agent Boyle. He stayed the course with me even after I warned that I was on the rebound and wasn't sure of my feelings for him.

I tried to love Hugh. I learned to cook lasagna for him; encouraged him to write *At Love's Door*, a book of poetry he had been incubating for years; and dressed him in cool khakis that made him strut. But we didn't make love and he didn't pressure me.

"You're practicing," Sooze, the wise wraith, announced one morning at the hospital.

"What?" I asked.

"Real give and take with a man. It's like singing scales in rehearsal. He may not be the one but you will sing arias in the great concert hall in your lifetime. You've made the decision."

"Thank you, Sweetie." I squeezed her hand.

Sooze's wizened face contorted. "It feels like harpies eating at my insides."

We rang for the nurse and arranged for more morphine. I held her hand and gently wiped droplets off her yellowed brow.

"It's all been pointless, the surgery, the chemo, those charade appointments with Phyllis," she gasped. Sooze's sunken cheeks had opened up her eye sockets so that her hazel eyes floated in her face.

"I'm dying, aren't I?"

She sat up and stared me in the eye.

Barely able to breathe, I thought, this is the moment.

"Yes," I whispered.

Remembering Raphaela's coaching, I added, "And I want you to go out in *Technicolor*, to choreograph your exit with style and grace."

I silently said my mantra as I waited to see how she would respond.

Sooze leaned back on her pillow, her face serene. Every muscle in her body let go and relaxed.

"And I am with you," I said as I took both of her hands in mine. "Until the last step, I mean, I can't go all the way."

"God, how can you be that heartless—it's always been me and you, Sooze and Janna," she teased. "How come you can't make this one last little trip with me?"

We laughed as tears streamed.

"Raphaela says *The purpose of your life is to become your own beloved warrior*. Now is the time to act from that place. Talk straight to the people you love. Heal stupid, petty conflicts, make reparations to those you've hurt." I bent over and gently kissed her forehead. "It's time for the warrior to live in love, love for yourself and all those around you."

I anointed Sooze with a second kiss.

Just then her parents came in and Sooze signaled me to be quiet. Clara had become a shell-shocked skeleton, whose boisterous outfits were gone, along with the melody in her voice. Byron appeared ashen and tight-lipped. But he had brought his only child a festive bouquet of pink and yellow flowers.

"Dear Heart, I've brought you a book about Paris in the Twenties and Thirties." Clara gave Sooze a violent hug.

"Gently, Mother," Sooze winced.

Byron leaned over stiffly and pecked at her brow.

"You look better today," he said blankly.

Clara hugged me and then painstakingly arranged the bouquet of pink carnations and yellow roses in a Waterford vase for Sooze's windowsill. Byron dragged two plastic chairs up to the bed.

"It's been so cold. Oh, let's all run away to Boca for Christmas," Clara started.

Remembering my coaching instructions, I intervened.

"Sooze, tell your mother what you really need from her."

Clara looked startled.

Sooze closed her eyes. "Mom, I'm dying. I know it's hard for you to accept, but better that we all face what's so. This is your last chance to tell me that I'm OK that I'm the daughter you always wanted."

Tears formed in the corners of her eyes.

Clara's face contorted in agony. "Dear Heart, no, I've called a world class oncologist at the Mayo…"

I interrupted quickly.

"Clara, let go. Just relate to Sooze right now. That's all we have. Can you see her perfection, Clara?" I asked. "That's all she's ever needed you to see."

Clara looked at me with tears falling hard. As they dripped onto her black wool turtleneck she studied Sooze.

"My darling, oh how I love you. More than life itself. And, yes, you are perfect. You are my perfect daughter."

Sooze smiled beatifically. "I forgive you, Mother. Underneath all the crap you were trying to help me."

"Oh angel." Clara took Sooze's bony hands and lost herself in violent, gut-wrenching sobs. My eyes misted over as Sooze whispered, "I'm happy I was your daughter."

At long last her mother quieted down and brought a newly filled water pitcher for the tray.

Byron had been standing by awkwardly watching the whole time. I looked over at him and back at Sooze. "What do you need from Dad?"

"I want to be alone with you…and I want you to hold me." She looked at him invitingly. "Come sit on the bed, Daddy. Janna, would you take Mom to the dining room for a cup of coffee?"

Byron clumsily arranged himself on the bed and took Sooze's frail body in his arms. She was gamely smiling up at him as we left the room. Clara and I cried our way down the hall to the cafeteria.

When we came back fifteen minutes later, Byron was still sitting on the bed gazing at Sooze. His words were barely audible. "…never forgive myself for taking you for granted, for thinking you'd always be here. When I retired I thought I'd be able to spend more time with you and now…" Teardrops fought to escape from the old man's eyes.

"Daddy, I forgive you. You're here with me right now." She stroked his arm.

"You'll always be with me, Suzanne," he croaked. She nodded and the four of us sat quietly.

Sooze broke the silence. "Say, I've got a new book title, *How to be 50 Pounds Lighter in a Day: the Forgiveness Diet.*"

Laughing through tears, I pushed ahead on my mission. "Sooze is being her own heroine, completing all her relationships and bringing peace to us all. Anything else, sweetheart?" I asked.

"Yes, this may sound silly…"

"Nothing is silly. You are scripting your life, just as you need it to be," I insisted.

"I want the Philly Folksong group to have their monthly sing here in my hospital room this Saturday." Sooze's wan face colored slightly.

"That's great. Herb sings with them and I'll ask him to arrange it."

Sooze's parents left and she looked gratefully at me. "Encroyable! Even my mother's happy. And she got what she always wanted—I'm thin now. One small problem: I'm also dying."

She guffawed and then I could see tendrils of fear take over.

I stroked her forehead. "I want you to meditate with me right now."

She closed her eyes and slowly all her features relaxed.

CHAPTER 20

Sweet Sorrow

Sooze died on the first night of Hanukkah, the holiday that commemorates a miracle of victory.

My family was sitting in the snug living room of Doris and Irv's plant-filled bungalow nibbling potato latkes. Dad's lady friend, Vivienne, the widow of one of his oldest and dearest clients, was a heavy-set, laughing *ballabusta*, who brought an unusual lightheartedness to our once dreary family play. Doris and Irv were pregnant with their first and had the special glow to prove it. And I was giddy from my recent triumphs over Greenway.

We sipped the sweet Manischewitz wine that Irv loved, each of us high and complete.

"It's a girl, I just feel it. I want to name her Sophie, after Mom," Doris said with a wistful look and a gentle pat to her stomach.

"A toast to that." Vivienne's full face twinkled, as she encouraged us to raise our glasses.

"Time for candles," the mom-to-be announced. We gathered at the kitchen table.

As soon as Doris lit the first candle on the Hanukkah, the holiday candelabra, an effulgent orange-white light spread out from the wick and filled the whole room. I knew instantly that Sooze had died. I sobbed with my whole body, each wave of grief swelling up from my coccyx, each wave saying, No, No, No.

"Janna, you're going off the deep end," Doris worried.

"Did you see the light?" I asked. Clapping hands to cheeks she slowly shook her head no.

I fled the house, jumped in the Volvo and raced over to HUP, hoping that I had just hallucinated. But as soon as I got to the ICU, I saw Sooze's distraught parents. The doctor on the floor sadly took us aside to confirm Sooze's passing. Clara wailed, "My baby, my baby," as she collapsed into Byron's arms. My stomach gripped.

I headed in slow motion toward her room. The room I never wanted to enter, the room of death. Her death, my death. Being Jewish, I had never seen a dead body—only closed caskets. The thought of seeing the corpse of my Sooze, my twin, filled me with nausea and stopped me cold right in front of the door. As I was trying to breathe and quiet myself, the clack, clack, clack of steel wheels announced the arrival of a gurney, pulled by two matter-a-fact orderlies. I barred the door. "NO, please. Give me a few minutes!" I begged. One shrugged, took out a pack of cigarettes and motioned for the other to go out for a smoke break.

All of Raphaela's lessons flashed back to help me, as I stared down my own fear and went in to face the biggest loss of all.

As I entered the room my heart beating wildly, I saw the small mound in the bed covered over with a sheet. "Fear lights the way, my darling warrior," I said to calm myself and her spirit. I went over and pulled the sheet back.

She was smiling.

I found myself quoting Wordsworth:

ॐ

But for those first affections, those shadowy recollections,

Which be they what they may, are yet the fountain light of all our day,

Are yet a master light of all our seeing,

Uphold us, cherish, and have power to make our noisy years

Seem moments in the being of the eternal silence.

And I knew in that moment that she would always be with me—her love was a fragment of the Divine all that is.

"Goodbye my precious angel," I whispered as I leaned over and kissed her cool forehead for the last time.

❦   ❦   ❦

The day after Sooze's funeral was the coldest Christmas on record. Sitting in my rocker, I stared at the ice weighing down the tangle of branches outside my bedroom window. Finally I opened a journal and poured out my thoughts:

To have been chosen as the midwife for Sooze's passage was a blessing of the highest order. I was able to see her become her own Beloved Heroine steeped in courage and love who swept us along in a river of caring. As her soulful eyes became portals to another world she spent more and more time in meditation and being-in-the-Now. Resonating with her, I came to know that we were meant to live in the eternal present in a fully conscious and creative way.

Sooze's thirst for spirituality and the Divine grew as her body wasted away. Sitting with her for long periods of meditation and silence, I had profound experiences of comfort, as if I was sitting on the lap of God. My long-held doubts and resentments about a Higher Power have completely melted away. Thank you, Sooze.

I put down the journal and unwrapped an Albert Einstein poster from Sooze's hospital wall that read:

ॐ

> To know that what is impenetrable to us really exists, manifesting itself as the highest wisdom and the most radiant beauty, which our dull faculties can comprehend only in the most primitive forms—this knowledge, this feeling, is at the center of all true religiousness.

How Sooze's face had lighted up when Herb burst into the room with his Jerry Garcia twinkle and presented her with that poster! The stark hospital space was so warmed by her great spirit. It was filled with rainbows from window crystals, white and red amaryllis, pink carnations and white roses, and the Georgia O'Keefe pastel that reflected the simple beauty that was Sooze. Just as Raphaela had predicted, her expansive self had changed the sterile room into a sacred place, as she dispensed blessings to all.

My courageous friend choreographed her own funeral, asking Herb, Morgenstern, her parents and me to speak. And she heard the eulogies first hand—she joked to us that she could hear them better in HUP than in heaven.

I read my part to her as the last rays of sunset flooded in through the hospital window. I spoke of the boundless love and service to others that were at her core and of her unstoppable humor, even in the face of tormenting pain. I ended with Gibran:

∞

For what is it to die but to stand naked

In the wind and to melt into the sun?

And what is it to cease breathing, but to free the breath from its restless tides,

That it may rise and expand and seek God unencumbered?

Flashes of Sooze's magnificent last days continued, as I tried to hold on her. I remembered her comforting Herb as he wept rather than the other way around, remembered her blessing her zombie-out parents and telling them she'd be their guardian angel.

I remembered her cracked voice happily warbling Joni Mitchell's *Circle Game*, "*And the seasons they go round and round and the painted ponies go up and down...we're captive on the carousel of time,*" with Herb and the Folk Song group strumming along. And afterwards, her triumphant grin as she announced that she had worked through her crazy bullshit about not being able to sing like Clara.

As the days passed, I was laden with grief that ebbed and flowed like tsunami that washed up and destroyed whole cities. Overwhelming sadness would strike in the shower; when I heard an old James Taylor tune that Sooze loved; when I saw the startling beauty of an amaryllis in the flower shop window; and, especially when I saw the number 8 on the elevator, the digit that marked the floor I would go to for solace and comfort.

But I noticed that the being-in-the-moment exercises allowed me to go through the swells of grief rapidly and completely. I saw more clearly that only resisted emotions cause suffering, not freely accepted feeling. Full-flowing grief sessions would rise up as I was innocently staring at a spruce or a cloud. I would simply hold my focus and be in communion with that one thing until the weeping passed. After that came a sense of being washed clean into the now, into stillness. During this process plants, trees, and streams blessed and healed me.

The paradox was, in spite of, or because of my pain, I saw heavenly beauty in all things, the whorls on a telephone pole, diamonds in the asphalt paving, white-blue auras of light around all sentient beings. A waking mantra came and resided in my soul: *I am easily present in the eternal divine now.*

CHAPTER 21

Doors Opened

"And $700,000 to Gilda's Place in New York City," my pale yellow flower pledged on the videotape of her will, "to publicize the ovarian cancer risk factors of asbestos, talc-based powders or the use of fertility drugs taken for more than three cycles."

Clara, Byron, and I sat watching the screen in a staid Center City brownstone on a cold Valentine's Day morning. We propped ourselves up against the pain at a huge oval mahogany conference table in Sooze's uncle's legal office. "I give $400,000 to the National Ovarian Cancer Coalition support group based in Pompano Beach for newsletters, media presentations and conferences to educate the public."

Clara dabbed at her death mask eyes with an embroidered handkerchief. "We're starting The Suzanne Banks Run for Ovarian Cancer in the spring."

Sooze looked at the camera. "And, with deepest gratitude, I give the bulk of my estate, $2 million plus or minus, to you, my friend and soul-mate, Janna Abel, to realize your dream, to enrich your life...get it Jan?...and for some serious shopping."

The room began to spin.

Byron grinned like a tired Cheshire cat. "You ministered to her until the very end."

I was unable to speak. After a few minutes I got up to walk around the table to thank them and tripped over a plush oriental rug. Clara jumped up to catch me and I hugged her tightly. "I love you both," I finally managed. "Anytime you need to talk or just be together, call me."

Clara held my shoulders. "You are the angel who brought us together. You deserve it. Thank you, My Darling."

Stunned I drove blankly up the Schuylkill, thinking I'm rich, I can buy whatever I want, go wherever I want, I don't ever need to work as a therapist anymore. I didn't know what to think. When I finally pulled up to Wissahickon Street, I came to my senses. It's just money, just money, I thought. Don't get carried away."

I slowly walked in the front door and greeted my sidekick.

"Milo, we're rich. You can order the gourmet doggie treats from Tailwaggers."

Scooping him up, I scratched his furry ears in exultation.

Next I rushed to call Hugh.

"Unbelievable. But you need to invest the money wisely."

"I'm thinking of investing in people."

"You mean Versace? Harry Winston?" Hugh guffawed.

"No," I laughed. "In women. What calls to me is a center to empower women, with groups on Raphaela's Lessons, a hotline, low-fee therapy. And we can be independent of those damned insurance companies."

"I'll incorporate you and be your counsel! Let's celebrate at Under the Blue Moon Friday night."

"You're on. Pick me up in the silver Mercedes, Dahling."

Hugh and I exuberantly drove to the cozy fish restaurant. When we were seated I studied his face. His chestnut eyes twinkled at me. I said softly, "I've wanted to say this for a while, but with Sooze and all…" Hugh bit his lip. "Right now is the first time I can catch my breath and be me, not me on the rebound, or midwiving death."

I took a deep breath and continued.

"Hugh, I love you. But I want to go really slow, with no expectations."

Hugh gave me a sexy smile. "What makes you think I want to go fast?"

❈   ❈   ❈

Raphaela's jade eyes glowed. We sat in the warmth of the Chadds Ford living room, our faces lit by a roaring fire in the walk-in stone fireplace. A late February snowfall dusted the windows with crystal flakes. The fire illuminated the room with splashes of aurum-violet light. Raphaela carefully arranged the folds of the orchid velvet dressing gown that draped over the carved legs of her chair. I unbuttoned the alabaster cape jacket that I had worn for the occasion and sat upright on the couch.

"I'm calling it *The Suzanne Banks Center for Women*," I announced.

Raphaela clapped with delight. "Right in our North Philly project! Thank you. And what about Greenway?"

I took *The Philadelphia Inquirer* clipping out of my bag and began to read the headline:

"Local Businessman Arrested by Federal Agents. Stephan Weisgart, along with his business partners, Brenda and Ed Kalter, were arrested last night at a rally for their nutritional business, Greenway, at Prudential Square in Boston. At the same time, FDA agents confiscated 'contaminated supplements' and financial records from Weisgart's apartment in Rittenhouse Square. According to agent Pat Boyle, who headed the investigation, Weisgart and the Kalters were charged with making false statements to a government agency, mail fraud, plus conspiracy to commit these two charges, and wire fraud. All are felonies punishable by prison terms and fines."

Raphaela high-fived me. We beamed at each other, sharing the moment.

"Joseph Campbell said it well," she began.

"We have not even to risk the adventure alone, for the heroes of all time have gone before us. The labyrinth is thoroughly known. We have only to follow the thread of the hero path, and where we had thought to slay another, we shall slay ourselves. Where we had thought to travel outward, we will come to the center of our own existence. And where we had thought to be alone, we will be with all the world." Raphaela made a graceful spiral wave with her bejeweled hand that sent tingles along my spine.

She disappeared into the kitchen and returned bearing a silver tray with two crystal champagne flutes and a bottle of sparkling cider. She poured the effervescent golden liquid and raised her glass to me.

"You have opened love's door!" Raphaela laughed. Then she became serious. "Love for yourself and others comes through mastering the first seven lessons. To your opening. As a woman, a spiritual being and as an apprentice," she toasted.

Tears of gratitude misted over me as I joyously saluted my teacher with the goblet.

"Raphaela, if only I were a poet, I could convey how much I cherish you. Is there anything I can do for you?"

"Share your knowledge with the world."

Epilogue

The original man in my life, my dad, got married on Mother's Day. Party girl Vivienne arranged an upscale soiree at Blue Bell Country Club for 50 friends with a minister for her and a reform rabbi for him. Vivienne's son, Roger, belted out Sinatra, Al Jarreau, and Motown classics with his band, The Blue Notes. Babba Pearl came up from Miami to give her blessing.

"Look, they're fooling around like a couple of teenagers," Aunt Irm exclaimed to me as my father and Vivienne waltzed from table to table. She put her arm around my waist. "Janna, you are truly the daughter I never had. You've become a woman in full."

"You've been reading Tom Wolfe," I laughed. "And thank you. I am your daughter," I added, as I encircled her waist and gave her a squeeze.

Uncle Morty, stooped with arthritis, nevertheless insisted on having a dance with me. And Doris, Sophie and I managed a two minute celebratory *Hora* that left us breathless with laughter.

Hugh was resplendent in a pinstripe navy suit and crisp dress shirt that set off the healthy sheen of his dark complexion. Dancing the night away with Hugh was like being surrounded by the warmest Caribbean sunshine. I could feel his eyes drink me in while I waltzed in the slinky lavender slip-dress with embroidered frangipani that he had bought me as a birthday surprise.

Babba Pearl didn't like Hugh, but, then again, she wouldn't like anyone who was only half-Jewish. This time her negative opinion didn't bother me.

At the end of a stellar evening, Hugh asked the Blue Notes to play the Smokey Robinson classic, *Being with You*. As we danced he sang the lyrics to me.

"I don't care what they think about me, I don't care what they say...I don't care about anything else but bein' with you, bein' with you..." He picked me up

in his well-muscled arms and twirled slowly around in circles. *"People can change, they always do. Haven't they noticed the changes in you?"* As I watched the ceiling and the other dancers go round and round my head started swimming and a child-like feeling of delight took over. Laughing full out, I took his head in my hands and kissed his soft sensual mouth. Maybe Hugh is the one, I thought, as his exquisitely sensitive lips met mine.

❧   ❧   ❧

That night I finally dreamt of Him again. We were sitting on my bed facing each other and He was holding an enormous crystal chalice. Raising the goblet to my lips, he gave me delicious sips of a warm elixir that tasted like milk, or cream laced with Kahlua. He seemed to know just when to put the chalice to my lips. Each time He gave me only the right amount, so that I could savor the drink to its fullest. The warming pleasure streamed through me, soothing and melting my body.

"Thank you," I whispered.

He put down the goblet and took my face in his hands. Radiant light sparkled in the blue of his eyes. "Who are you?" I wondered.

He winked at me.

"My animus? You mean Jung was right…" I began to answer. He put a finger to his lips to silence me.

Then he held my face in his hands and we melted together into the fiery light of a thousand suns.

The End

THE LESSONS

I. Fear lights the way to mastery.

II. When you face loss, love blossoms.

III. The Divine awaits your daily invitation.

IV. Falling in love with yourself is the first step to finding the love you seek.

V. Your path is a dance of two steps forward, one step back.

VI. You can go home again.

VII. The purpose of your life is to become your own beloved warrior.

More Information

❦   ❦   ❦

For more *Opening Love's Door* transformational work go to www.OpeningLovesDoor.com to order:

Opening Love's Door **Workbook**: Let go of your resistances, your fears, your old wounds and losses and build renewed power, love and grace in your life. This e-book helps you transform with step-by-step in-depth coaching on each of the Lessons. Guided exercises take you through and beyond the thoughts and feelings that plague your thinking and into affirmative beliefs and spiritual openings that create a life that is just right for you.

Opening Love's Door **Special Reports:** These on-line reports deal with specific strategies and goals. Topics include *Opening the Doors of Love, Fear and Mastery, Facing Loss,* and *Being-in-the-Moment.*

Opening Love's Door **Newsletter:** Subscribe to a monthly on-line newsletter that helps you stay connected with the Lessons in your everyday life.

Opening Love's Door **Teleseminars:** Call in from the comfort of your own home to take seminars on *Personal Power, Love, or Embracing the Divine* with the author, Diana Kirschner, Ph.D.

❦   ❦   ❦

Please email me at **DrDiana@OpeningLovesDoor.com** with your own personal experiences in using the Opening Love's Door lessons!

See our website at http:www.OpeningLovesDoor.com

Order more copies of *Opening Love's Door* at **www.OpeningLovesDoor.com** or by calling **Toll Free 1 (888) LESSON-8 (1-888-537-7668).**

0-595-33386-9

Printed in the United States
31620LVS00003B/49-60